"Where the hell did you come from?"

Aaelefein extrapolated from sense to meaning, meaning to sound, and learned the complex sounds, but lacked the vocabulary to respond.

"What's the idea, sneakin' up that way?". The human bristled, then peered closely at him. "Hey, what are you made up for, anyway? This some kind of a joke?" When the Caian did not respond, the human took another step backward. "Now look, buddy. I'm just goin' my own way, not hurtin' anybody. Hell, it's a free road, but if you're hopped up on somethin' you just back off, okay?"

Aaelefein tried the language. It was short on tonal variation but surprisingly complex within its narrow auditory range. "I'm just goin' my own way not hurtin' anybody," he mimicked.

The human relaxed a bit. "Well now, that's better. Hey, how come you're dressed up like that? You an actor or somethin'?"

"Some kind of a joke," Aaelefein said.

"O-o-kay," the man said. "Tell you, though, you're not goin' to flag a lift lookin' like that, and if some eighteen-wheeler comes by, I'd appreciate it if you could just sort of fade while I get myself a ride. I'm goin' on in to Clover," he said. "Where you goin'?"

"On in to Clover. I'm not goin' to flag any lift."

"Damn right you're not. That's what I said." He paused. "You sound like you're from California," he said. "That's where I'm from. California. I can always tell a 'Frisco native by the way he talks. 'Frisco, right?"

"Right," Aaelefein replied.

"Me, too."

By the time lights of a large vehicle showed behind them, Aaelefein had a working knowledge of basic California. As requested, he "faded" before the truck pulled up and watched unnoticed as the creature flagged a ride.

By the time the trucker let them off in Clover—the creature riding inside and the Caian on top—Aaelefein had added to his California and picked up a good bit of Texas.

STARSONG

A Science-Fantasy Love Story

Dan Parkinson

Cover Art
NEAL McPHEETERS

TSR, Inc.

For Randy and Jenny Scott,
who are the future

STARSONG

This book is protected under the copyright laws of the United States of America. Any reproduction or other unauthorized use of the material or artwork contained herein is prohibited without the express written permission of TSR, Inc.

Distributed to the book trade in the United States by Random House, Inc. and in Canada by Random House of Canada, Ltd.

Distributed in the United Kingdom by TSR UK Ltd.

Distributed to the toy and hobby trade by regional distributors.

DRAGONLANCE is a registered trademark owned by TSR, Inc. FORGOTTEN REALMS is a trademark owned by TSR, Inc.

First Printing, June, 1988
Printed in the United States of America.
Library of Congress Catalog Card Number: 87-51261

9 8 7 6 5 4 3 2 1

ISBN: 0-88038-536-7

TSR, Inc.
P.O. Box 756
Lake Geneva, WI 53147 U.S.A.

TSR UK Ltd.
The Mill, Rathmore Road
Cambridge CB14AD
United Kingdom

They were five, these people of the ancient Cai. But now, in chord, the five were one. Harmonic senses attuned, their song a shifting brilliance in the void, they clung and sang and flashed across emptiness toward the world their people had abandoned thousands of millenia before.

They were five in concert—four select adepts, hands clasped in a ring of vibrant empathy, and in their midst the one who was Feya. Aaelefein, the strongest of will, concentrated vast resonances on the song of transference. Almond eyes alight, seven senses tuned to a perfection of pitch, he sang the ranges of harmonic thrust that drove them toward their destination. At his throat the senester, seven perfect crystals alive and vibrant, responded to his pulses and amplified them. He concentrated on destination and directed the mindsong of the chord. The five who were one were a dazzle in the void. Massed harmonics drove outward, transcending distance.

Ahead, on the galaxy's fringe, planets orbited a small sun. The third planet was cloaked in living mantle. The chord flashed toward it. Aaelefein sang to the senester, and stars crawled away behind them.

At his left was Sefraeonia La-Cos, her slim hand close

in his as she perceived his song and built upon it the structure of resonance that was the form and body of the chord. She was the percept, drawn from clan Cos that the chord might be complete. Better than the rest, Sefraeonia could perceive the intricate patterns of resonance.

She in turn clasped the strong right hand of sturdy Haralan, adoptee from the devastated Eldretten realms, last of the clan Canenden. Haralan, solid as the rock of worlds, was continuity to the chord. His strong underwave of empathy was steady and deep, a rhythm to sing by. Haralan would not fail them. Only he among them had tasted the Corad, and the crystal blade at his side pulsed and glowed with dark intent.

On Aaelefein's right, and always in his mind, was the scintillant Nataea. Her bright eyes danced as she sparkled radiant overtones across the fabric of the song. Her hand in his was small and alive with an empathy so strong that it supported all the rest. Brilliant empath, her skill the very soul of her, Nataea had been the final choice for the chord, and Aaelefein had known dread. The mission was dangerous, and she was so very vulnerable. And he loved her. But now she soothed him. Within each lyric trill that he added to the chord were special notes put there just for him. The entire chord responded, a fullness of bright harmony sparkling in the void.

In the center, the Feya, tiny and radiant, clutched her diadem and encompassed them all with shielding harmonics. Winifraeda Feya, incredibly old and incredibly beautiful, sang to her diadem in ranges that were low and constant, tightly woven to hold about them a cocoon of comfort, a shield against the emptiness just beyond its ringing sphere.

The five were one. They were the chord, and the one

last, desperate hope for the world Nendacaida, final home of the Cai. None knew what thing or quality on ancient Caiendon had repelled the Corad, but these five—if they survived—would seek it there. For all that remained of Caidom, it was the only chance.

The mindsong flowed and Aaelefein touched it with minor tones of longing. He knew—they all knew—that they would reach Caiendon, sad old world once vital-bright. But they knew as well that they might not return. The chord hummed bittersweet.

From the beginning, there had been a trace of lonely dread in the harmonics. The old lore told how it had been on Caiendon at the time of the transference, but that had been so long ago that even the lore grew dim. Now, only distant perceptions of the Feyadeen, glimmers from across the void, hinted at what they would find. The troubled ones, the Raporoi—they who had brought the darkness—were gone now. But their children remained, their descendants, and the soul-darkness that emanated from them was intense.

None of the five in chord had ever tasted that darkness. They knew its nature from the old lore, but not its flavor or its power. How much would it hurt them? And how suddenly would it hit them? The chord was strong but terribly fragile. Could they, unaccustomed, contend with the thing that had driven their people away epochs before?

Shield yourself, my Nataea, Aaelefein wove into the song. Empathy is the striking path of the darkness. You above all are vulnerable.

Soft trills of shared concern ran around the chord and came back to him, brightened by Nataea's reassurance . . . and the sparkle of her love for him.

Quick bell-tones danced in the fabric, silver lyric

strong and stern. The Feya's eyes danced. Tend the chord and keep it strong. For now, the chord is all that matters. We must reach Caiendon. We must bring back a Corad shield. Concentrate.

A Corad shield. They didn't know what it might be, but they knew where it was. Somewhere on the planet that was their ancient ancestral home. They would seek it. They must find it. Haralan's blade had tasted Corad, and Winifraeda knew the skills of search. Sefraeonia might perceive its essence, or Nataea's empathy tell them where to look. Somewhere on old Caiendon—lost home world—was a thing . . . or a substance or blend, or a pattern of harmonics . . . that was bane to the Corad. Something that drove the life-drainer away.

The Feya suspected that the Corad was as old as the void itself, and some felt it was the soul of the void. It was a presence cold and deadly, and it had no song. Where it went it sought the living essences, and where it touched it left dead stone.

Without a shield, Nendacaida would die.

The thought pervaded, and a deep melancholy settled upon the chord. Aaelefein hastened to correct it, damping the minor strains and weaving bright notes among them. Nataea reacted instantly, lacing the new refrain with flecks of brilliance. Aaelefein squeezed her small, warm hand.

She was his own select, a lovely Cai girl in whose blood flowed traces of a kindred race. Lithe and high-breasted, with the compact stature and laughing dark eyes of Cai-kindred, she enthralled him. This special one, this Nataea, was as much a part of him as the sun of Nenda-caida. Their special harmony strengthened the chord and stilled its tremors. The mindsong carried true, the will of Aaelefein and the special empathy of Nataea enfolding it.

Even among a people for whom empathy was as natural as the tasting of resonances, hers was remarkable. It was thought by some that Nataea might be a leaper, one of those rare few with the power, in their last moment, to leap to a receptive host. Yet if so, Aaelefein realized, then her sacrifice in joining the chord was the greatest of all. The rest gambled only their lives. Only she was gambling immortality.

She sensed his concern—she always sensed everything about him—and pressed his hand. Star-notes dusted the fabric of the chord. Teasingly, Haralan stepped his steady rhythm to a momentary, erotic half-beat and the percept Sefraeonia giggled. Aaelefein steeled himself, overrode and steadied the chord. The cocoon of resonance brightened and coalesced as Winifraeda Feya reinforced her shield-harmonics. She was tired and intense and had no time for distraction. It was only by her concentration that they lived. Just beyond her willed resonance—only a hair from each of them—was the killing void. Aaelefein responded, raising the pitch.

The five who were one in chord flashed across emptiness, a tiny, bright flow of lyric resonance brilliant in darkness where dull stars crawled away in distance as they passed.

Distance meant nothing in chord, only duration. Still, the vastness of space had begun to tell on them by the time Aaelefein sensed approach. He tensed at the imminence of destination, and his urgency reflected around and around the chord. The soul-searing darkness of the old world was near. When would they feel it? What would happen then? Would it jar their harmony, even for an instant?

If so, Haralan thought, we die.

Winifraeda's diadem flared stern bell-tones. Concentrate! The harmonies tightened, quickened to a series of trills, seeking ahead.

With five times seven senses they saw it, looming to become a great ball in the vastness, a planet of full mantle with a single moon. It loomed and grew, and its sun became a coronet beyond its darkling disk.

On its night side were clusters of light and strange resonances. Above its sky, here and there, were objects in orbit, metal-sensed and lifeless yet with resonances of their own. The Cai perceived them and wondered what they were.

Reaching, searching senses knew the touch of tenuous atmosphere, the savor of seas and forests, of icecaps and tropics, of spiced vapors across broad plains. A longing took them. Here was the place of legend, lost home world, strange and alien now, but still alluring as no other could ever be.

I sense Cai harmonics, Sefraeonia thought, her percept skills at full. There and there, in hidden places . . . so very dim, but there. But the rest . . . strange . . . such strong essence. . . so troubled . . .

In response, Aaelefein felt Nataea's empathy open to receive. No, Nataea! His pulse was urgency. No! Shield yourself! . . .

Then it hit them, and Nataea screamed, battered by the savageness of it. The darkness rose up around them, and they knew, in undefended agony, what their race had fled.

The chord faltered, its harmonies shredded. Clutching her diadem, Winifraeda fought to maintain the shield of resonance. Beyond was still the void, and it could kill. Aaelefein felt her struggle but could not help. He was engaged in a struggle of his own. The senester rang powerfully in seven broad spectra of resonance as he strove to reestablish the chord. He overrode, pressed his will to its limits, and felt Haralan's continuity of rhythm supporting him, shaken by fear and an awful grief. A moment more, he commanded. One moment more of harmony . . .

The ancient skill of Winifraeda Feya was mortally tired, and for an instant there was a rend in the cocoon. Only for an instant. She willed harmonies to the diadem, and the rend was mended. But now there was a hole in the structure of resonances. There was no scintillation, no hint of brilliance. Among the spectra of struggling harmonics were no bright stars of overtone.

Aaelefein squeezed the small hand to his right. It was cold and did not respond. His driven control became a scream of rage and terror. He reached for Nataea with all his senses, willing her well, willing destination . . . now! The chord dissolved.

They tumbled in a jolting mass upon cool grass between peaks. Aaelefein lit on his back, and the bulk of Haralan thudded onto him and rolled away. Sefraeonia gasped with pain. Winifraeda Feya, deft on tiny feet, flailed for balance. They were no longer one. The chord was broken. They were on the world that once was old Caiendon, and its mortal darkness pressed hard about them.

With senses probing, Aaelefein roved them, touching them, and counted only three plus himself. He extended his senses, found a pitiful spark, and ran to it.

She lay by a tree, limp and broken, her pixie vitality only a memory. As he knelt to touch her, anguish welled in his almond-gold eyes and fell in heavy drops on her cold breast. With every sense, with every ounce of will, he searched for Nataea in the broken body in his arms, knowing, in that instant when the cocoon parted, she had had no shield.

He found a dim spark and clung to it, feeding it. Just for a moment it flared, and her great dark eyes opened and looked up at him. Her voice was as faint as expelled breath.

"My love, my Aaelefein. I will try. But you must find me."

Then the spark was gone. Aaelefein knelt beneath an alien tree, rocking in his grief, clutching the dead body of his beloved. Nataea the empath, scintillant pixie-girl of clan Reget of the Brightwaters, was gone.

2

The high sun of old Caiendon came and went and came again, and through it all the Cai knew the darkness. It clung to this lost world like a shroud. It permeated everything, a hard, dark substance of black despair, and their Cai empathies had little defense against it. It was a grief, a sorrow, a terrible loneliness that sang the soul of this old world. They could only endure it and suffer.

Through it all, Aaelefein sat broken by his grief, withdrawn. It was stolid Haralan who carried away the body that had been Nataea. He found a clearing in a grove where a trace of ancient resonance remained and gave the body to the soil. It would add to the little Cai-essence that clung to this remote place.

The others tried to reach out to Aaelefein, to comfort him, but they had to withdraw. His grief was too much like the awful soul-darkness that hung over this world. They could bear no more of it. Sefraeonia turned her senses inward, concentrating on the healing of her broken arm. On this world where her will was so damped, her senses so battered by all-pervading sorrow, it might take days to mend. Winifraeda paced and peered, casting about for a trace of hope, for a means to the impossible—a means to restore the broken chord. It seemed hopeless. A chord is five, or fives, but never only four.

And yet, now there were only four of them on this hostile world.

From a high place the Feya watched as evening descended over a valley below. Clusters of little lights winked on. She reached out her senses, then drew back, stung by the aching sorrow that emanated from them. Those, she knew, were the abodes of the people of this planet, children of the Raporoi of ancient times. It was from them that the darkness came.

What sort of people could they be? Her heart cried out for the misery of creatures whose awful loneliness could shroud a world in sorrow. She damped her empathy and turned away. She was still too weak to long endure it.

But she had tasted it now, the darkness of old Caiendon. She knew what it was. These people had come to sentience lacking the thing that made sentience endurable—the ability to share and to comfort. If they had any of that at all, she could not perceive it within the immersing, constant individual loneliness that made up the darkness. And the darkness was pain. The haunted aloneness of those people was intense, and the empathic Caians shared their pain. They could not help sharing it. To be Caian was to know.

Another day came and went. Haralan brought food from the forest where it was plentiful and water from a high spring where it was pure.

Sefraeonia concentrated on the healing of her arm. And Aaelefein Fe-Ruast, willmaster, singer of the senester and leader of the expedition, sat apart and remote, lost in a bleak world of his own. Winifraeda Feya relieved her own sadness by coating it with exasperation. When again the sun rose and Aaelefein had not moved, she brought water from the spring and threw it on him. The abused, hurt look he gave her was better than his silent grief.

"There is work to do," she told him. "We are here. Now we must find a Corad-bane for Nendacaida."

His sadness heavy on him, Aaelefein arose and stood over her, looking down at her ancient, tiny face. "Feya, it is no use. Whatever we might find, the chord is broken. Without five . . . without Nataea . . . we can never leave here. Nendacaida is doomed, and so are we." He looked at the alien ground beneath his feet, and his shoulders sagged. "Without Nataea . . ." He did not finish the thought. Without Nataea, nothing really mattered.

Winifraeda planted her hands on her hips. With eyes and mind she stung him. "If you grieve so, Aaelefein, how can you sit and do nothing? How can you ignore what Nataea asked of you in her last moment?"

"What she asked?" He stared dumbly at her. Then he understood. How had he forgotten? Had he been so lost that even his senses had departed? *Find me*, Nataea had whispered. *I will try. But you must find me.*

Winifraeda's lustrous eyes held him. "Yes. She tried to leap."

"But . . . here? To whom? Sefraeonia did not receive her, and who else could? She could not reach a male . . . or a Feya. Besides, we were all too close."

Still her eyes held him, her mind-song strong and intense. He wondered, as always, what such a mind might see. But what she suggested . . . how could it be possible?

"There is no one else here, Winifraeda," he pointed out.

"There is a world here, Aaelefein." She swept her

arms outward. "Out there, all over, there are intelligent creatures. Maybe only the children of Raporoi, but we are not certain of that. Once there were Cai-kindred on this world. Is it not possible, then, that there may yet be? Is it not possible that even one of the dark ones might have received her? Can you declare absolutely that our Nataea found no one . . . that she leaped to void?"

Aaelefein looked about him at this strange, old world and sensed its encumbering mind-darkness as a pervasive, numbing ache. He felt the Feya encouraging him, with, in the background, Haralan and Sefraeonia supporting. Such a forlorn hope she presented, that somewhere, in some lost corner, there might be a pixie descendant, who happened to be receptive at the moment Nataea died . . . who might now be, in part, his beloved. That Nataea's depth of empathy might have been so great that even on this soul-dark world she could have found such a one—a receptive female sentient with the empathy to receive a cast spirit.

Impossible, his mind told him. If the people of this world had empathy, there would be no such darkness. But could he be certain that all of them were so? He concentrated on the possibilities, so remote, and felt the support of Winifraeda and Sefraeonia, even of Haralan up at the spring. It is a hope, they assured him. It is the only hope we have.

Without Nataea there could be no chord, and no returning. Nor would there be other chords. Of all the Feyadeen, only Winifraeda had been able to grasp the ancient lore. Without Nataea . . . Grief washed over him again, dulling his senses.

"You have the senester," Winifraeda told him. "And you have the song. You must try, Aaelefein."

"I will try," he decided. "I will go among the people

of this world . . . if I can tolerate it . . . and learn how to begin. Then, if I can, I will go and search."

"Toward the rising sun," Winifraeda reminded him. "Those who have leaped have always cast in the direction of rotation, and the distances are similar. Fifty horizons."

"We don't know how such things would occur here . . . if they could occur at all."

"It is a place to start your search."

"I will go," he said. "I will try. The rest of you can begin here. Maybe you can discover what it is on this world that fends off the Corad."

Haralan came down from the spring, and they joined hands, the four of them, to sense the song of parting. Their desperation was a shared thing. They all knew how remote was the possibility that Aaelefein could find Nataea's spirit. And they all knew he might never return. But there was no other course to follow.

They blessed him with their harmonies. They wished him well. Then Aaelefein Fe-Ruast, leader of the first expedition to this world from another, set out to search for the tiny spark of scintillance that was the spirit of his lost love.

Behind him he heard Winifraeda's voice. "Put that water down, Haralan. And you, Sefraeonia, your arm is healed enough. You no longer need to sing to it. We have work to do."

* * * * *

The place where they had landed was high on a mountain, a cove where rock outcrops nestled a little valley rich in flora and deep with loam. Aaelefein's strong fingers clung to rock faces as he clambered down a cliff. From its base he descended a series of shelves in as many jumps, resonating momentum into the rock beneath his feet each time he landed, draining the shock of impact. It was not his best skill, this balancing of inertia through the harmonics of muscle and bone, absorbing impact and resonating it back into surfaces. Haralan was much better at such things; the sturdy Eldretten had a natural affinity for momentum and a mastery of inertia. But with the aid of the senester at his throat, sorting and amplifying his cast harmonics, Aaelefein could manage.

Finally the mountain sloped out in a long shoulder, and he began to run, each long stride covering distances on the downhill grade. He held his pace, absorbing and storing momentum against the rises, using it when he needed it. The inertia-balancing taxed him. He had to concentrate on it. A Caian who stored too much momentum and released it at the wrong moment could splatter himself . . . or run right into the ground. It was a dangerous practice for the unskilled.

But as he put the thrust of the mountain behind him, the task became simpler. On the last long, gentle downward slope he collected enough momentum to carry him far out onto the facing plain before the sun had set behind the peak.

He noticed creatures around him, placid dumb brutes and wild things, many of them mammalian like himself, and in great variety. Their existence was a surprise. On Nendacaida, only people were mammalian—Cai and all the kindred races. All other creatures were egg-layers or spore-bearers—just as the lore said had inhabited this world in very ancient times.

Yet here he saw feathered flying things as well, as on Nendacaida, and quick, small replicas of the reptiles and serpents that were familiar to him. He slowed enough to race a herd of prong-horned animals that shied away at first, then returned at his call to cavort around him for a time. Their innocent, presentient company was a slight relief from the constant, eroding darkness.

Then, as he drew nearer to the places of the children of the Raporoi, the darkness seemed to build. It grew more intense. It was not the darkness of night coming on. Aaelefein could see perfectly well in the absence of day-light. This other darkness was a weight on the soul, a feeling of grief so strong and so general that it dimmed the senses.

The old lore was hazy about the Raporoi, except that they had resembled Cai in physical ways. When Aaele-fein finally found his first human, he learned that the resemblance was uncanny. The creature walked along a road, peering into the night. It wore garments of woven fiber and carried a parcel. Undetected, Aaelefein fol-lowed the creature, studying it. It was a male of mature years, and it appeared startlingly Caian except for minor details. The hair on its head was too long, and the ends of the hairs had been cut. Its eyes and mouth were oddly straight-set, its nose slightly too protrudent—a face a Caian could have worn but not with any degree of pride. The planes of the face were flat . . . blocky. The ears were small and round, set slightly low. The creature was a hand-length shorter than Aaelefein, and heavier through the body.

Coming close, Aaelefein sensed the terrible . . . blind-ness of the creature. It had eyes, ears, a nose, taste, and touch that functioned in limited ranges, but that was all. It lacked any perception of the ranges between what its ears heard and what its eyes saw, or those beyond. And it had almost no empathy. It lived within itself, a prisoner in its own body, trapped and lonely in a working mind, unable to range beyond it.

This close to the creature, Aaelefein could separate the components of the awful darkness it generated, could analyze them. Fear was part of it, remorse and the pain of understood mortality. Greed and guilt, anger and loneliness vied and balanced, in a dance of torment. And shadowing it all was a hopeless longing, a blind drive to somehow be better, to be more. The turmoil of the thing's psyche was a tangle of fragile balances encased in a lonely shell.

Surprisingly though, there was more. Within the fiber Aaelefein sensed a humor as hard and quick as any he had known and strengths of determination that awed him. Sensing the strange, tragic creature, feeling its feelings, Aaelefein felt deep sadness for it. He understood now what had driven his own people's ancestors away.

But now there was work to do. He must learn the local forms of communication. He knew from the creature's sensory limitations the ranges of pulse in which to search. Empathy as tightly under control as he could manage, the willmaster reached for meanings and let himself be noticed.

The creature looked around, jerked, and stepped back. As it spoke, Aaelefein compared its intents to the sounds it uttered, the visual messages it gave.

"Where the hell did you come from?"

Aaelefein extrapolated from sense to meaning, meaning to sound, and learned the complex sounds, but lacked the vocabulary to respond.

"What's the idea, sneakin' up that way?" The human bristled, then peered closely at him. "Hey, what are you made up for, anyway? This some kind of a joke?" When the Caian did not respond, the human took another step backward. "Now look, buddy. I'm just goin' my own way, not hurtin' anybody. Hell, it's a free road, but if you're hopped up on somethin' you just back off, okay?"

Aaelefein tried the language. It was short on tonal variation but surprisingly complex within its narrow auditory range. "I'm just goin' my own way not hurtin' anybody," he mimicked.

The creature relaxed a bit. "Well now, that's better. Hey, how come you're dressed up like that? You an actor or somethin'?"

"Some kind of a joke," Aaelefein said.

"The hell you say." It looked around. "What kind?" When Aaelefein didn't answer, it peered at him again. "What's the matter? Why don't you talk to me?"

Excellent. Aaelefein was gaining key phrases. "Why don't you talk to me?" he encouraged and started walking. The creature hesitated, then came along with him.

"O-o-kay," it said. "I don't know what the hell this is all about, but I guess we're goin' the same direction. Tell you, though, you're not goin' to flag a lift lookin' like that, and if some eighteen-wheeler comes by, I'd appreciate it if you could just sort of fade while I get myself a ride. Okay?"

"Okay."

"I'm goin' on in to Clover," it said. "Where you goin'?"

"On in to Clover. I'm not goin' to flag any lift."

"Damn right you're not. That's what I said. You'll have a long walk, though. Things look close out in this country, but they're not. Lots of bare miles out here. You been here before?"

Aaelefein had not yet found the respondent negative. He said nothing.

"You sound like you're from California," the creature said. "That's where I'm from. California. I can always tell a 'Frisco native by the way he talks. 'Frisco, right?"

"Right."

"Me, too."

By the time lights of a large vehicle showed behind them, Aaelefein had a working knowledge of basic California. As requested, he "faded" before the truck pulled up and watched unnoticed as the creature flagged a ride.

By the time the trucker let them off in Clover—the creature riding inside and the Caian on top—Aaelefein had added to his California and picked up a good bit of Texas.

3

Margaret Mary Harrison awoke to a world of splendor so profound that it took several waking moments to realize that it was, more or less, the same old world she had awakened to each morning for the past thirty-one years. Yet in no way was it the same.

She pressed her eyes, then sat up and looked around, dazzled. It was her room—the room in her parents' house that had been hers since the breakup with John four years ago. The things around her were her own things. The morning streaming through her window was just a morning. But never in her life had she known such color, heard such music, felt so . . . exalted. Bright eyes wide with wonder, tremulous with confusion, she gasped and felt her heart racing. The worn bureau by the door seemed alive with subtle colors, a thousand shades of woodtone radiating from deep within its varnished oak. The mirror with its age-flecked edges was a wondrous, enticing thing, beckoning to other worlds beyond its crystal surface. Textured walls above their paneled fascia were no longer dead white. Myriad diffusions of pastel highlight tinted each peak and valley. The picture by the lamp—a dusty old Georgian thing she had salvaged from her marriage only because John wanted to keep it— suddenly was a riot of colors, a festival of tender shades

and subtle meanings. She felt she could become lost in
it.

Birds welcomed the morning, and she counted them.
A mockingbird sang his territorial prerogative . . . how
did she know that? She knew. The muffled chirps of
three sparrow fledglings still in the nest, and she read the
demand and the desperation in their tiny voices. Two
would live to fly away. . . .

She bit her lip. Stop it, she commanded herself. Just
stop this. Throwing back the covers (the quilt on top carried traces of scents long forgotten, a cedar chest, her
grandmother's sachet), she dashed to the bathroom and
turned on the water at the sink. Its flow-song was velvet
brilliance, infinite gradations of bell-like tones. Desperately she splashed the cold water over her face, noticing
even in her confusion that the tip of her tongue sampled
and dwelt on each of the hundred tiny tastes that make
up water. She splashed again and found herself count-
ing, through sensitive fingertips, the lashes of her eyes.
She was trembling. She looked in the mirror. The face
there was completely her own but as she had never seen it
before. She had never noticed those amber-to-rouge
highlights in her dark hair. Thirty-one years of mirrors
and none had ever shown her the variety of shadings in
her dark eyes, the fluid texture of irises, the dark depth
of pupils imaging herself. How had she never noticed
such things? They were so obvious.

Stop it! Stop it this minute, please!

Sudden fear as she thought the plea. My God, am I
dead? Am I a ghost? Is this what it's like? She whirled
and looked back through the bathroom door. Relief diz-
zied her. Her bed was empty. She had almost expected to
see herself . . . her body . . . lying there.

Back to the mirror. She peered into her reflected eyes.

There were radiances there. Drops of water hitting water was a minute lyric. From the wall lamp came a soothing sixty-cycle hum. Tile beneath her bare feet was cool and resilient. Everything was bright clarity. Her awareness stunned and frightened her. It was as though she had been born this morning.

Dread thoughts suddenly whirled through her mind. Had she suffered a stroke in the night? Was some terrible thing eating her brain cells? Had she somehow been drugged? But it didn't feel wrong, just . . . wondrously new, a revel of marvelous awareness with a hint of bitter-sweet longing at its roots.

Hesitantly she spoke to her reflection, noticing as she did the infinite qualities of her own soft voice. "Meg? Is this you? Are you . . . am I me? I . . ." She lowered her eyes, feeling suddenly ridiculous. "Damn it!" she shouted. "Stop it!"

As suddenly as she had found it, the intense awareness receded, seeming somehow startled and apologetic. She slumped, head down, leaning on the sink for support. She felt dazed . . . confused, disoriented. She breathed deeply several times, shaking her head. Avoiding her eyes in the mirror, she turned away, squaring her shoulders. Her awareness still seemed acutely vivid, but by comparison to a moment before, she seemed back to normal.

What in God's name, she asked herself, had happened to her? Nothing in her life had ever so shaken her as . . . as what? What had it been? Deep down, she knew that whatever it was remained, held somehow in check, and that she could let it return if she chose. She slipped into her old robe and went to sit on the edge of her bed.

"What happened to me?" she muttered. "It's as if I . . . but nothing 'happened.' I just woke up." She jerked upright. There had been a response. Something, some part of her, it seemed, had agreed. There was a faint tingling behind her forehead, just above her nose. The dread came again. A brain tumor? *No*, something assured her, *nothing dreadful at all*. There was a note of apology.

"For Christ's sake!" Margaret shouted. "What is this, a conversation? Who's talking to me?"

In the silence she heard her mother's distant voice. "Meg? Meg, are you all right?" When she didn't answer, there was the familiar creak of the third step. She hurried to her door and opened it.

"I'm all right, Mother. I'm just talking to myself. I'll be down in a few minutes."

"Oh. All right, dear. Breakfast is almost ready." The step creaked again.

She went to her window and opened it wide. Morning sun had cleared the top of the Fletcher house across the street. It spangled through the walnut tree. She felt its dancing radiances on her skin and was startled at the joy she felt. Hesitantly she unhooked the screen, leaned out, and peered upward. There it was, right up under the eave, a clumsy nest of twigs and straw. Deep sympathy welled in her for the hungry baby bird that would not survive. Biting her lip, fighting to retain her self-control, she closed the screen and hooked it.

She had dreamed, she told herself. She was still wrapped in the clinging wisps of a dream. That was all. It was a dream. But then, what was the dream? She tried to sort it out. Suddenly there was an image, a face. She willed and, obediently, the image came clear. A man's face, but . . . odd. A face she had never seen but seemed instantly to recognize in some way. A slightly triangular face—broad forehead, clean planes of cheek tapering to a strong, sensitive chin, wide-set slanting eyes the color of dark rose-gold, so gentle and so masculine that she felt her breathing go ragged. They looked at her, into her, knowing her. Arched brows and a wide, sensitive mouth with a trace of gentle smile . . . it was the strangest, most compelling face she had ever seen. With an effort of will she turned it off, wrenched herself from the image. It had left her feeling vibrant, with a delicious melting sensation.

"My God, Meg," she scolded herself, "you're as horny as a school girl."

Some unsuspected part of her, some tiny part, giggled. She would have sworn it. She suppressed it. How could she have dreamed such a face . . . such an unimaginable face? I wish I hadn't stopped painting, she thought. If I could paint him, I could sell him for a bundle. He's beautiful.

She was glad it was Saturday, a holiday weekend. She wasn't sure she was in any condition to cope with the mundane tribulations of a real estate office. Guiltily she realized she was glad Roy would be gone another week. She didn't want to have to cope with Roy today, either.

Oh, Roy, she thought, if only you had a face like that . . . eyes like that. She wasn't sure how much she loved Roy Holloway. She did love him, in a way. She probably would marry him one day, but not for a while yet. One day she would feel better about her failure with John . . . better about herself in general. Roy would wait. In his way he understood. Four years seemed a long time to pull oneself together, but she was getting there. Roy had been alone just a year now. They had started seeing each other after his wife was killed. They could wait a while longer.

She folded her robe, took off her nightshirt—one of

John's old shirts which came to her knees—and looked at herself again in the mirror. The woman she saw there was trim and compact, the right curves in the right places and all slightly exaggerated by the fact that she had to stretch to reach five feet tall. She thought of herself as an average-sized person despite that.

They said she was the image of her great-grandmother on the O'Toole side, a tiny, feisty woman who had lived to be ninety-seven. Well, she thought now, if that's true, then you weren't so bad, old Maude. The mirror showed her a round, pretty face, high breasts, flat stomach, a small, resilient frame that had never failed to catch its share of attention from the male population. She knew she was still seeing with a heightened awareness, but she nodded, satisfied. Not bad, Meg old girl. Again that tiny, unsuspected presence radiated agreement, and she blinked and shook her head.

Henry O'Toole was at the table letting his cereal soak while he read the comic strips. Hazel was finishing the bacon. Margaret looked at her parents and realized with unusual intensity just how deeply she loved them. Her heart reached out to them, cherishing, and suddenly she recoiled. Her eyes went wide. She had . . . tasted them, somehow, these people she loved. In that instant she had known her parents as never before, and the suffering was there along with the joy. She had *tasted* them, and they were bittersweet. Again she felt the vague tingling behind her brow.

She set down her half-poured coffee. "Mother, I don't want to eat right now. Save mine, and I'll have it later." She walked through the living room and out the front door. She felt choked. She felt as though she wanted to cry, and she needed to be outside.

She walked, soaking up the morning, letting it sing to

her. Turning at the library, she hesitated. Judy Garvey
was coming toward her.

"Oh, no," she muttered to herself. "Not now. No
soap-commerical conversation this morning. Don't let
her notice me."

Margaret knew that the thought was silly. At this hour,
they were the only people on the sidewalk walking
toward each other. But she felt again that tiny tingling
behind her brow. As Judy approached, there was no sign
of recognition. They passed. Margaret turned, puzzled,
and watched the woman go on her way. Then the enormity of it came.

"Good Lord in Heaven," she said aloud. "She *didn't*
notice me."

But that was ridiculous. How could she not have? . . . I
did something, she told herself. I wished she wouldn't
notice me, and then I did something. What was it?

All she could remember was . . . a shift of the eyes, a
shunting away, just at the instant when Judy became
aware of her presence. A blink, and a shift of the eyes,
redirecting line of sight . . . redirecting attention.

And Judy had passed by as though Meg were invisible.

Again Meg felt the tingling, just behind her forehead,
and a sort of apologetic query—not a question, simply a
feeling. *It was all right, wasn't it? It was what you . . .
you? . . . it was what I wanted. Wasn't it?*

Puzzlement that bordered on panic tore at her. What
has happened to me? she asked herself. What is it? Tentatively she loosened the clamp-hold on her senses. The
bright world gloried around her, nuances of color and
texture caressing her, light that was more than light,
shadow that was more than shadow. Tones on the
breeze, dimly heard, brightened and became a singing
radiance of sound. Blossoms whispered to her, a tapestry

of scent-range that bordered on sight and sound. Sunlight in her hair murmured signals of pleasure.

What is happening to me? She wanted to scream the question aloud, but even as it formed itself there was that response again, assurance from within.

Nothing terrible has happened. Maybe something wonderful, but nothing bad. Don't be frightened. And the last was a plea. Fear hurt . . . something . . . in her. Fear punished. There was no need to fear.

She wished away the brilliance, and it receded obediently.

That shifting of the eyes, to pass unnoticed . . . it was a visible signal, but the response had been astounding. Judy Garvey hadn't ignored her. It wasn't like that. Judy had literally not known that she was there. She explored the idea, needing to focus on just one phenomenon. A shifting of the eyes, redirecting . . . but at exactly the right instant.

How did I know when to do that? Even if I had known how, how did I know when?

It was when she started to be aware of me, just before she was.

But how could I know that?

The response that formed then was puzzled. How could I not know? She was there. How could I not have known her perceptions?

Meg shook her head, so confused that she felt dazed. As she moved past the post office, she saw Tom Gentry and Hap Hastings standing in front of Hastings' restaurant, chatting. Hastings would be opening his doors soon to get ready for the afternoon trade. Meg hesitated, then approached them. Both were facing away. As she drew near, they turned, and she let her senses guide her as she did the eye-shift thing again. The men turned, looked past her, and turned away again.

Neither of them had noticed that she was there. She passed them and went on, unseen.

What was Hap Hastings worried about? Something to do with his son . . . She had an image of Corky Hastings, an impression of a classroom, a feeling of dread . . . failure . . . twice . . . Corky had failed two summer-school courses. His father had just learned of it.

How do I know that?

How? The man is standing there, and I passed within a foot of him. How could I not know?

Meg returned home when the sun was high. Ravenous, she finished the remains of breakfast, assembled a sandwich, and went out to the sunporch. Hazel was at the pantry, looking for insecticide.

"It's at the back of the second shelf," Margaret said. "Behind the bleach."

Hazel glanced at her, puzzled, then retrieved the insecticide. "How did you know what I was looking for?"

"The same way I knew where it was, Mother." Her mother, walking back to the kitchen, did not respond.

Meg sat on the quilted daybed. As far back as she could remember, the porch had been her favorite place—sunny in the morning, breezy cool in the afternoon, cozy and shuttered in winter. Tentatively, she eased the restraints on her new perception—just a bit—and savored the fantastic riot of colors, sounds, scents, and textures about her. She drank it in, then subdued it and found she missed it. It was as though the world had gone from color to dull shades of gray. She tried it again, and subdued it again. She was getting the hang of it—whatever *it* was.

Hazel came from the kitchen. "Meg, are you feeling

all right?" she asked, noting an odd expression on her daughter's face.

"I feel fine, Mother." Strange, she thought, how true that was. She couldn't remember ever feeling better.

"Well, you looked sort of . . . distracted, I guess. No problems?"

Problems? Without warning, her world had suddenly introduced itself to living color and stereophonic orchestration, but was it a problem? She didn't know what it was. She needed time to explore it, to think about it. Hazel was worried—the sense of her worry came sharply to Meg.

"No problems," she assured her mother, aware of an overtone in her voice that soothed and reassured. "I was just thinking."

"Oh," Hazel turned away, her worry gone. "By the way, I don't suppose you know where the—"

"Upstairs by the bathroom sink. Dad left it there when he fixed the faucet."

"Your father never puts anything away," Hazel fussed. Then she stopped and turned curious eyes on her daughter. "Meg, what are you doing, reading my mind?"

"No." There was no banter in the response, though she knew her mother's question was rhetorical. "I can't do that. I don't know what you're thinking. But I do know what you want when you want it, and how you feel. . . . Why didn't you tell me your back was bothering you again?"

They stared at each other. Suddenly, desperately, Meg wanted to talk with her mother, to explain . . . but explain what? She didn't know what had happened to her. How could she explain anything? Nothing she could say would do more than make her mother worry.

On impulse, she blinked and shifted her eyes, the

thing she had done before, but Hazel was still looking at her. *It doesn't work if a person is concentrating on you,* she explained to herself. Overwhelmed, she wouldn't let herself dwell on how she knew that.

"It's all right, Mother," she said. "I'm just doing some soul-searching, but everything is fine."

4

For a time Aaelefein remained hidden, watching the people who were visible on the night-dark streets of the little town. There were only a few, and as time passed he noticed a perceptible lessening of the pressing soul-darkness of the place. Cautiously he reached out, probing here and there with his senses, seeking out first one human and then another, testing their emanations.

Most of them were asleep. In sleep their awareness of their loneliness diminished, and so the weight of darkness was less. He roved among the places where the people slept, sampling them, learning more about them. This close among them he did not use the senester. It was not needed. The resonances of the people around him pressed him from all sides, so many that it was difficult to sort them out. He had an impression that, in sleep, their minds created worlds unlike the world of reality. In some of those worlds they were less alone, and in some more so, but much of the dream-sense that came to him focused on aloneness. He probed here and there for deeper meanings, wanting to understand them.

He probed . . . then withdrew abruptly, startled. Response resonance had met his. One of them had felt his probe and answered. He crouched in shadows and tried it again, warily. The person was asleep, but dreaming, had felt his resonance and reacted to it. The person seemed to welcome him.

Carefully, avoiding the range of resonance that had brought response, he searched out that one. It was a cub. A child. And in its sleeping mind he found empathy. Not strong or developed, as in a Caian, but it was empathy nonetheless.

An animal came stiff-legged, ready to challenge him. With quick, high trills he found its perceptive range and soothed it. It came to him and wagged its tail, and he marveled at it. Approximately the size of a woodnymph, the creature was mammalian, quadruped, carnivorous, and of about the order of intelligence of a sprite. Its essence bore overtones of friendliness, loyalty, and tenacity, and it wanted its ears scratched. It licked his hand and communicated acceptance in a broad range of harmonics both above and below the apparent auditory ranges of the people with whom it cohabited.

For a time the animal followed him as he scouted the town, and he was pleased at the company. But then another smaller and slightly different creature crossed its path. Giving a yelp of delight, the quadruped left him to chase and threaten it, its resonance combining frolic and inherent ferocity.

Wheeled things, metal-cased, stood here and there, vehicles like the "eighteen-wheeler" on which he had ridden, but smaller, a variety of sizes and shapes. One of them, resting at the side of a dark street, he investigated. He studied it from all sides, above and below, then deciphered its door and studied it from inside. Much of what he found had obvious function, but he found no clue as to how or why it worked. He was driven from it when another vehicle rounded a corner, almost catching him in its headlights. The two creatures inside this one were male, alert and suspicious. Their essence radiated darkly.

He walked a well-lit street where most of the structures had large sheets of clear crystal emplaced in their faces and stopped at one that had garments displayed inside. If he were going to walk among these people, he decided, he should be garbed like them. It would be best not to be noticed.

The structure had a portal with a metal lock. He stood before it, resonating up and down the electromagnetic spectrum, close-focusing his song upon the locking device until its bolt clicked back and he could open it. Once inside he explored the enclosure and its contents, fingering fabrics, tasting their content, awed at the variety of weave and texture achieved by a people who lacked the harmonics even to draw flosses from the vapors or to grow crystal devices pitched to their own resonances. Sensing their limitations, he was puzzled by the magics they achieved despite them.

I have much to learn of these people, he told himself.

Various artificial replicas of the forms of males of their breed stood here and there, fitted out in garments. By studying these he learned the uses of various garments, then outfitted himself with one full set of clothing and put it on. It was terribly uncomfortable, stiff and constraining, but a reflecting crystal on a wall assured him that in these garments he might pass relatively unnoticed among the creatures on this world.

Through the front crystal pane, he spotted the same moving vehicle he had seen before. It stopped in the street before the building, and its occupants emerged, resonating intent. He stood in shadows among racks hung with garments and studied the beings. There was distinct menace about them. Staying two strides apart, hands hovering at dark objects on their hips, they

approached the enclosure. One shined a light through
the crystal, flicking about the interior, while the other
tested the portal and opened it. Then they were both
inside with him, and their darkness pressed painfully
upon him.

At a table near the door, Aaelefein found a stack of
fabric containers with strap handles. He took one to carry
his Caian garb in. Methodically, the two men moved
through the enclosure, pointing their lights and searching. When they had both moved away from the portal,
he stepped out and closed it behind him, resonating its
lock back into positive mode.

Their vehicle stood in the street, alive, singing a mindless harmony of machine sounds, and he was tempted to
explore it, but he did not have time.

Some distance away, the creature with the wagging tail
found him again and padded along at his heels, panting
happily. Its companion of a time ago, the animal let him
know, had climbed a tree and refused to come down and
play.

Singing to it as he walked, holding the harmonics to
the animal's auditory range, he learned several combina-
tions of sounds in the human vocal range to which it
responded readily, and he puzzled over these, wondering what they meant. Most of them had no real meaning
to the creature. They were only codes to which it
responded by rote. They included "damdog," "scat,"
"attaboy," and "getoffth'couch." But there was one
combination that had great meaning to the animal. He
voiced it, testing, and the creature's joy was absolute. Its
name was Hobo.

For a long time it stayed with him, helping him to
explore, showing him alleys and hideholes, trashbins
and safe paths through vacant lots, and warning off oth-

ers of its kind who offered to join them.

Hobo left him, finally, when the moon was high and the town was very still. The creature emanated apology, but there was a place where it was supposed to be now, and its duty was clear. It invited him to come with it and promised him comfort and security, a soft place to sleep and food in a dish, and creatures who undoubtedly would scratch his ears and adopt him.

Then, sad at his refusal, the animal turned away and headed for home. Aaelefein felt the weight of loneliness upon him all the more for its departure.

On the roof of a tall building, above the worst of the horizontal resonances of the street, Aaelefein sat and watched the sky lighten in the east and wondered whether the Feya might have been right. Could Nataea have leaped? Even on Nendacaida, where anyone would welcome and absorb a cast spirit, the leaping was extremely rare, a feat achieved by only the most brilliant of empaths under the best of conditions in a receptive world. Was it possible that Nataea had somehow achieved it? Here on this soul-dark world where blindness reigned and the harmonies were songs of mourning, could she have found even one soul to shelter her precious tiny spirit in its final, faltering moment?

Nataea. Softly, he sang the name, voicing its full harmonic range, and the dull atmospheres of a sad world shimmered momentarily, quickened by the beauty of it.

He slept then, the brief, healing rest of the Cai, and awoke to a bright morning dulled and haunted by the intense dark resonances of thousands of people no longer asleep.

The intensity of their darkness stunned him, and he damped his senses to tight small ranges, shutting out as much of it as he could. How could they survive? he wondered. How could such a race have come to be, that had such fullness of the mind and such blindness of the senses? How could they exist, each locked forever within itself, alone and longing, yet incapable of rapport? What sort of insane world would produce such a race?

Still, he reminded himself, it was the same world that had, so long ago, produced the Cai. This very same planet had once gloried in the singing radiance of harmonic rhapsody and brought forth a people who could sing with it. These who now were old Caiendon's people had no song . . . and yet within the dark emanations of them there was something that called to him. Beneath the pall of distress that beat at him, the intense, agonizing loneliness that punished his senses and made him mourn for them, he found there was much more.

Even in their appalling darkness, these were creatures of keen intelligence—vigorous minds always seeking the unknown, searching for ways around their blindness. They were a strong race, strong in ways strange to the Caian. They could be violent, he sensed. They could be hostile and deadly if aroused. He had sensed that from the pair of males who searched for him in the place of garments. And still, beyond it all, he found in their resonances a capacity for love.

Perched on his rooftop, unnoticed, Aaelefein studied the waking town below and found himself, suddenly, to be deeply attracted to these odd creatures. It was an attraction that shook him, seeming to come from elemental realms of himself that he had never explored.

I have, he told himself, a great deal to learn.

Cautiously, then, he loosed the clamps on his wide-ranging senses, steeling himself against the pain of perception of massed, myriad alonenesses. With large-orbed eyes that saw ranges of spectrum beyond

human sight, he watched the creatures passing below
and marveled at them. Tapered ears attuned to frequencies both lower and higher than human hearing, he listened to their voices, the pulsing of their hearts, the
working of their bodies, and the subtle overtones of their
vocal projection, some of which influenced them
although they could not hear them. And with vast, aching parsing-sense, spanning the ranges of harmonics
between sight and sound—those ranges in which they
emanated all their hopes and griefs, their response to
beauty and their terrible, blind longings—he scanned
them and experienced a grief greater than theirs. Few
among them had any receptivity at all in those ranges,
and those who did were only vaguely aware. So, in those
ranges that spoke of longings and sought understanding, the resonances that were the stuff of empathy, they
cried out in their blindness and never knew that they
called.

Aaelefein knew, and their mute torment wrenched at
his throat and brought tears to his eyes.

It would be worse, he knew, when he went among
them . . . when he touched them. Then he would have
to deal with the infrasonics and would know the full
power of their darkness.

He steeled himself and concentrated on his task,
pushing to its limits the steadfast will that made him
leader of the chord. He must accustom himself to associ-
ation with the tragic people of this world. He must transcend the darkness or learn to tolerate it. He must go
among them then and learn their ways. Only by knowing them could he know the limits of their tolerance,
and only then could he unleash the power of the senester
and go in search of the spirit of Nataea.

He had to believe the improbable—that she had

found a receptive sentient and made her leap. He *must* believe it. He must cling to that belief, because without it, there was nothing. Without Nataea the chord was doomed, and without the chord Caidom was doomed.

And—the realization haunted him—without Nataea, he wasn't sure whether he cared.

He put the thought away and concentrated on believing.

In the bright sky above him, a bird dipped low and chirped its song, crystal-drops of resonance heralding the morning. On impulse he spoke to it, trilling a quick code of tones in its range, hearing it absorb them into its own song. Possibly, as with the feathered creatures of Nendacaida, it might pass the code along to others, a hint of Caiansong in birdcall that might reach the Feya and the others and let them know that he was well.

In the distance, he heard the bird trill again, its song imbued with hints of Caiansong, and he heard another bird mimic the sparkling tiny tones of it.

It wasn't just the people here who sang darkness, he realized. The world itself, the very essence of it, was their resonance. The people and the planet were in concert, and their essences fed back and forth, reinforcing the strange, dark harmonies of the living mantle.

What would happen, he wondered, if the music of Caidom could somehow be reintroduced here? If these tight, angry harmonics could be rewoven, expanded, overlaid with the rich singing resonances of Caidom . . . How could there be darkness among infinite glories?

But it was a thought without substance. Such a thing could never be possible. Caidom had once, on Nendacaida, imbued a world with its essence, but that had taken millennia to accomplish, and there they had started with a silent, unresonated orb. To induce resonant lyric into the very mantle of a world that already had its own harmonic weave . . . such a thing was beyond possibility. An entire resonant world . . . no lore of Caidom, not even the mighty power of the senester at its broadest range, could ever override more than the smallest fraction of it.

Haunted by longing, battered by darkness, Aaelefein Fe-Ruast concentrated on the people passing below, learning them, preparing himself to go among them.

5

Margaret dreamed of dazzling colors and heavenly music and woke again to splendors that diminished promptly when she willed them to. The rioting colors faded and stabilized, the eldritch harmonies muted, and she closed her eyes again and stretched luxuriously. She had apparently overslept. She had that rested, muddled, and slightly guilty feeling that always came from sleeping longer than her usual seven hours. A delicious feeling, actually, though disorienting.

She tried to remember her dreams but could put not form to them. They seemed odd, though . . . as though she had not been alone in them. Her throat ached slightly, and her scalp had a warm, tingly feeling. Yet even as she noticed these, they also diminished, and she had the feeling again that someone had just apologized to her, though there had been no words.

All these things registered vaguely, sleepily . . . then she remembered and came instantly awake. All the meaningless, frightening, wondrous, and unique experiences of yesterday came flooding back, and her eyes opened wide. She lay staring at the ceiling, her mind racing. Yes, it was real. It had happened, whatever it was. Almost afraid to breathe, she wondered whether it was gone. Was it still with her . . . that expanding of the senses, that feeling of being visited by something other than herself?

Did she want to find out?

She let the question hang before her, puzzling at it as her eyes puzzled at the patterns of color on her ceiling— a funny, not quite symmetrical checkerboard pattern of dim pastels, large rectangles of deep lavender bordered by wide lines of violet. She traced the patterns with her eyes and felt a creeping dread. Her ceiling had no such colors. There was only plain white latex paint.

She sat up and looked around, her eyes widening even more. The wall across from her bed was the same color as the ceiling, except that the pattern was vertical stripes. Below it, the fascia panel glowed a rich vermillion with darker shadows in it suggesting a continuation of the violet stripes above. The worn old bureau was various shadings of mauve, purple, and blue. The mirror was deep blue, darkly reflecting the wall above and behind her. The picture by the lamp was a blank canvas of deep purple within a shimmering violet frame.

My God . . . The words echoed in the stunned silence of her mind. My God.

The bed where she lay was shades of deep purple, except where she was. Around her, outlining her, was an aura of rose tint increasing to bright magenta. She threw back the covers abruptly. Her legs glowed warmly, even through the fabric of her nightshirt. In panic, she rolled from the bed and stood, then caught her breath when she saw herself in the mirror. She glowed, brighter by far than the other light in the room. She seemed to light up the surfaces around her with bright magenta highlights. She was alight! She shone with an unearthly pink radiance, a neon person standing in a purple-pastel room.

This time she screamed it aloud. "Oh, my God!" She

whirled to the window, aware of sounds elsewhere in the house, keenly aware of sounds outside, aware of something—some surprised-tasting something inside herself, seemingly trying to calm and soothe her.

It was the same outside—blue trees and deep blue lawns, houses glowing dimly in various shades of lavender and lilac, a pink bird flitting in a sky of midnight blue, the Fletcher's dog at its purple gate across the street, looking toward her window . . . and shining with a magenta glow.

She heard/sensed her father hurrying across the hall, heard her door open, turned and saw him shining there, another neon person, squinting into the room and reaching for her light switch.

It clicked. Abruptly the room and everything in it returned to normal—or nearly so. Still there were the strange colors, the sense of glowing, but now they were just faint highlights adding luster to plain white walls.

Henry, blinking away sleep from concerned eyes, stared at her. His sleepy, questioning presence was an aura that she could taste.

"Meg? What's the matter, honey? What happened?"

She sensed her mother in the hall behind him, hurrying. Across the street the Fletcher's dog began to bark, and she felt that she could almost understand what it was saying.

"I . . . I don't know," she said softly. "It was like . . . like . . ."

Hazel was there then, at Henry's shoulder. "Meg? What's the matter? You screamed."

It's all right, something inside assured. *Forgive me, but there is nothing wrong.*

"It's all right," Meg mumbled, dazed. "I don't know what it was . . . something I . . ."

"Are you ill, dear?" Hazel's concern, like Henry's, had a sharp taste.

They came to her as when she was a child, she realized suddenly, wondering and reassuring, a whirl of parental response. She hadn't noticed the reaction in years, but it was there.

"Did you have a bad dream, honey?" Henry asked. Hazel's hand touched her forehead, then withdrew abruptly as though she had felt a shock. Her eyes widened and Meg felt her fright like a blow. Behind her forehead was that familiar tingling.

"I'll bet you had a nightmare," Henry reassured her, glancing at the bedside clock. Meg looked, too, and was surprised to see that it was just past two in the morning.

Hazel was staring at her, rubbing her hand where it had touched her. Again she reached, and Meg clamped down tight on the sensations within her. Deep down, something agreed and responded and the lusters dimmed. Hazel's hand on her forehead was warm, and even through the tight restraints Meg felt . . . or tasted, somehow . . . strangeness in her concern . . . a puzzlement.

"I guess that was it," she told them. "I had a bad dream."

"Yeah, I thought maybe you did," Henry agreed. But there was a sudden, quick curiosity in his eyes, and his presence tasted of abrupt intuition. "Uh, do you want to talk about it?" he asked. "The dream, I mean . . . or anything?"

Something in her wanted to respond to his intuition, but there were no words.

"I thought it was morning," she said lamely.

That faint tingling then, seeping through, and Hazel's concerned hand withdrew from her forehead again, as though shocked. "Henry," she said, wide-eyed, "feel her head."

"Do you have a fever, honey?" He raised his hand and touched her, jerked away, then slowly touched her again. His eyes narrowed, studying her, his lips pursed in thought. But to Hazel he said only "Static electricity, hon. It's been dry. But she doesn't have a temperature."

"I'm fine," Meg assured them. "I simply had a bad dream. Everything's fine. Honest." She felt a fullness in her throat and sensed . . . something . . . adding overtones of reassurance to her voice. Her parents' love was a tangible aura, touching her, and hers for them was a wash of calming reassurance that somehow went out to them. She was aware of calming them. Inside, something reacted with tiny elation. *Well done*, a voice seemed to say. *You learn quickly.*

"Go back to bed," she told them. "For Heaven's sake, it's two in the morning."

Even after they had returned to their room, she could hear the murmur of their voices. Odd, she thought, how acute her senses had become. She had never heard so well before.

Thoughts flowed in her mind, random segments that had no words, only snatches of meaning. Sensory limitations . . . some extendable . . . (something) latent, adjust (something else) . . . harmonics . . . wider spectra . . . The words were her own, but they fit the thoughts somehow.

What is happening to me? On impulse she crossed to the switch and turned off the room light. Instantly, the eerie colors returned. She glowed in the dark, bright shades of pink. Everything glowed. She went to the window and looked out. Despite the fear that shrouded her—fear of an unknown so bizarre that there were no explanations—despite all that, she was enthralled at the beauty of it. A glowing, iridescent pastel world of blues and purples and hot pinks. Night shades such as had never been seen . . . no, she—or something—corrected herself, such as *I* have not seen.

Below on the lawn, movement caught her eye. Confused and fascinated, she watched a pair of neon-bright cats night-stalking beneath the dark purple foliage of a lilac hedge, their footprints tiny trails of violet that faded behind them on deep blue grass.

Her eyes began to ache, and she thought—oddly— please, not so fast! I'm only human.

Why did I think that? She caught herself. What a strange idea.

A wisp of memory tugged at her, and she groped for it and found it. Pictures in a magazine, an article on home insulation, infrared pictures of heat escape. She looked at her walls and ceiling. The stripes might be studs behind sheetrock, the ceiling patterns those of beams and joists.

I'm seeing in the infrared, she told herself. Or else I'm imagining that I am.

In the bathroom she turned the hot tap. Purple water spun in an indigo basin, and she watched it—again noting the lyric bell-tones of its music as it flowed. Moments passed, and the color of the water began to change. Blue-violet to dark lavender to violet to magenta, brightening and glowing. The indigo basin also began to change, purple radiance creeping up its sides. When the water was crimson bright and she felt the heat of it radiating, she turned off the tap.

That's exactly what I'm doing, she explained to herself, slowly, trying to make sense of it. I am seeing colors in the infrared spectrum. People can't see infrared. But that *is* what I'm doing.

Her eyes ached and again the vagrant thought: Don't push me too far. I'm only human. A command, as though to someone else. Obediently, the brightnesses dimmed, but still she could see. In a dark room in the dark of night, she could see.

Within her was a sense of . . . something . . . wishing her well and laboring to give her a precious gift.

Four hours of sleep had left her fully rested, alert and wide awake. She put on her robe and went downstairs, avoiding the squeaking third tread, aware of the sleep to which her parents had returned.

She went outside, and the night stillness was a song of perceived resonances, a concert of sounds, scents, and colors that bathed her in radiance. She sat on the front porch steps, deep in thought, trying to find a logical explanation for the events of the last day.

One of the neon cats came shining from the dark lilac hedge, and on impulse she called to it, a strange, soft crooning at the edge of hearing. The cat looked toward her, alert, then bounded across the glowing blue lawn to rub against her. She stroked it, enchanted by the unrestrained pleasure it emanated. The creature looked up at her, cat eyes wide-pupilled from dim light, and she wondered what it saw with those lustrous eyes. Did it see what she was seeing now?

The eyes were large, oval, subtly slanted. They reminded her of the dream face, and immediately his image came to mind, vital and clear-focused: broad, rounded brows, slope of cheeks, upturned V-shaped mouth, and those almond-gold eyes looking at her . . . seeing her and knowing her with a gentle, certain knowledge that made her want to cry. It was more than just dream recall, that face. It was as though the image was presented to her, held there by someone else and presented for her to see.

For a moment she permitted the glories again and reveled in the beauties of a world come brilliantly alive. But she felt she could drown in it, so she tightened the clamps again.

Despite that, something in her—that otherness that seemed to be there, sharing her mind and body—seemed gratified that she had allowed a moment of it.

What is happening to me? The question was a constant, underlying thought. And with it was a constant response: *Nothing dreadful. Strange, yes, but not dreadful at all.*

And gratitude. A feeling of gratitude, as of someone else giving thanks to her, profoundly and sincerely.

For hours she sat on the steps, deep in thought, aware of far more than a human being could be aware of, frightened yet repeatedly soothed by those awarenesses that were part of her. She tried to understand, and the tiny otherness within her tried to help her understand, but there were neither words nor concepts for it.

More and more, she was certain that it *was* an otherness . . . almost like another person there, part of her but very different and separate. Thoughts came, and she followed them, trying to find slots for them in the world as she knew it. Few of these thoughts produced anything but confusion.

She found a trick, though, that seemed to produce a sort of dialogue. She relaxed and let questions float in her mind—simple questions, yes or no, agree or disagree—and the otherness responded (or she imagined that it did) with feelings of positive or negative.

Are you something other than me? *Positive.* Are you a ghost? *Puzzlement, no concept.* Are you alive? *Positive.*

Are you me? *Uncertainty.* But you are someone else? *Positive.* Am I going crazy? *Negative.* Am I imagining all this? *Tentative negative.* If so, I am imagining this part, too. Why are you with me? *No clear response, feeling of great sadness, of loss.* Did you die? *Positive.* But you're still alive? *Positive.*

Her thoughts went around and around.

Are you changing me? *Positive.* Can I make you stop? *Positive . . . hint of pleading.* Can I be rid of you? *Hesitant positive, bittersweet . . .* then a thought with words, sudden, desperate, and pleading: *Please let me stay. He needs me—they need me.*

And again the vision of the face—that beautiful, exotic, almost unearthly face of her dream.

Oh God, she moaned inwardly, exasperated, I think I'm going mad. I'm talking to myself in my mind, and I don't even understand my answers. What's happening to me?

Wait, the tiny thereness pleaded. *Wait. We can be closer. You will know more. It is very hard . . . we are so different, yet alike. Please wait. Let me stay.*

As dawn tinted the sky and the nightcolors receded before other hues that Margaret had never seen before, Henry O'Toole came out and sat beside his daughter. He gently touched a hand to her forehead . . . only for a moment, then he looked at her with eyes full of wonder. "What is it, Meg? What is *that*?"

"I don't know," she said. "Something has happened."

"Can you tell me about it?"

She shook her head. "I don't know what it is."

As though to assist her, the otherness in her found a word and presented it. A word, it seemed, that had to do with how she and . . . it . . . were alike. Meg blinked, confused. *You?* she asked in her mind.

Yes, partly, the thought said. *And you. And him, too.*

Him . . . my father?

Yes.

The word hung there, wanting her to consider it. The word was "pixie."

Henry was looking at her, concerned. "Is it something you can handle, Meggy?"

"People say I'm like Grandmother Maude," she said suddenly, slowly.

"Your great-grandmother? Yes, I suppose you are. You look like old pictures of her."

"Are you like her, too?"

He shrugged. "People always told me I was. I don't know. She liked music, and the deep woods, and laughter, and birdsong, and bright colors. She loved to dance, and she loved her family, and she couldn't stand liars and cheats. I can think of worse people to be like."

Meg sat in silence for a time, then turned to him. "Dad, what does the word 'pixie' mean to you?"

He paused, then chuckled. "I don't know, but it's probably a good description of your great-grandmother . . . and of you, too, for that matter. Why? Does this have something to do with what's on your mind?"

"I don't know. But it seems as though it might."

6

Soothed and comforted in a way she didn't understand, still deeply puzzled but with her anxieties lulled by a sense of well-being, Hazel had slept. Through the hours of the night, Margaret was aware of her mother's rest, glad that it was so. She knew the depths of Hazel's concern for her. Somehow it seemed she had tasted/heard each anxious nuance of it. She had wanted to explain. But explain what? She didn't know what was happening, only that it was unique and that she herself needed some answers soon.

She sensed the same concern from her father, but with Henry it was different. More than ever before, with her puzzling newfound perceptions, she realized how different her parents were . . . and the marvelous way their differences blended to make a complete couple.

She had always known this of them, but never so intensely. Her father's patience, his wit that seemed always to encourage but never to harm, his sense of enduring devotion to those he loved, these things now showed themselves to her as deep strengths. Henry didn't have to understand a thing to accept it. All he required was assurance that there was no harm in it.

But Hazel was the opposite. Not knowing made her fret, and the more she questioned the more she saw a puzzle as being somehow ominous. Hazel required explanations; it was her nature.

So different, yet so alike in their difference. They cared about her, and the taste of their concern had a familiar flavor.

Familiar sound? Feel? As Margaret stood on the walk, bathing in the unearthly radiance of another unexplainable morning, she frowned at the inadequacy of terms. How to describe the things she was seeing . . . hearing . . . sensing? How to describe them, even to herself? There were no words.

Hazel and Henry—they were like the clear voices of two dissimilar instruments blended in perfect harmony . . . like air and water that meet and meld and between them form a mist of rainbow hues.

What could she tell them? That someone was talking to her in her head and showing her fantastic things she had never seen before? How could they accept such a notion? How could *she* accept it? Yet, for the moment, she did, because it was so lovely in so many ways . . . and because—so far—there hadn't been the slightest hint of threat or jeopardy.

No harm, the sensed presence seemed to say. *Never harm, only what I can give to you.*

She felt that the presence wanted to make everything clear to her, but didn't know how because she didn't know how to understand.

But I have to tell them something, she chided herself. They have eyes. They can tell that something has happened.

Wait, the presence seemed to urge. *Just a little longer. We will* . . . what? Communicate? Understand? The feeling was that there was more to know and that she . . . they . . . were making progress.

She and whom? Or what? Somehow she was being affected, and she felt as though it were a person doing it. She thought of witchcraft, and the response was a puzzlement. The concept meant nothing to . . . it. She thought of telepathy, and the response was almost one of amusement. No, it was not "out there" somewhere broadcasting its feelings. It was here. With Meg.

At dawn, Henry had put on his go-to-hell hat and loaded his fishing tackle into the car. He waved to Meg as he backed out of the drive. It was his summer Sunday ritual, an hour or two spent wetting lures at Rock Creek. He rarely caught anything, but that didn't matter. As he drove away, Meg noticed how strong his resonance was. She was aware of him even when he was out of sight. Yet for a moment the otherness within her ignored that awareness, apparently absorbed instead in an intense curiosity—almost a fascination. She opened her barriers a little, sensing it, and realized that its fascination was with the car itself, and its reaction to the car was akin to the feelings she had when she thought of witchcraft.

The odd, giddy sense of other-worldliness struck her again, and she put it aside. That was too much to think about, on top of everything else.

Sunlight sang to her. Trees heavy with sweet life rustled their branches in the morning breeze, and the sound was a chorus of a million tiny wind-chimes, a tapestry of richness laced through with birdsong and the shimmer of insect wings. In the wafting scent of flowers she tasted the promise of their nectar and the caress of the soil on their roots.

Will this last? she wondered. Something inside her hoped desperately that it would, but its reponse was a mute acceptance. *That is for you to decide*, it seemed to say.

When Meg went back into the house, her mother was waiting for her, sipping her morning coffee. "You're up early," Hazel said, curious eyes studying her daughter. "Do you want to talk about what's bothering you?"

Meg poured coffee for herself, noticing for the first time in her life the vastly complex patterns of resonant scent that made up the smell of coffee. She turned and leaned against the countertop. "I don't mind talking, Mother. I just don't know what to tell you. Something . . . well, something strange has happened and I don't know how to describe it."

"Is something the matter?" Hazel looked at her more closely. "Do you feel all right?"

"As a matter of fact, yes. I feel wonderful. Just strange, that's all."

"Strange how?"

"I don't know. Aware, maybe." Like someone who has lived life in a cellar and just seen sunlight for the first time is aware, she thought, but how to explain such things?

"That wasn't just a bad dream last night, was it?"

She felt Hazel's concern probing at her, almost a physical impact. *So that's how intuition sounds,* some part of her observed.

She shook her head. "No. It wasn't a bad dream. It wasn't anything bad at all. I was just startled."

"Were you startled yesterday, too?"

"When?"

"All day. I noticed. Are you and Roy having problems, Meg?"

"No, nothing like that. It's just . . . Mother, I'll tell you about it when I get it all sorted out. Right now I don't know what to say." (I could say somebody is talking to me in my head and showing me colors that I can hear and sounds that I can see, she thought.) She changed the subject. "Isn't this the day you're supposed to help Christine move her furniture?"

Hazel nodded, reluctant to be put off a hot trail. "We told her we'd be there about eleven. She'll serve lunch, then we'll listen to Henry complain about how much her piano weighs."

"Which room does she want it in this time?"

"I doubt whether she's decided. Meg, have you seen the doctor lately?"

"Oh, Mother! You're such a worry-wart. I told you, there's nothing wrong with me. Don't worry. I'll tell you all about it later. I just need to think for a while. You and Dad go on to Indianapolis and have a nice time. I'll see you when you get home."

"You could go with us."

"I don't think so. I need some time to think."

Henry returned an hour later, empty-handed and grinning. "Some fellow caught five big ones right across from me. I told him he's using the wrong lure, because now he has to clean the smelly things." He carried his toolbox out to the car, then came in the back way. Hazel was upstairs, and he paused, looking at Meg. "Any answers yet, kid?"

"Not yet. I'm working on it."

"Your mother is worried about you, you know."

"And you aren't." Meg smiled.

"Of course not. But when you figure it out, let's talk. Okay?"

"Okay. Have a nice time in Indianapolis."

"Sure. I'll bet that woman doesn't know which room she wants the piano in. Doesn't she know that thing weighs a ton?"

Meg grinned as he went to call for Hazel, and within

her the otherness glowed happily. Again it did something, and the word came to mind . . . *pixie*.

When her parents has gone, Meg puttered around the house for a time, doing busy-work while she tried to catalog what had happened in the past two days. The ache in her throat had subsided, but she felt that something there had changed. Her eyes no longer burned, but they still felt odd. And she noticed that everything she saw looked clearer than in the past. She put on her glasses, and things looked blurred and distorted. She took them off. It was as though her body was . . . correcting itself, somehow. Sorting out its little defects and mending them.

Somehow, there had to be an explanation.

The live, vibrant otherness was with her constantly, but it seemed to respect her demand for privacy in her own thoughts. It seemed to try not to intrude. It was just . . . there.

Burdens were lighter when shared, and she wanted to share all of this with her parents. And maybe with Roy, when he returned. Her uncertainty puzzled her. She had pretty well decided that she would marry Roy one day, and yet . . . how to share this thing with her parents seemed a simple problem when she compared it to sharing with Roy. He was so pragmatic, so resistant to any sort of change. And of course the tragedy of losing his wife and son—and the way he had lost them—had left deep scars. No, trying to explain something unexplainable to Roy was going to be difficult.

Why is this happening to me?

A tiny response reassured her.

If you are someone else and you're part of me, why can't you explain it to me?

A hesitation. Puzzlement. She had an impression of

distance, of spaces between people, that should not exist but somehow did . . . of barriers.

Meg was going to need time.

In the kitchen, the telephone hung in its arch under the company china. She dialed, heard the ring and the response.

"Peggy? Hi, this is Meg. Is Mark there? Sure." Waiting, she noted, oddly, that there was nothing unusual about the telephone. Strange. When the world changes, why does the telephone remain unchanged? Its blue plastic case and curled cord had a fine luster she hadn't seen before—just as everything now seemed to have vibrances and lusters she had never noticed—but the mechanism . . . the mechanical diddling of things in the circuit, the voice at the other end of the line . . . these were just as before. Just dead mechanical sounds on a telephone. Just clicks and voices. It was puzzling. She heard Mark answer twice before she responded.

"Mark? Meg. Say, something has come up. I need some time off . . . I don't know, a few days. I'll let you know. . . . No, everything is okay. It's just a personal matter. . . . Sure, I'm fine. Look, the books are posted, those closings are on your desk, and that letter to Mr. Caldwell—yes, the specs are with it . . . Worthan? No, I don't know about him, but if he's on file, June can find him. . . yeah . . . no, don't worry. Everything's fine. I'll see you in a few days, okay? Yeah, sure. You, too, Mark. Thanks."

For long moments she stood by the phone. Then slowly, curiously, she eased the mental restrictions on the . . . the glory inside her. As before, it responded and the world became a dazzling place of infinite color, fantastic texture, bright scents, and sparkling planes. Each time, it seemed to be stronger and more intense, as her perceptions widened to accommodate it. It was marvelous, unbelievable . . . and terrifying. But she let it be there and concentrated on sounds—the musical drip of a leaky faucet, the rainbow bells in the ticking of the hall clock, the chorus of hushed summer outside—and lifted the receiver again. She dialed, and the contrast was shocking. Amid the myriad splendors that surrounded her, the sounds at her ear were dull, dead electronic ditherings. There was no splendor.

"For all your banking needs," the mechanical voice told her, "you can rely on the Peoples National Bank, serving Rockville and Martin County for more than seventy years. Time twelve-oh-four. Temperature seventy-nine degrees." She hung up.

It's like being in two worlds at once, she thought. But the telephone is only in one of them. Even with these . . . perceptions . . . a voice on the phone is just a voice.

Closing her eyes, she fought back the splendor, forcing it to recede to the edge of awareness. She was afraid of it, afraid she might become lost in it and never find her way back. She was afraid she might not even want to.

It receded, and the world became almost commonplace. Then a small sound caught her ear, and something inside her seemed to twitch, to come abruptly alert. In the shrubbery outside the open living-room window, a blackbird preened iridescent feathers. Its bill clicked rhythmically as it worked. It paused and chirped, and suddenly the liveness behind her brow was a frenzy. The second world sprang full around her, stronger than ever before, and she almost screamed at the awesome beauty of it. Please, she thought. No. Stop, I can't stand it! But it continued, unheeding, with a wave of fierce desperation behind it.

She found herself walking around the arch and across

to the window, powerless to control herself. As she approached it, the bird watched her, alarmed, and tensed to fly away. But she opened her mouth, her throat quivered, and the sound that came was a high, lyric trill at the edge of hearing. The bird relaxed and stood tall, watching her with bead-bright eyes. Again she sang, cowering inside herself, confused and terrified. She had no control. Her brow tingled frantically, and her body acted alone. She heard herself trill again, soothing the bird, and caught essences of meaning in the strange, high notes. She opened the screen and reached out. The bird hopped onto her hand, and she sang to it, a crooning treble cascade of sounds like water in a brook, sounds that had form and color and texture and intense meaning. The image of the face of her dream came again, unbidden, and she sang its likeness to the bird perched on her thumb. It tipped its head, listening. The image in her mind studied her—great, gentle gold eyes in a sloping, beautiful face, a rhapsody of masculinity with eyes that seemed to see her and to know her.

Aaelefein, she sang in bird-trill, somehow sensing the meaning, *find me. Find me. Aaelefein* . . . the bird responded in a trill that had within it the key notes of the name. Then it spread scintillant wings and was gone.

Gradually the tingling subsided. The perceptions dimmed, and things became as they had been. The awful splendor receded purposefully, until it was almost gone. Sobbing, Meg dropped to her knees by the window, crying with relief and horror. She had been possessed. She had been controlled. Something inside her, a will other than her own, had taken charge of her and manipulated her through those unbelievable minutes, and there had been nothing she could do.

But now came an odder thing. She felt that she was

being begged to forgive, and with the plea came comfort and a strong, gentle reassurance. With an effort she got to her feet, walked back into the kitchen, and dialed the telephone.

"For all your banking needs, you can rely on the Peoples National Bank . . ." When it was done, she dialed it again.

Aaelefein. Aaelefein. A lyric of sounds and more-than-sounds, embroidered with complex harmonies. A song. An orchestrated symphony, yet somehow it was a name. It went with the face, and like the face it made her tremble. Somehow, having a name, the face became real. Somewhere he—Aaelefein—was. And by some sorcery beyond recall she had beckoned him.

"Oh, God," she whispered.

Terrified, she sought the refuge of the daybed and huddled there, small and trembling. She felt all of her realities slipping away, and she clung to them. Like the sound of the telephone, they offered comfort. Beyond was the unknown. She felt terribly alone.

Alone. She felt it, and the tiny thing within her—the otherness—seemed to recoil. As though it feared . . . Lonely, she thought, reacting to the feeling, testing it. She thought of loneliness, expanding on the concept— mortality amidst infinity, desolation, brevity of life, hopeless, lost! The otherness within her suffered and drew in upon itself. Lonely! She concentrated. With cruel, deft thoughts she punished it, testing it. It had frightened her, and she reacted. Loneliness hurt it, somehow . . . made it suffer and cringe and plead. She called up melancholia, forlorn misery until her throat tightened and her eyes stung. Inside her, something whimpered and began to die. And now there were words in its plea. *Please,* it begged her. *Please stop the dark-*

ness. Darkness? *Yes, loneliness is darkness. Please! I have not hurt you.*

You frightened me, she told herself. You? What are you? What is this thing? Sobs wracked her. Who am I? Roy, why aren't you here? I don't care if you can't understand, neither can I. I need you!

From deep within her, the otherness responded, a deep wave of sympathy. Aaelefein . . . it came again, the image rising in her mind, tentative against her will but still somehow a shield, protecting the part of her—the thing within her—that she wanted to punish. Yet, more than that, a shield for both of them, for her and it, to fend against the harm she was doing to both of them. The terrible shroud of loneliness she had woven collapsed. She wept.

Half-blind with confusion, small and hurt, a child needing the comfort of remembered reality, she curled herself into a ball on the daybed and wept.

I am so sorry, a part of her whispered, and she couldn't tell which part it was.

But that was terrifying, she thought. That . . . thing with the bird. And yet, except for the terror of possession, what had occurred had not been awful at all. Only strange, and in a way very beautiful. The act itself, that poignant communion with a blackbird, had been entrancing. There were no words for it. There had been a terrible, desperate need, a great love so encompassing that nothing else mattered, but with it a feeling of enormous desperation for someone else . . . for others, many others . . . of something begun that must be completed. And she had sung a rhapsody that was a name, and the bird had somehow understood the song of it. It had flown away carrying trill-tones of love. It had flown with purpose, a bird with a mission, grateful for the tiny portion of that love that was its fare.

For an hour or more Meg lay there, drained and confused. Then she sat up, took a deep breath, and thought a question.

Can you explain to me what this is all about?

Hesitation . . . a sense of distance and of barriers.

Do you want to explain?

Positive.

Can you show me more than I have seen?

Positive.

If you show me, can I be the same again?

Negative. A sadness.

Can I still be in charge of my life . . . after?

Positive. An apology.

Will I still be me?

No response, only a sense of compassion.

Will you and I be one?

Long hesitation . . . a sense of desperate need to be one with her, of something incomplete, unresolved. Then . . . *negative.*

I'm not ready for this, she thought. I'm frightened. How can I accept something I don't understand? Are there really two of me here? Me and . . . something else? Do I really want to know? But I can, I suppose.

Positive, the concept responded.

All I have to do is open up and take a look.

Positive.

Damn it, she thought, I have my life on course—at least I did until yesterday. I don't want any changes. But I can't go on like this. I have to know. Or else I have to get rid of this . . . this thing inside me.

Please, if you cast me out, I will die. He needs me.

But I can get rid of you if I want to, can't I?

Positive.

With a severity that caught her throat, she brought herself under control. She couldn't just avoid it, she knew herself better than that. She had to see what there was to see.

She drew herself upright, pulse racing. Somehow she was certain that she was saying goodbye to her tidy world. It would not be the same again.

Show me, she decided, and let the clamps fall away.

It came, the heart-rending beauty, but this time soft and comforting and with a touch of sad acceptance. It sang within her, sweet-soft minor melodies full of night-song and heartbreak, flecks of sweet brilliance dusted across a dark tapestry of desperate need. A personality was there, a personality entirely apart from her own but encapsuled within her, a being somehow not quite human, but complex and compassionate and wholly beautiful, a being desperate, determined and totally vulnerable to her. It let itself be known to her, opened itself wide to her, and in so doing gave up its last defense. It would require only an act of will on her part, she knew, and the being would be gone. Only the slightest nudge of will . . . but it pleaded with her, helpless in its surrender but wanting desperately to stay. She felt its plea and heard her voice whispering the words of the other: "If you drive me out, I will die. He needs me. Please let me stay."

It accepted her prerogative and her right to choose. Acceptance and a lonely plea. It was a whole personality, incredibly beautiful, real and alive. And yet it was no more than a tiny spark of existence within her, a mote of desperate need alone in emptiness. It had shown her all it could. The being was desperate and it had no power to coalesce further with her. It had given her all it could, had bared itself to her, and she could snuff it out if she chose.

"I'm in charge of my life," she whispered fiercely. And in the tiny brilliance, there was acceptance.

Margaret Mary O'Toole Harrison stood, stretching her small body. The glories of perception washed around her, bathing her in harmonics and radiances beyond anything she could ever have conceived. With a hard lump in her throat, she said good-bye to a future she had accepted and accepted a different future she could not imagine. Inside, she felt a tiny, deep gratitude.

The image came again, offered as a gift, a thing to share. She studied the triangular face, the knowing, dancing, almond eyes, the hint of a smile on the upturned mouth.

Aaelefein.

He might never come. But she knew he would try.

7

They had stayed late at Christine's house, and Henry's choice of time-saving routes through Indianapolis had stalled them in traffic tie-ups on the Burdsal Parkway and again at Lynnhurt and Tenth. As a result it was dusk when they left the city, the sunset fading over the hills ahead, and it was dark when they reached Rockville.

"You and your shortcuts!" Hazel fussed. "Meg was expecting us home hours ago."

"Consider it an adventure," Henry said, grinning, as he negotiated a corner. "Besides, our daughter has trusted us to be out alone since she was twenty." He leaned forward, peering ahead. "Will you look at that?"

Hazel was already looking. Still some distance away, little dark forms swooped and circled around a street light. "What are they?"

"Bats," Henry said. "Lord, there must be fifty or sixty of them. I've never seen so many at one time."

"Bats?" Hazel peered, realizing that he was right. "What are they doing in front of our house?"

"What bats do, I imagine. Catching bugs."

He slowed as they approached, and rolled down his window. On both sides of the street, people were standing in their yards watching the performance. A neighbor waved as they passed. "Hi, Henry! You folks in the bat business these days?"

Henry grinned at him and raised his hand in an elaborate shrug. As he drew abreast of the street light, the dark sky seemed a kaleidoscope of winged creatures, whirling in choreographed patterns of flight. He pulled into the driveway, passed the house, and drove into the garage. Several cats scurried gracefully aside.

"What on earth is going on?" Hazel said.

Somewhere nearby a dog howled, and others joined it in its song.

They got out of the car, stepped from the garage, and Henry pulled down the overhead door. A cat twined around his legs, leaning against one leg after the other, purring audibly. He leaned to scratch its ears, then followed Hazel toward the back door. No lights showed from the house, only the little photoelectric-activated lamp outside the sunporch.

As they approached the door, Hazel stopped, listening intently. Somewhere a symphony of tiny silver bells was playing, notes at the edge of hearing, ringing in exquisite harmony. For a moment the O'Tooles looked around, trying to find the source. Then Henry pointed. "It's coming from the house."

"What is it?"

"Who knows? But it's pretty, isn't it?"

"I never heard anything like it."

The back door was unlocked. As he pulled it open, the faerie music ceased and Meg's voice came from the darkness beyond. "Hi. How was the trip?"

Hazel peered through the door. "Margaret? What in . . ."

Henry stepped into the house.

"Dad, watch out!"

He stopped.

"Oh, for heaven's sake," Meg said. "I forgot to turn on the light. Just a minute."

They heard her steps, then the kitchen light clicked on.

A card table stood in front of the daybed, its surface covered from edge to edge with crystalware. Wine glasses, goblets, bowls, and cups—every piece of crystal Hazel had carefully collected seemed to be there. She stared at the array. "What in the world are you doing?"

"Didn't you hear it?" Meg asked. "The music?"

"We heard something," Henry said. "What was it?"

"These. Have you ever heard anything so lovely?"

"You were playing the crystal?" Hazel felt giddy, trying to comprehend. Meg had been sitting here in the dark . . . doing something with all this . . . and didn't know the light wasn't on?

"Gorgeous," Henry agreed. "How'd you do it?"

"Well, I just sort of . . . oh, come on, both of you. Sit down. We need to talk."

"We certainly do," Hazel breathed.

"What's been going on outside?" Henry asked. "All those bats. And cats. And dogs howling."

Meg blinked at him, then grinned shyly. "Oh. I'll bet they heard it."

"Heard what? The crystal?"

"More likely they heard me . . . well, us . . . singing to it. That's what makes it work. She's been showing me how . . . oh, Mother, sit down! I guess I'd better take it from the beginning."

Meg paused, sighed, and ran a hand through her hair. "There's someone here with me . . . no, I mean right here." She held a finger to her heart. "Inside me. Yes, I know. It sounds weird. I'm just beginning to understand. But, really . . . "

Hazel and Henry sat down slowly.

It was, beyond doubt, the strangest conversation any of them had ever had. Meg had decided that the only way to tell them what had happened was to simply tell them and hope they understood. She herself understood little of it, but she could describe the sensations of the past two days . . . the awakening to splendors unimaginable, the presence—apparently within her—of someone else, someone so utterly different that they could rarely communicate even in thought, but who nonetheless had shown her glories.

Hazel sat and listened as one stunned, but only for a time. Then all of the concerns of the past two days focused themselves on a single question. "Meg, when was the last time you saw the doctor?"

Meg gave a bittersweet smile. "It isn't something a doctor would know about, Mother," she said softly. "And it isn't imaginary. It's as though this person, this someone who is with me, needs sanctuary and chose me. It's . . . oh, lord, I don't know how to describe it. But she really is here."

"Where?" Henry asked, looking about.

"In me . . . with me." She raised a tentative hand and touched her brow. "Here, it seems like, but I think that's just where I feel her."

"I can't believe this," Hazel said. Her voice was strained. "Margaret, do you know what you're saying? I've never heard of anything like this. I think we should make an appointment . . ."

Henry was tugging at his lip thoughtfully. "Meg, last night . . . when you woke up, what did you see?"

"I saw . . ." She hesitated, then grinned at him. "I guess I saw the world in a different light." She felt the otherness within her giggle.

Help me, she thought. I want them to understand.

The being inside her seemed to explore her feelings for her parents and to bask in the love that was there. *You are all beautiful,* it seemed to say. *But you have never shared as (something) do. It might be painful.*

Help me, she thought again. She felt its agreement. As though on impulse, she sat between her parents and took their hands, her father's solid hand in her right, her mother's softer hand in her left. "Let me show you," she said.

She loosed the clamps and the glories came, rich and soft, a splendor of light and music and love and concern passing from flesh to flesh. In that moment Margaret knew her parents as she had never known them before, and she understood why the otherness had hesitated. The pulses of touch-sense work both ways, and she knew them—her mother and father—as no generation should know another. All the joys and the hurts, the tapestry of all the years, were there.

The harmonics of knowing flowed, released gently, a thread at a time, by the strange spark that had come to be a part of Meg. Deep, rhythmic waves of pure feeling carried messages of beauty on their crests and an intense knowing just beneath, and Margaret felt tears come to her eyes. Desperately, she restrained it, holding back the whole huge, stunning glory of it and releasing only glimpses because she could not stand more.

She knew what they were seeing . . . or feeling, or hearing. They were seeing the heart of her, as she was seeing theirs. And just beyond her, or within her, they were glimpsing another person—tiny in the tone-shadows, a poignant, exquisite other personality, a symphony of subtle pitches and orchestrated shades . . . a rapture enshrouded in bittersweet regret.

She held it for them as long as she could, then she
pulled her hands away and wiped her streaming eyes,
choking sobs.

They sat in silence, and when she looked at them there
were tears on their faces, too. But they weren't looking at
her. Their eyes were for each other, and each was seeing
in the other what they both had always known was there
but had never seen so vividly.

Inside her, the tiny otherness crooned gently, calming
and reassuring her, and there was a sense of elation within it. It had learned something, too, and it felt joy.
Somehow, she felt it had discovered that they—and
she—were more akin to it than it had conceived.

And that thought quelled the sobs and widened her
eyes—eyes that were slightly larger than they had been
two days before, and which now had a subtle elongation
to their pupils. Meg had resolved that the . . . thing . . .
within her was, somehow, another person. It could be
nothing else. But if it were a person, then how could it
be surprised at qualities natural to people? The question
sent a shiver up her spine. Who was it? Who was *she?*

And where had she come from?

8

An eagle told the Feya that Aaelefein was well. The bird came as she draped vaporfloss on a frame of living willow she'd made. The creature's call was touched with Caiansong. It had come far, she knew, and others before it farther, all with resonances attuned so that Cai who heard their song might know that Aaelefein lived and pressed his search.

The ancient one was deeply grateful. She called the eagle down, and Haralan brought fish from a brook to reward its efforts. While it ate she touched its mind. Many of the creatures from her home planet, Nendacaida, had tonal affinity. Things of instinct only, still they could retain and carry simple messages for the Cai. But the creatures of old Caiendon were too far removed from the guiding essences of Caidom. Their perception was limited to narrow bands of resonance. It was a mark of Aaelefein's genius that he had been able to touch the feathered ones and impart to them his signal. It was the sort of thing their lost and mourned one, Nataea, might have attempted. Her empathy had been profound. That Aaelefein had achieved it was surprising. Once intonated, the creatures would retain the codes of song and pass it on. But to impress the mind of that first bird was an achievement. Such empathy was not one of Aaelefein's major skills.

The bird knew nothing of its impress, of course. It was only a bird. It carried no meanings beyond its own, but its call overtones were message enough. Aaelefein lived.

They watched the bird depart. Then Sefraeonia and Haralan lent their skills to Winifraeda as the vaporfloss, so nearly air as to be almost invisible, danced in the willow frame.

Haralan knew the essence of the Corad. He had seen it on Nendacaida when it came, destroying all save him of his entire clan. Sefraeonia was a percept of high degree. If there was a sign, she would observe it.

Their hands joined, they stood before the draped floss and Winifraeda knew, from Haralan through Sefraeonia, the nature of the Corad. She built within her mind, in seven senses, an image of the life-eater that was as complete as the three could will it. She concentrated, searching the image for those characteristics that were its essence of being. When she had it, she willed it into the gossamer floss.

What was bane to the Corad would now be bane to this floss.

The power of the floss lay in its total acceptance of patterns of resonance and its retention of them. Strands gleaned from the atmosphere, compacted by a single note of magnetic harmony, the stuff was alive in a sense, but it had no impress of its own. It was a perfect medium for the complex resonances of creature essence. The floss became whatever essence it was given.

Akin in its manner of creation to the resilient fibers of blended substance that made up her own robe and doublet, Sefraeonia's filmy gown and wrapped girdle, and Haralan's red kilt and flowing cape, and to the sturdy fabric of their footwear and of Haralan's corselet, the vaporfloss was the finest and most fragile of resonated strands. It barely existed. Still, it was alive, and once given an essence it became that essence, totally. Given the essence of the Corad, it became Corad. It would seek what the Corad sought, and be repelled by what repelled the Corad.

Haralan's crystal blade had touched Corad essence. Now Sefraeonia perceived that essence, and the Feya sang it to the floss and the floss was Corad.

Concentrating through Sefraeonia's percept senses, the Feya watched the barely visible stuff for sign. It danced in the frame, but its movements had no meaning.

"Haralan," the Feya willed, "if your blade will attune to these pulses in the air, make them still."

Haralan drew his blade. Its shaft of black crystal went milky gray, then white, then diamond-clear as he sang to it. The blade hummed a wide range of frequencies up and down its edges, and Haralan held it high. The dancing floss calmed, then went limp on its frame. Winifraeda closed her eyes and concentrated. Through Sefraeonia they watched. In stillness the floss hung and writhed in agony. Then it darkened, shriveled, and was gone. Without life, it ceased to exist.

Winifraeda opened her eyes, loosed Sefraeonia's hand, and turned away, deep in thought. Haralan sheathed his sword. Its blade was once again dead-black crystal.

In the dim regions about them, wolves howled frantically, ferrets milled in confusion, and bats clinging in dark caves fought to regain their equilibrium. At Dubois on the Wind River, a ham radio operator logged two minutes of atmospheric interference and credited it to sunspots. Several hundred people watching a national sports event on television lost the signal for those same two minutes. Scanning military satellites registered a two-minute "blip" of all-frequency silence over the lower Absaroka range, and startled monitors called in their technicians.

Weary and disappointed, the Cai rested on cool grass beside a stream, and the Feya puzzled over what they had learned. The floss, living fiber sung from the air, had held the spirit of the Corad. Being Corad now, on this planet where the Corad could not come, it had died. But it had not given a direction.

"The Corad-bane is here," she said at last. "The floss died of it, but it did not seek escape. Therefore the bane is in all directions."

"Then we have not found it," Haralan grunted.

"Even if we do"—Sefraeonia's bright eyes glistened—"we are but three. We cannot go back. There is no chord."

"Trust Aaelefein," the Feya admonished. "He will find a way. Meanwhile, since the floss tells nothing here, we shall go elsewhere. Somewhere, if we keep trying, a Corad-attuned floss will find the bane stronger in one direction than in others. Then we will have a path."

"I hate to leave this place," Haralan said. "At least there is a trace of Caiansong here. We may not find such comfort elsewhere."

"If you wanted comfort, stout one, you should have stayed on Nendacaida," the Feya said. Haralan did not answer.

There was little to make ready. They had brought little except themselves. Yet when Sefraeonia unwrapped her girdle and made a waterbag to carry, Haralan came and gently took it from her. Her arm had mended, but it was weak. He knew it still pained her. His back was strong;

he would carry her load. Winifraeda, who missed nothing, turned away to lead them. Being Feya did not cause one to forget the nature of youth.

They did not go as Aaelefein had, toward the rising sun. Instead they traveled southward, keeping to the high places, avoiding the habitats of men. Nor did they travel rapidly, as Cai are able to. Few canyons did they see that robust Haralan could not have crossed in a trice. And for the most part, slim Sefraeonia could have kept pace with him. But such feats were not for Winifraeda. Tiny and ancient, she demanded a sedate pace and reasonable routes. And because she was Feya and they loved her, they complied.

Few enough Cai ever became Feyadeen. More than age was required, for with the Feyadeen rested all the lore of the ancient race. Winifraeda's skills went far beyond those of her companions. The drawing of vaporfloss from the substance of air was but the least of her abilities. Within her tiny person rested all the skills Caidom had ever mastered, retained through ages of persistent study. So much of her former self had she spent becoming Feya that she was barely more than three feet tall, and the long hair on her doll-like head was the color of spun silver.

Few Cai ever became Feyadeen. Few ever wanted to.

As they traveled, Winifraeda wondered at the darkness they perceived. It was a constant burden to all of them. It wore down their wills, made their rest fitful, shrouded their senses with its aura of hopeless grief. Even in the high meadow far from the children of the Raporoi, the sense of lonely darkness was always present. The earth itself had absorbed its strain, and it was part of the planet's mantle, a dark harmony in the vibrance of a living world.

The Feya felt a deep melancholy, a longing for things so far past that she herself had never known them. This sad place, peopled now by the sad children of the Raporoi, had once been fabled Caiendon. She imagined it as it had been then, through the long, bright ages of the time of Cai, before the ancestors of humanity awakened.

Beautiful Caiendon, lore recalled it, motherhome of the singing world, changing through the ages but changeless, quick with the essence of Caidom, Caikindred, and the creatures that thrived in their harmonies. Some of the creature kinds remained, though most now were gone, replaced by others attuned to different songs. And even those that were descendent from the last of their kinds to have heard Caisong now were mute, dumb things unattuned to glory.

She wondered if any of the Cai-kindred lived. Certainly their kind must have survived long ages after the Cai had gone—the beautiful, thoughtless nymphs, quick sprites in their hidden places, the countless varieties of winged or finned or hooved beings . . . and above all, the pixies, playful and sympathetic, going where they would. What Cai lad, first blush of adulthood strong within him, had never loved a pixie?

Of all the kindred left behind, Winifraeda prayed most that the pixies had never suffered. They above all existed to love and to be loved. And if their kind lacked the all-knowledge of true Cai, was that so bad? No happier people had ever stepped forth under a golden sun.

Fervently, Winifraeda hoped there might yet be pixies on this sad, old world that once was Caiendon.

The darkness, so devastating to Caians in their knowledge, had never affected the Cai-kindred. Some had gone with the Cai to Nendacaida, and their descendants flourished there. Others had remained behind. Let them, the Feya prayed, have found the joy they always gave so freely. Let no pixie ever have known torment.

According to the lore, one full Caian had also remained behind. Old Rigil Fen-Belen, armsmaster of clan Belen of the Smoking Peaks, had been so crippled by a beast that he was unable to strike chord. Yet so proud an old warrior was he that he refused a place as passenger among a chord of five fives.

Rigil Fen-Belen. Countless legends lived on about him. He had preferred darkness to dependence.

Winifraeda wondered how long he had lived and how he had fared. Had the pixies cared for him? Of course they would have, and shielded him as best they could.

As they moved south, Haralan ranged far out, bringing Winifraeda and Sefraeonia food and water, studying the lands ahead. Several times they detoured wide to avoid settlements of the Raporoi creatures. The darkness radiating from such places was painful. Then, far ahead, Haralan found a great city. It sprawled over miles of mountain land, and by the time they could sense its magnitude their very souls ached from the weight of crushing darkness.

Yet even as Haralan scouted for a way around the city, Sefraeonia the percept, her bright eyes missing nothing, pointed upward toward a peak to the west. "There," she told Winifraeda. "Up there, nearly to the snows, there is yet a little essence. A place that remembers the Cai. Its song can help us."

"I can understand how it has remained," Winifraeda said after studying the distant place. "There is no easy access to that brave height, and the Raporoi were never nimble."

The harmonic echo lingering on the peak was ancient, but it would make it easier for Winifraeda to weave her floss. They had gone a way toward it when Haralan overtook them. Winifraeda showed him where they were going, and he led the way as before. At a secluded canyon, they paused to watch a human male and his cub disporting on the bank of a graveled stream. The adult held an elaborate switch. An attached spool held spun thread which was captured in rings along the length of the switch and extruded from its end. At the thread's end was a device of little feathers. Flicking the switch adroitly, the creature caused the feather bit to touch the water in various places.

"He attempts to entice fish," Winifraeda decided. "He is teaching the cub his art."

As the Feya's senses probed, the human cub turned abruptly and stared at the Cai. Its mouth dropped open, it stared for a moment, and then rose and came toward them. Haralan bristled in alarm.

"Let it approach," Winifraeda said. With mindsong she diverted the father's attention for a moment. The cub came closer.

When the child was near, the Feya reached out a delicate hand and touched its cheek. The child stared at her, its eyes huge with wonder. The child was almost her height, and its hair was the color of sunshine.

"It could almost be a Cai-child," Haralan observed.

"But look at its ears," Sefraeoni pointed. "And its face is so round, and its throat oddly contoured. Yet, it is not so different from a Cai babe, at that. Do you suppose? . . ."

Winifraeda hushed them. She held the cub's hand in her own and gazed into its eyes. Finally she turned away. "Remarkable," she said. "Among the very young, it seems there is no darkness. I had suspected as much, and it is true. Now I know why. This cub has no sense of mortality yet, and it has a diminished but very real empathy." To the cub she said in Caiansong, "Go to your father now and show him how to entice fish."

The child ran away, and they watched as it held out its hand to its father. The adult hesitated, then handed it the switch. Within moments the child, flicking its feather lure as dextrously as had the father, had two good fish upon the bank. The Cai could hear the little one's song.

As they set out again for the distant peaks, Winifraeda said, "The cub will never have to go hungry."

9

The place they sought was a small, deep cove behind a shielding croft of mountain, fended against the great stone body of the peak itself. It was a hidden place, steeped in time. Only Sefraeonia's sharp senses could have found it. Echoes of the ancient harmonics of Caidom lingered there, but were hidden enough to deceive lesser skills.

Its floor was rich in loam and succulence, where Winifraeda found willow to yield her withes. There was sustenance at hand for them, and a sense of comfort, of a burden lessened. The touch of lingering lyric about the place strove with them against the darkness.

"A roost," Haralan announced. "A true Cai-roost. Had I this place on a gentler world, I would hew the heart from this stone and make of it a castle."

"On a gentler world," Sefraeonia concurred, "such would be a castle fit for a noble clan."

"Bring water," Winifraeda told them.

Through the passing of a sun she toiled, with their assistance, drawing from the thin air the fiber of the floss, imbuing it with simple essence that it might live until she had enough to use.

Finally it was ready, and once again she fashioned a frame of living withes and draped the floss from it. This time it was done by night, beneath a moon that was the last great symbol of what had once been Caiendon. Winifraeda knew the Corad-bane could be anywhere, and anything, that was of this world. She must alter the test to various conditions.

She took their hands, and they stood in stillness before the hanging floss. Again, Haralan perceived the nature of the Corad, and Sefraeonia passed the perception to Winifraeda. Their three sevens of senses attuned, they fed the essence of the life-eater into the floss. It stirred, seemed to ripple in the moonlight, its myriad strands seeking, reacting. Sefraeonia fixed upon it, and Winifraeda drew from her. The eldritch stuff flowed, first this way and then that, writhing from its frame.

The floss tried to escape, Sefraeonia felt, and Winifraeda knew. The floss was truly Corad. It was attuned. It perceived its bane, sought a direction to flee . . . and stopped. It darkened and shriveled and was gone.

The Cai slumped in exhaustion. Again, it had given no direction. They sat in weariness until the moon was gone. Then the Feya sent Haralan for water and Sefraeonia for withes. When they were gone she began again the tedious drawing of floss from the vapors of the air.

"The next time," she told them later, "we will withdraw from the mantle of Caiendon. There, atop that croft, we will test the floss where it must face upon the world that is and not the one that was."

Haralan was restless. There was little enough for him to do. Through the days, as Winifraeda worked and Sefraeonia watched, he busied himself at the base of the shielding croft, working with his sword of crystal. The blade shimmered and sang as it sliced the rock, hewing slabs as he crafted them. With Eldretten skill he carved pillars of eye-deceiving beauty, arches that seemed only faceless rock unless viewed from the proper angle, soffits whose inner faces were alive with designs of flowing vines and rampant foliage.

When the Feya and Sefraeonia paused to consider his work, Winifraeda nodded and Sefraeonia was aglow with delight. "You have mastery of the stone," she said. "It is beautiful."

"No mastery of the stone, fair one. But I am from a clan of builders. The mastery is in knowing what to remove so that what remains will be pleasing. I toy with this. It is better than watching our Feya's fingers produce nothing from nothing."

"Will your castle find Corad-bane, oaf?" Winifraeda scolded. "That, after all, is why we are here. Still, I expect it is better to leave you playing with the mountain than to have you sit and sigh with boredom while I am trying to work. So proceed. It will not harm this poor world to have something of beauty upon it, even if it is hidden in this place."

"Then you do agree Haralan's craft is beautiful?" Sefraeonia pressed, defending the scolded Haralan.

"Did I say otherwise?" With a frown, the Feya returned to her weaving.

"She loves us too much," Sefraeonia explained to the sulking warrior. "And she loves our people too much to consider giving up."

The touch of her soft hand on his shoulder eased the pulse of anger in Haralan's neck. "I know, little one. Nor would I even think of giving up. It is just that her labor is so tedious, and I know so little of it. Give me a castle to build, and I am more content."

"It is beautiful work, Haralan Caharel-Ruast." Admiring, Sefraeonia stepped through the carved portal and looked around at the arched vault now four strides deep into the living rock. Finished, it would be a grand entry chamber.

"I know I am Caharel of clan Ruast—an adoptee," Haralan admitted. "But there was a time I was full Fe of clan Candenen of the Spires. As proud a clan as was in Caidom. The Feya knows I will not fail in my mission, even if it is hopeless. I have seen the Corad and what it left of Eldretten. My people are gone, Sefraeonia, but I would give my arms and my eyes to turn the life-eater away. I thank clan Ruast for accepting me as Caharel. I am satisfied with the status."

It was the longest speech Sefraeonia had ever heard the stolid male make, and she turned and looked up at him. "My clan is Cos, Haralan. My people are inter-singers for the Eldreyen clans. We have little awareness of status among us. It interferes with perception. I see little difference between Caharel and Fe. Both are only people."

Her eyes were so bright, her empathy so luminous, that Haralan turned away. "Would a princess of the Cos enjoy a castle such as this might be . . . if it were on a gentle world?"

"She might." Sefraeonia pursed her lips and looked around again. "It would depend on whose essence suffused it."

She went away then, to learn from the Feya, and Haralan drew his sword of crystal and peered around in the moonlight. On the inner face of the entry arch, where rock-sculpted vinery grew from wide pillars to face in the center in a swirl of granite leaves, he crafted a small, perfect flower of seven petals. It was the clansign of Cos. He lacked the temerity to inscribe the cross of Ruast, and did not even consider the twin spires of clan Canenden. He

was the last of the Canenden. The spires would not be
scribed again until the Corad was gone from Nendacaida.

Early sun sought the floor of the roost when Winifraeda completed her task. "We will seek again," she
said. "This time at the top of the croft."

The climb was almost straight up, and Haralan carried
the little Feya clinging to his back most of the way. She
was too busy to climb herself; she concentrated on her
tiny handful of floss, nourishing its dim life.

From the top of the peak, the world spread radiant
around them. In the distance was the city, its bright
buildings clustered tall on a central rise and spreading to
the horizon beyond. The darkness of massed loneliness
smote the Cai there, making their spirits weep. Even the
floss, when the Feya draped it, seemed to draw back
from the place of the haunted ones. Its tiny essence
sensed the darkness, as did their empathy.

"Calm the pulses," Winifraeda told Haralan. He drew
his blade. The air still, they joined hands and again
focused the essence of Corad into the wisp of floss. Haralan recalled, Sefraeonia perceived, Winifraeda focused.
And the floss became the stuff of Corad.

It twitched. Then with a violence that seemed pure
terror, it streamed outward from its frame, twisting and
writhing, pointing straight back at the looming mountain peak beyond the hidden place . . . away from the
city.

It struggled, strained against its frame of withes, darkened. Then it was gone, its lifeless elements absorbed
back into the air from which they had come.

With horror, the three Cai turned from the floss to
stare out over the miles at the sprawling, brightening city
of the children of the Raporoi. The message was clear.

The floss had told its tale. In that direction lay the Corad-bane. They would find it in the city itself . . . right in the midst of the emanating, agonizing darkness from which their Caian souls recoiled.

"Among the haunted ones," Sefraeonia breathed. Even from this distance, the radiating darkness was an agony.

Haralan turned to the Feya. His gaze was dismal. "If we go among them, Feya, what then? Will the floss even work in so much darkness?"

Winifraeda shrugged, her head hanging. "I don't know. But I know nothing else to try. Come, let us go back down. I need to think."

All the way down the jutting crag, as she clung to Haralan's strong back, Winifraeda's mind was spinning. She searched the lore of ages and found no wisdom to match this situation. There was no precedent. She had seen the floss, as Cai-essence, shy from the darkness in pain. But she had seen it too, as Corad, recoil and die. The darkness was there. But there, too, lay the Corad-bane, and they must find it.

Back in the cove she wandered about, deep in thought, while Haralan went to sit in silence on the portico of his castle facade.

At eventime, the Feya called them. "We do not know enough, not nearly enough. And in the city of humans it will be difficult to learn. Therefore we need to learn as much as we can here before we venture there."

They waited upon her words.

"Among all those haunted ones," she continued, "I fear my spirit will be muffled by the darkness. I may be too old to withstand that much pain and still function properly. And yet we must learn from them what we need to know."

"Aaelefein is among the humans," Haralan pointed out. "He is suffering it, and yet he lives . . . somewhere."

Winifraeda nodded. It was true. But of them all, Aaelefein was the strongest of will. Even the Feya was no match for him in that respect. And what she must know—the clues to where and what was the Coradbane—would require that all her skill be untroubled by enveloping darkness.

"Aaelefein does what he must, Haralan. And we do what we must. We may have to go among them there, but let us go fully prepared. It has occurred to me that there may be, among those poor creatures, some who, in their own way, have become Feyadeen. Those are intelligent creatures down there, children. There may be wise ones among them."

"Not wise as we know."

"Only because they are not as we are, Haralan. Be not mistaken, though. We think of those creatures as Raporoi because it was the Raporoi our people left behind in the evil time. But the Raporoi are gone. These are the children of the Raporoi, and they have grown. There is still the darkness, but these are creatures much like us in their souls.

"I would commune with a wise one of these people," she continued. "There may be an accord we can find. But it would be best done here, not down there. Therefore, Haralan, you must go down among them, seek out a wise one, and bring it to me."

Haralan brightened. Even the prospect of descending into the maw of the darkness was better than sitting around doing nothing. "I will go, Feya. How will I choose a wise one if they have not the aura of Feyadeen?"

"We have been in accord, Haralan, you and I. You

have touched Feyadeen wisdom. You know its taste. Seek it out. But have great care, armsman. The creatures are fragile. Select one, but do not hurt it."

10

The children of the Raporoi have come far, he mused as he leaned back on padded cushions and felt the vehicle surge with machine vibrance. Senses damped hard against the seeping darkness that shrouded the humans around him, Aaelefein pondered the complexities of the strange race that had spread across the ancient, abandoned world of the Cai.

Five fives of days he had spent learning something of the arts of these alien folk, that he might blend among them. He passed easily now, but cautiously. His alienness might not pass any too close scrutiny.

He had observed the varieties and blends among them. They were a young race, still largely unconsolidated in their geographic specialties. Differing in physique, language, skin color, and custom far more than did the Cai, they were a homogen of kinds. It was the key to his blending among them. To those of European extraction he would appear vaguely oriental except for his height, possibly Eurasian. To the various orientals, he might seem nordic. His coloration, though distinctly not that of any race on this world, might seem to each to be somewhat like another. He knew his ears drew attention, as did the slant of his cheeks, but among a race of so many separate breeds these features would seem merely unusual.

Some among them had a distinct—though undeveloped—empathy. These he usually avoided, the girl beside him now being an exception. Among empaths there could be little deception.

The thing he rode was a passenger coach. A bus. It droned along a strip of dark pavement, a sight-straight line segmenting moon-bright vistas of ripe grain that receded to the horizons. He would have preferred to ride on top of it, rather than inside. The metal enclosures so favored by these people distorted and damped his senses. Still, he realized that to the people of this world, such limitations meant nothing. Unlike Caians, their physical senses were so limited that being enclosed by anti-resonant materials rarely seemed to bother them. Whereas Cai instinctively sought the high places, these people could be happy in holes.

Such realizations left him more enthralled than ever by the magnitude of human endeavors. Never had the Cai so broadly utilized their world. But then, never had there been so many Cai. These people flourished in the billions.

The girl beside him slept, stirred, and slept again, her head coming to nestle on his shoulder. Her presence was strong upon him. Aaelefein had found her in the town of Clover. She was a stranger there, just like him. A local male in rut, clouded by distilled spirits, had accosted her on a night-quiet street. Her fear had called, and the Caian had come. The fear-sense had been a shock to him, it was so much like that of a Caian girl threatened by the great carnivorous lizards that roamed Nendacaida—descendants of those that had roamed old Caiendon in ancient times.

She had emanated fear, and Aaelefein had acted decisively. If the rutting male never understood how he came to be bruised, hurt, and head-down in a garbage container, it was no more than his due. The girl was no Caian, but she was female and deserved to not be abused.

For most of his days in Clover, the girl had tagged after him, adopting him. More than she could know, she had helped him in his learning of the ways and customs of the people of this world, and of how to blend among them.

She identified him as a foreigner, as alone as she, and she helped him to learn. Her name was Carrie Hummingbird, and her only relative, a grandfather, was far away on a reservation.

From that detail, Aaelefein discovered a remarkable quality about Carrie Hummingbird. Even though the old man was far away—more than fifty horizons, he estimated from her talk and her concepts—still she felt close to him, almost as though the distance had nothing to do with their feelings for each other.

It was not a Caian thing, in that it involved no projected resonance and no actual communication. But it surprised him, in seeming so opposite to the lonely soul-darkness he found among the people of this world. Carrie was alone, and Carrie was lonely, but she was aware of her loneliness and she drew a warmth from it.

Once when she was helping him learn words, he asked her—partly through words, partly through the subliminal infrasonics as they held hands—why she was different from so many others. She had laughed at that, and her acceptance of being different was a happy thing laced with tinges of regret.

"I am a Native American," she told him, having him repeat the words. "Sometimes we have our own way of thinking."

He understood, in a way. There had been separations and conflicts between her ancestors and those of others. The passions of one generation were passed on to the next. Still, he thought there was something more. She was so quick to respond to the simple resonances, the basic ranges of empathy, he felt that somewhere in her ancestry there must have been pixie lineage.

She had helped him learn to go among humans. And somehow he could never quite tell whether she suspected he was not one of them.

Most surprising to him of all, he realized that more than his empathy responded to her. He had a strong physical attraction to her. The pheromones of call-scent were astonishingly similar to Caian. He would never have guessed that two separate races so far removed as Cai and human could find each other so attractive. But it was so.

Among humans, he found, many took lightly the coupling of pairs. Gratification of five senses was less demanding than the pairing of seven. Few Cai ever paired more than once, and that for life. Still, he appreciated the presence of Carrie Hummingbird. He cherished her as one might cherish a favorite sprite on Nendacaida. And he concentrated on the sweet memory of Nataea and on his mission.

The girl stirred again in the dim light, and her hand rested on his. He opened his senses, tolerating for a moment the buffeting of omnipresent darkness, and soothed her with touch-song. She slept serenely.

A small, sleepy town crept past the window. Here and there, lights shone, little globes of fire in the night.

These humans, the children of the ancient Raporoi, were a race of earth and fire. Deprived by nature of the broad-spectrum senses—and thus of the mastery of harmonics and resonance—this race of humans had resorted to the primal elements. They used fire for everything. They drew from the earth to build elaborate vials of iron, and these vials they implanted with fire. The vessels contained the fire and responded to its ambience, powering mechanisms that moved over land and sea, even through the sky.

Unable to bend the solid elements to their wills, humans overcame them. With their fire-in-iron tools, they made cold places warm and warm places cool, reshaped earth, and pushed water from place to place. They even tapped the primal rhythms of the planet's living mantle to generate burning bolts of stifled magnetism. They translated ambience into fire. They fed fire into threads of sunmetal and transmitted it from place to place as pulses. If Caidom had thought the Raporoi would succumb to their grief, Caidom had been mistaken. These children of the haunted ones were a tough, implacable race and had built upon their limitations to accomplish magics.

Always among the Cai there had been those who dabbled in the arcane arts, who suspected fixed relationships among all things. But they had never mastered it. Caian philosophers toyed with the idea of disciplines in which a phenomenon of mechanics could be repeated infinitely, in which the elements themselves could be harnessed. Such magic was beyond Cai lore. But the children of the lonely ones in their awful blindness had found ways. Their magic awed him.

Carrie Hummingbird's dreams melded into awareness. She opened dark eyes and looked at him. "Are you all right, Alvin?"

"I'm all right, Carrie. Go back to sleep."

She cuddled closer. A soft breast pressed against his

arm. Her girl-scent, her living rhythms, were enticing.
He smiled to himself and put his arm around her, making her more comfortable. She might be threatened
among human males, but not so with a Caian. Her inno-
cence itself was her shield. Gently, he touched her with
mindsong, and she drifted back into peaceful sleep. It
was sad; though they could not generate mindsong, the
creatures—at least some of them—responded to it as
though they were starved for it.

What would they be—these strange, determined,
lonely people—if they could share senses as Cai did?

A few seats behind him a young couple sat very close,
their hands clasped together, and he sorted out their
murmurs from the other resonances in that range.

". . . have to find an apartment there, Johnny. I don't
know how we're going to live in the meantime. We'll
need some money."

"We'll make out, I guess. Tom—you remember Tom?
The guy with the computer outfit? He said there are jobs
in Cleveland. Said if a guy's willin' to work, he can make
a livin' there. Don't worry, honey. We'll get by."

Aaelefein felt the shared anxiety of them, their fear of
tomorrow and the dreams of someday. Overlaying it was
an understanding between them. Whatever happened
tomorrow, they would be together, back to back against
a hostile world or side by side striding forth into a bright
one. The love they had for each other was a compelling,
living thing within each of them, a song they could not
sing because they had no words for it. All they could do
was cling together and hope . . . and trust themselves
and each other.

The more he studied humans, the more he was awed
by them. They could not share, but they compensated.
Lacking the Cai blending of resonances, they created

substitutes, always seeking to transcend their limited senses. They forged elaborate languages of voice and tongue, of gesture, expression, and touch. It was awesome, the nuances they could convey with inflected words alone.

The love those two frightened young people shared was not different from the love he had shared with Nataea, it only lacked the means of expression.

A large, dark-skinned woman with two little girls sat across the aisle from him. They shared a grief, and the woman concentrated on comforting the children. The littlest one snuggled against her, the child's mind puzzled and troubled.

"When I die, will I go to Heaven, too, Aunt Judy?"

"Hush, child. Sure you will."

"Will I like it there?"

Aaelefein didn't have to turn his head to sense the hot tears forming in the woman's eyes. The tightness in her throat was echoed in his own.

"You sure will, child, 'cause your momma is there right this minute, fixin' it up just for you."

More and more, as he immersed himself numbly in the awful darkness generated by their presence, Aaelefein was drawn to these people . . . these humans of old Caiendon. They were alien to him, so different, yet in so many more ways alike.

The magical things they did with their tools, things that to Aaelefein were purest witchcraft, they called science. But those endeavors by which they tried to surmount their darkness, they called art. He recalled one, a duplication of a painting by a man named Rockwell—an aged woman and a young boy sat at a table by a window, heads bowed on clasped hands. An act of faith in the presence of others. The Caian had been deeply touched by it. The artist had sought transcendence by depicting others seeking the same.

". . . and blue curtains with white lace in our bedroom," the young woman behind him was murmuring sleepily. "Would you like that, Johnny?"

"You ain't gonna die, too, are you, Aunt Judy? Missie an' me ain't got anybody else."

". . . we'll have to have a car, I guess. I can work overtime for the down payment."

"Hush, child. Aunt Judy won't ever leave you two alone. Didn't I promise your momma?"

Toward the front of the bus, a man alone and lonely told himself, "She'll be there . . . I know she will . . . she'll give me another chance . . . I don't deserve it, but she will . . . just one more chance . . ."

". . . and we'll have pretty pictures of daisies on the walls . . ."

Aaelefein felt a swelling tightness in his throat. In his days among them he had come to feel a deep, gentle pity. They were blind, and they sought to see. They were deaf, and they sought to hear. Colors on fabric, audible harmonies played in concert, thoughts and shapes hewn from living rock—and without resonant blades!—words written and spoken, elaborate pretenses . . . with these arts the children of the haunted ones sought the undefinable. Whole souls imprisoned by limited senses, still they strove to be free.

He felt the soft breath of the girl beside him. He brushed her cheek with gentle fingertips. Mindsong caressed her. Be at peace, Carrie Hummingbird. For this moment, be free of the darkness. He hoped she would remember her dreams. They were as beautiful as any Cai's could be.

* * * * *

They had breakfast in western Nebraska in a little hamlet huddled among immense fields of grain. The place was full of rumpled passengers and sleepy locals. A freckled waitress glanced at him and then looked again, moon-eyed. He was relieved when she touched his hand while accepting the menu. There was no suspicion, just the ordinary reactions he seemed to generate among humans. He relaxed, damping the ache of human aura around him. In blue jeans and plaid shirt, loafers on his feet, and a scarf concealing the senester at his throat, he was a human among humans . . . or close enough to pass.

Carrie raised an eyebrow, her ebony eyes bright with humor.

"Women can't leave you alone," she teased.

He smiled at her, and, toying with the nuances of human speech, said, "I do my best."

At ease, he let his hearing and parse-sense range outward, searching in the low to medium ultrasonic lengths. It had become habit with him. Caiansong carried in those ranges above audible human frequencies. Never had his Nataea said his name that the accompanying mid-frequency harmonics had not carried their own special code, their secret song to each other.

"You do funny things, Alvin," Carrie said. "Sometimes when people look at you closely, you do a . . . a sort of thing with your eyes, and it's as though they stop noticing you. I wish I knew how you do that. Sometimes I'd give a lot not to be noticed."

"People are easily distracted," he said. "It's hard to concentrate on someone you don't know. But you can learn that trick, if you want to."

She shrugged. She was never quite sure whether he

was telling the truth or just playing with words. Alvin
Frost was the strangest man she had ever known. And
maybe the nicest. She knew he was attracted to her, but
she also knew there was an iron reserve about him. He
would never take advantage. She knew she had teased
him cruelly a time or two, testing, almost offering, but
he had kept his distance. She should feel rejected, she
supposed. But the response had never seemed like rejec-
tion. It was kind and loving. But a relationship just
wasn't to be.

They ate in silence, and Aaelefein was aware of the
occasional attentions of others in the place. People who
looked at them looked twice, but there was only curiosity
in them. That and a kind of wistfulness. People saw a
pretty Indian girl and a distinctive-looking man. Some
who looked wished, vaguely, that they could be them.

"You know something?" Carrie asked. "You always
smell good. Sort of like cinnamon and cloves."

"Thank you," he said, suddenly distracted. Far in the
distance among the meaningless background of ultrasonics was a pattern—no more than a hint, but it caught
his attention. "Come on, Carrie. We're finished here.
Let's wait outside."

The bus stood empty in the morning street. Few people were aboard. She watched him raise his head, seem
to taste the air. Then he turned purposefully and walked
toward the new sun. She tagged after him. At a corner
where time-worn bricks formed a head-high cornice
below blind windows, he stopped, raised his head, and
whistled. Carrie stood puzzled. The sound was sad and
eerie, yet she felt she had heard only part of it.

Aaelefein stared into the morning sky. Fascinated, she
peered there and at first saw nothing. Then there was a
mote against the sky which grew until she could distin-

guish beating wings. It was a meadowlark, coming
directly toward them. The bird continued on, and its
trill was a tiny duplicate of the whistle she had heard.
With a thrust and flutter, it landed on the brick ledge.
Alvin held out his hand, and the bird hopped onto his
finger.

The lark sang to him, weaving a medley of incredible
brillance just for him. Aaelefein tipped his head in concentration.

Suddenly, Carrie felt a strange dread. Something odd
was happening, and it frightened her. Moving close to
Alvin, she slipped her hand into his. He seemed not to
notice, but as their fingers met, it was as though her
heart touched his. Sadness washed across her. She felt a
terrible hurt and a deep determination that she knew
were not her own. Terrible grief tore at her . . . a sense of
beckoning, of searching. Alvin's fingers twitched, and
the perceptions dwindled. Carrie heard a soft flutter of
wings, and she looked up. Through the tears in her eyes,
she could barely make out the bird flying away.

Alvin looked down at her, took her hand in both of
his. "I'm sorry, Carrie. I wouldn't have done that to you.
But I was concentrating. I didn't notice."

"The bird . . . it spoke to you?"

"No. It's only a dumb creature. But its song is . . .
more than song. Somewhere it learned new notes."

"You are searching for something, aren't you?"

"Yes, Carrie."

She didn't understand any of it. She didn't try. She
had felt the love within him and the awful grief that
drove him.

"She must have been very beautiful, Alvin."

11

The mail truck from the Colorado School of Mines protested as its driver backed it jarringly over the curb in front of Jacob Laurel's A-frame bungalow. The crate standing alone on the truck bed shuddered.

Laurel, his aging face gone white, bounded from his railed porch and onto the lawn, waving his arms. "Watch what you're doing, for Heaven's sake! That specimen is irreplaceable!"

Grinning unconcernedly, the driver wrenched his wheel over, squealed his tires on the incline, and brought the truck to rest six feet from Laurel's garage door. The driver and his assistant swung down, placed ramps, and unbuckled a heavy-duty dolly. Sweating in the high, bright sunlight the pair hoisted the wooden crate and strapped it in place. Laurel hurried to open the garage door.

Inside was no garage at all, but a neat laboratory dominated by a wide, clean center table. An array of devices lined the walls. Laurel ran nervous fingers through the wisp of white hair at his temples as the two deliverymen trundled the crate jauntily down the narrow ramp and into his domain. "This side up" was stenciled upside down on the slat sides. Laurel bit his lip.

"Careful, please," he scolded. "Those stones are a

hundred million years old. Can you, ah, right it without breaking it?"

"Right it?" The driver looked at the crate. "Oh, right side up. Okay. Lay it over, Will."

"Careful!" Laurel almost danced in his concern. But for all their disinterest, the two were gentle. They eased the crate over onto its side, then upended it properly, and finally slid it to the end of the table. On its top, in prim letters, was the origin, "Sul Ross University, Alpine, Texas," and the forwarding label, "Dr. Jacob Laurel, Paleontology, Colorado School of Mines." Laurel found he was perspiring. He had waited a year for these samples. And they had waited for him for a hundred million years. The deliveryman secured the straps on the dolly and trundled it back onto the truck. The driver looked expectantly at Laurel.

"Thank you," Laurel said distractedly as he signed his name to the receipt and accepted the yellow copy. He quickly closed his door as the man left, oblivious to the driver's scowl at not receiving a tip.

For a time he simply stared at the crate. Then he took a deep breath, rubbed cold hands together, and went to find a tool to cut the straps.

At seventy-seven years of age, Jacob Laurel, Ph.D., was twelve years into technical retirement from the teaching of archeology, paleontology, and anthropology. But as consultant-emeritus to four universities and the holder of a pair of open research grants from foundations in New Jersey and Michigan, he still had the contacts he needed to pursue the several quests that intrigued him. Foremost among these was the cataloging of thousands of anachronisms which, despite all evidence, seemed to place manlike creatures in the midst of the Mesozoic era, one hundred million years ago! Throughout the century and a half of modern science, such things had been found . . . puzzling evidences quite without verification in corollary fact, but puzzling nonetheless. There was the triceratops femur in Arizona with a bit of what seemed to be shaped quartz embedded in the bone. There was that bit of impressed fossil in Switzerland, the imprint of an ankylosaur skull that appeared bound in woven hemp. There was the thing from the LaBrea pits, a remnant of a reptilian creature with a crystal "blade" in the midst of it.

And there was the damned track—his own discovery, forty years ago, which had earned him only derision from his peers. It was a footprint, for all the world the print of a man with a size 10 quadruple-A foot. It was in undisturbed strata on the shoulder of an Illinois wash. He placed it in the middle Cretaceous period, documented and published it. For forty years, he had regretted that move. His only comfort even now was that most of those who had not let him live it down weren't around to crow anymore. He had outlived them. Jacob Laurel intended to live long enough to corroborate his discovery.

With hands that should have trembled but did not, he snipped the bands and pried the lid off the crate. He snorted. They didn't pack with excelsior any more. The crate was full of white polystyrene peanuts. Planting his glasses firmly on his thin nose, he began digging.

There were three samples, slabs of ancient limestone several inches thick and cut to sizes ranging from eighteen inches square to the largest, almost two by three feet. Holding his breath, he hoisted the last of them across onto the table, then removed his glasses and mopped his face with a handkerchief. His glasses were waterfalls. Wiping them, he wandered into the kitchen, looking for his pitcher of iced tea. The newspaper was spread on the dinette where he had left it when the truck honked, and for a moment he gazed again at the image of a man printed a half-page high in the local feature section. The Centurion again. Or so they had taken to calling him.

For the past three days or so, news media had been having a field day with that one. He appeared and reappeared in various parts of the city, walking along a street, climbing through a library window, sitting on top of a transit bus, acting, for all the world, like a bizarre and erratic tourist. He wore a red theatrical costume of some sort, reminiscent of the garb of a soldier of the Roman Empire. That was why they had started calling him the Centurion.

For three days he had been the most sought after, most photographed, and most mysterious figure in Denver. He had even bumped the water resources controversy and the Southmoor Slasher from the front pages. He was a sensation. Obviously he was a hoax, but certainly an original one, and Laurel was intrigued with the special effects. The man appeared and disappeared at will, even among crowds of people. A local radio station had offered a reward of $1,040—matching its frequency—for proof of his identity and his purpose.

The picture in today's *Post* was excellent. The Centurion seemed to have no reluctance to cooperate with photographers. He was a tall, athletic man with broad shoulders and a strangely striking face—all inclined planes and slanted lines beneath a close-cropped cap of light brown hair. He had arresting eyes. Women commentators never failed to mention them. Their male counterparts more often mentioned the decorative blade, like a shortsword, at his belt, and the scarlet cape he wore over his . . . body armor? It was hard to tell. The cape was ankle length and of such silk-fine stuff that it seemed to spread and flow with every breeze.

The latest ten-day wonder, Laurel mused. There was always something. At least the Centurion hadn't hurt anyone. Sooner or later the truth would come out. He would be advertising a new brand of toothpaste or some new form of checkbook savings. Some advertising agency was having its moment of glory.

He found his iced tea and went back to the garage. For several minutes he adjusted lights, studied dig placements on the chart on his wall, and generally got his thinking into the proper state of discipline. Then, resolutely, he began the study of his prizes.

He started with the grid-47-A40 piece. It was beautiful, a near-perfect imprint of a saurian foot. He picked up a rule, frowned in distaste, and tossed it aside. It was metric. He found another that measured in inches. The track was twenty-one inches in length overall, with the thick, bird-toed impress of a grazing reptile. An excellent fossil. It could have been made yesterday.

The second slab, the smallest, was a puzzler. It seemed to be a human footprint—modern man, narrow foot, high arch, and five distinct toemarks blurred as though impressed through cloth. It would take study. Second toe longest, he noted. Classic foot.

But the largest slab was the anomaly. On it were two of the distinct human prints and another of the dinosaur prints, smaller than the twenty-one-inch specimen. This one was slim-toed and measured seventeen inches in length. The "human" prints were, respectively, seven inches and eleven inches in length. Different creatures. But on this slab, quite clearly, the smaller "human" print had been overprinted by the demonichus. And the larger "human" print slightly overlapped the saurian's track. There could be no doubt. No doubt at all. Somewhere in what was now Texas, creatures with humanlike feet had co-existed with dinosaurs. He took a deep breath and leaned on the table, his slight shoulders hunched.

It would take a long time, possibly months of tedious work, to substantiate what he believed to be true. But he knew. As he stood there, he knew. The three prints on that slab of ancient chalk had been made within moments of each other.

The specimens were all that he had been told. They were more. Dr. Jacob Laurel had not known awe in forty years. But he knew it now. One hundred million years ago something with the advanced anthropoid foot of modern man had been pursued by a great carnivorous lizard. And the lizard in turn had been pursued by another, larger thing that had a human foot.

By the end of the day, his awe had turned to a burning hunger that obliterated the aches in his aging shoulders, the pain of standing too long on his feet. He had measured and photographed, done a dozen separate depth-analyses, stress-tested the rock itself, and scraped its edges for corroborating analysis of its makeup. Tired and hungry, he finally tore himself away from the work. He was becoming fuzzy around the edges.

I'll think on it again tomorrow, he told himself. But I'll find the same thing. It's true. By God, it's true!

Forty years before, Jacob Laurel had sensed destiny—the feeling of pieces coming together to form a whole, the solving of a puzzle of such magnitude it staggered the imagination. Forty years ago he had not had hard evidence. But he had *known*. Awe flooded through him again, and destiny gloried around him. One hundred million years ago! Man! True man.

Slumped and weary but with great excitement raging in him, Laurel trudged into the kitchen, poured a glass an inch deep with white rum, and added as much water. He carried the glass into the living room, set it on the table beside his recliner, dropped into the chair, and let his scant weight sag into it. He wished he knew how to sing. Hell, he even wished he remembered how to cry.

* * * * *

Three and one-half miles away, on the roof of a lumber shed beneath a darkling sky, Haralan Caharel-Ruast raised his head and opened his senses. The darkness sombered him, but he ignored it. His nostrils twitched and his almond eyes widened as he ranged his senses outward. He turned slowly, then stopped, focusing. For a long moment he stood, fixing in his awareness the taste of Feyadeen and its source. Then, clamping his will down again against the encroaching darkness, he leaped to the ground and strode away along a northbound street. As he went, his stride lengthened to a ground-covering lope.

* * * * *

During the past few days, the Denver police department had built a large file on the character called Centurion. But it was one of the nut files. It classed with Sasquatch reports and giant birds—except that the Centurion was undeniably real. The call desk at DPD Central had been so swamped with Centurion calls that the switchboard now automatically routed them to a clerk. They would find the joker eventually and slap him with about a hundred misdemeanor charges. He hadn't bothered anyone particularly, but he was one hell of a nuisance.

This time, though, it was different. The clerk took the first call and shot it back to Central desk. The Centurion had appeared again. He had walked into a private home and walked out with an old man wrapped in a blanket. Several neighbors had seen the incident.

The missing man was a retired professor associated with the School of Mines. The Centurion no longer was the property of the misdemeanor-nut section. Kidnapping was a felony offense.

12

Roy Holloway was tired. The trip had been exhausting. It had left him with more uncertainties than answers, and with a sour taste in his mouth from having to deal with a system that demanded high dues of anyone trying to run an honest business. The project was a simple one—drainage structures for a proposed highway extension west of Mandel. But it had proved not so simple. The drainage, it turned out, would cause ponding in a lowland some miles away, and the environmental spooks had seen a chance for some high-profile confrontation.

His bid had been an honest bid. It had been the best bid. But then things had begun to go sour. The freaks hollered, and the politicians in Illinois reacted, and the plans were revised. That changed project plans in Indiana, and suddenly his little drainage job was in limbo.

He had spent two days in Chicago, trying to get the work sorted out, then some more days in Springfield, trying to get a line on the mess there, and finally a long week in Washington at hearings. And still the situation wasn't straightened out. And if it ever got straightened out, the project would go back to bid, and he would have to start all over again.

He felt like spending a little time with Meg. She could always take his mind off things. She was a light in the darkness. In the past year, he had grown to love her, to depend on her. It puzzled him. The disappearance of Teddy, and the sudden death of Dorothy, still haunted him. The nightmares tormented him every night. And yet, despite that, Meg could raise his spirits and quicken his pulse. He wouldn't have believed, a year ago, that any woman ever would appeal to him again. But Meg had come along. His Meg.

He landed at Indianapolis, retrieved his pickup, and drove the thirty-plus miles to Rockville, tired and irritable and confused. There had been no good days lately. Only bad ones. He wondered if he shouldn't go straight to the O'Toole house—just stop by for a few minutes. Just seeing Meg might lift his spirits.

Roy Holloway was a simple, straightforward man. His measure of life was simple, too . . . a balance of the good days against the bad. Mostly, through the seventeen years with Dorothy, they had been good days. The bad times had come when Teddy disappeared.

Roy had suspected for a long time that there was something wrong with his son—the silent reserve that had grown between parents and child, the unpredictable behavior, the flaring temper, and the times of sullen secrecy. Dorothy and he had worried about it. There had been the freakish, mindless, blaring music, snatches of lyric that were not the words of song but the rantings of juvenile lunacy. There had been the wary, dull-seeming friends who came at odd hours to hide with Teddy behind his closed door. They had seen it, and worried, and done nothing because they didn't know what to do.

The day came, though, when Roy walked into Teddy's room and caught him with the apparatus. From that

moment, pretense was gone. There followed the recrimi-
nations, the shouting and the tears, the demands and
refusals, the agony. Roy hadn't really tried to find out
where Teddy got the stuff. He hadn't really wanted to
know . . . because he knew that if he did find the pusher,
he would kill him with his bare hands.

Then one morning Teddy was gone, and they didn't
even know how to search for him. On that day, Roy suspected he would never see his son again. Worse, he knew
he had lost him a long time before.

The agony had never left him. There had to have been
something he could have done . . . something that
would have kept it all from ever happening. That was
where the nightmares came from. He should have done
something, but he had never known what to do. So
Teddy—poor, altered kid—was gone. The pushers and
the freaks had pounced on him, had led him, and now
he was gone.

It had been even tougher on Dorothy, he knew. She
couldn't overcome the might-have-beens either, and she
couldn't live with them. The night he learned that her
car had gone off the Elm Creek bridge, there had been
almost no grief left for him to mourn her. He had not
expected ever to love anyone again.

But then he met Margaret . . . little Meg. Oh, she had
always been around, first as Margaret O'Toole and then
as Margaret Harrison. He had noticed her—pretty,
laughing little pixie of a girl who kept things going in
Mark Froman's real estate office. But only after Dorothy
was gone—anguished months after—had he ever really
looked at her.

He hadn't courted her, exactly. They simply met, and
then they met again, and after a while, he found that he
could not do without her for long. It was as though all

the lights had gone out for him . . . and then she came along and offered him a candle.

Yes, he decided, he would stop by the O'Tooles' before he went home. Just seeing her might be the best thing he could do right now. It had been a long, dark two weeks, and he needed a candle.

Nearing Elm Creek, he passed the old fairgrounds. There were tents there, in the pasture by the creek—a big top and a motley cluster of smaller tents. Vans, campers, and trailers lined the creek and the entrance road. Many of the people were oddly dressed. There were men with dark robes and long hair, women wearing strange, dull saris and dark caps. He slowed as he passed, and suddenly all the old hurts rose in him again, and with them the anger.

What idiot, he wondered, had allowed a bunch of freaks to set up shop on county property? Some nut cult was having a mystical experience there at the expense of the taxpayers who would have to foot the bill to clean up after them, and he knew the signs. Since Teddy, he knew the signs. A nut cult. Freaks and drugs. He made a mental note to do some chewing out. The place for freaks was California, not Indiana. This was *his* part of the world, and he had lost too much to the freaks ever to be able to tolerate them again. Let them go someplace where he didn't have to see them. They didn't belong here.

Before him the light was red. When he stopped, someone approached the pickup . . . one of the robed ones, trying to hand him a leaflet through the open window.

"Brother," the creature said, "the way is truth."

Roy regarded the dirty whiskers sprouting from the pimply face, the rheumy, too-old eyes with the pinpoint pupils. He thought of Teddy. "If you stick that arm in here, I'll break it off," he growled.

The creature stared at him dully, eyes not quite focusing. "Cast off blindness, Brother. In truth is the light out of darkness."

Roy turned away, sickened. The light was still red, but he hit the gas and steered the pickup onto the main road, gritting his teeth. Someone was going to catch hell for this!

He was still fuming when he pulled up in front of the O'Toole house, but his spirits lifted when Meg met him at the door. Her smile dazzled him, a radiance that was almost a tangible force. I've been away too long, he thought. Have I ever seen her look so lovely?

Her eyes looked up at him. Her eyes, yet so . . . striking! How could he have just now noticed?

"Roy!" she said. "I didn't expect you today. When did you get back? Don't just stand there gawking, for Heaven's sake. Come in." She reached for his hand, then suddenly recoiled, her smile faltering. Her eyes widened, as though he had suddenly hurt her.

Puzzled, he entered and turned as she closed the door. "What's the matter, Meg?" Her eyes held him. They seemed larger, somehow . . . luminous and deep. They were different. He blinked the thought away. He was tired.

"You're so angry," she said. "You—it surprised me. Did something happen?"

How had she known he was angry? "Oh, nothing. There's a mess at the fairgrounds. I guess I'm just in a bad mood."

"Yes." Her smile returned, tentative now. "You are." Again she took his hand, and she seemed to wince. But she held it. Then she said, "Oh. Those people. I heard. But they aren't hurting anybody, Roy."

"Well, they can go someplace else and not hurt anybody. I don't want to see them." The old hurts welled again in his chest, and he saw real pain in her eyes. Physical pain, as though his anger had pierced her, had made her bleed. What was it about her that seemed so different? Suddenly she was suffering, and abruptly Roy had the eerie feeling that some other part of her—some part he had never met—was pushing forth to shield her. He looked away for a moment, then turned back, and Meg seemed almost normal again.

"Please sit, Roy," she invited. "Tell me about your trip. Are you all right?"

"I'm fine," he assured her. "I guess I'm just more tired than I thought. For a minute there, I felt like I was asleep on my feet."

It was a strange, uncomfortable visit. They sat on the sunporch and chatted. He told her about his trip, the frustrations and disappointments of it. A time or two he started to mention the nut cult at the fairgrounds—that had really topped off his day—but each time she interrupted, veering from that as though it hurt her, seeming to practically read his mind, to alter course before the course was set. He shrugged it off. She didn't want to hear about such things.

He had imagined that radiance, that dazzling welcome at her door. He must have imagined it. She seemed pleasant enough now, but somehow reserved. Distant? It was nothing he could put a finger on. Maybe she was tired, too. He knew he was.

"I need to get home, Meg. I just stopped by to let you know I'm back. I'm a little tired. Maybe we can talk tomorrow. Okay?"

"Of course, Roy." She smiled again, and there was a trace of that dazzle in it. Just for a second she was looking at his eyes, and he blinked. If he had imagined some change there—in her eyes—he was still imagining it. But he couldn't identify what it was.

A frame-taut canvas stood on the canning table, propped against some books. He stepped around to look at it. "What's this?"

"Oh, I'm just playing with an idea. I may try to paint it."

There were pencil lines on the treated canvas—an ovoid shape, like the outline of a face but slightly wide at the top and oddly sloped toward the bottom. A straight line bisected it from top to bottom and arcs crossed it, dividing its height into approximate thirds. "A portrait?" He tipped his head. There was something unusual about the shape drawn there, something not quite . . . normal. But he couldn't grasp it. "Who's it going to be?"

"I really don't know yet. I just started."

"Well, let me know when you decide." She smiled at that, a quick, irrepressible smile. He really didn't remember her being so damned pretty. "I see you're working on a suntan," he added.

"I'm what?"

"A tan. You've been getting some sun."

She looked at her bare arms. She seemed surprised. "Oh. I suppose I have."

He noticed something about her eyes then that he hadn't noticed before. The pupils were not exactly round. They were slightly elongated. How had he missed that? The effect was pleasing, but . . . odd.

"Tomorrow, then," he said, grinning. "Bye, Meg."

* * * * *

Roy had second thoughts about raising hell after he got some sleep and thought about it over coffee. Something Meg had said made him think. Were those freaks really bothering anybody?

Maybe not, a part of him said. But then the old, hard anger hit him again. What was he thinking? Turn and look the other way? Again? Never again. Maybe that's the problem, everybody just looks the other way, he thought. But right or wrong, he knew he could never look away again.

He made some phone calls and then went to the courthourse. He wasn't the only one there.

"How in hell," he demanded, "can you justify letting a bunch of creeps like that on county property? How many sheriff's officers are assigned to keep them in line? How much is it going to cost to pick up their garbage? And how many decent local kids are going to get a dose of something while they're here? Do you want that kind of liability?"

"Roy . . . all of you . . . we can't just rescind a permit. What are the grounds?"

"The hell you can't." Roy towered over the man at the desk. "You get some deputies out there and lift a few floorboards. Check some tirewells and vent covers. See what you find."

He had support, and he had his way. By noon, the sheriff's property office had a fair stash of illegal substances in custody, and the jail had a few robed loonies on charges. The rest of the camp was dismantled and gone by two.

Roy drove out to the fairgrounds to satisfy himself that they were gone. A pair of deputies waved at him as he drove through, then shrugged at each other as he left. Roy Holloway had certainly got that straightened out.

And, of course, he was right, and who could blame him? Holloway was a decent guy, and everyone knew what had happened to his boy . . . and to his wife. Some idiot down at the courthouse had his neck on the line for ever issuing that permit in the first place.

But Roy Holloway wouldn't push the matter. He was a decent guy. He wasn't vindictive or cruel. There was just no more room in his world for freaks.

13

Aaelefein traveled far enough south from Pipestone, Minnesota, that the resonance of Carrie Hummingbird would not interfere with his mindsong. He had to travel until she was simply a memory to him and not an awareness of presence. The place he found, where his senses no longer detected her, was a smallish town in Iowa, and he got off at the bus station there and walked back along Highway 59 to a little motel he had seen from the bus.

It was late evening, nearly night. The girl watching television behind the desk in the cubbyhole office was a pleasant-faced blonde, both willowy and ample in a black jersey and shorts. Humans, he had noted, came in more interesting variety than did the Cai. They were, of course, a far newer race.

A bell tinkled as he opened the door. For a moment the girl concentrated on her television, then grudgingly tore herself away and turned to him. Her eyes went wide and starry.

He waited for her to speak. When she seemed unable to, he asked. "Do you have a vacant room?"

She jolted to awareness. "Oh . . . yes, sir, we do."

"Thank you. I'd like it. Just for tonight."

"For tonight. Yes, sir." She continued to stare at him. He knew by now it wasn't the manner of his dress. He.

wore dark trousers, a gray turtleneck shirt, and a sport coat, and carried a valise. All proper. No, the problem was one he was growing used to. No matter how he tried, he could not avoid having such effects on human females. He understood it. Any human male seeing his first Cai girl would be just as dazzled. The creatures were limited to five senses, with the result that those five fed the entirety of human awareness, just as seven senses fed Cai awareness. Moreover, the girl's entire reaction was to the sight of him. She found his features strange and pleasing. So she reacted totally to a single sense at a power of seven-fifths. In short, she was thirty-five times as strongly struck by his presence as a Cai girl would have been.

It seemed a reasonable theory, at least. And observation verified it. What it failed to explain was why a Caian, in turn, should find humans so . . . interestingly attractive. When he smiled at her, he thought for a moment that she would fall out through her eyes. He picked up the guest cards and handed them to her, breaking the trance.

"My name is Alvin Frost." He pointed to the appropriate space on the card. "Put down San Francisco, California. I have no car. I will stay only tonight. I'll pay in advance."

Looking over her shoulders, he noticed the television set. The voice of a commentator droned. The picture on the screen was an image of Haralan. Aaelefein found it a good likeness, considering that it was a likeness only of sight. He hoped some bird, touched with his song, had reached his friends so that they would know he still lived. Haralan, the announcer told him, was in Denver. That was in Colorado. He imaged the land mass and its delineations and placed the site. They were there, then, in search of the Corad-bane. He wished them well, and some part of his love-aura must have touched the human girl. She almost melted. He had to be more careful about that. Not all humans were totally devoid of empathy. Carrie Hummingbird had taught him that, and with it had come a resurgent hope. If there were human females with empathy, that was one more hope for Nataea. The bird-song had been a clue. Human empathy offered a hope.

The girl offered—desperately wanted—to show him the way to his room, but he soothed her, and gentle, probing mindsong sent her back to her television set, only a little puzzled at the secretions still working within her.

In seven fives of days Aaelefein had absorbed a great deal of understanding of the human race. It was his choice to pass among them unnoticed, and he had become skilled at it. If they found him remarkable, it was only as a remarkable human. He was almost enjoying the deception. Among the Cai, so little deception was possible that the skills were not inherent. He noted that Haralan, apparently becoming quite famous in Denver, had made no attempt at deception. That was like the big Caian. It simply would not have occurred to him. Gentle warrior, he thought, my blessing to you in what our Feya has set you to.

The room was a cubicle with a bath stall, bed, and various human apparatus. He turned on the television set. Two women were commiserating over the condition of a soiled garment. One pulled a box of compound from a bag, and the two launched into a discourse on its merits. Aaelefein watched, entranced. The poor creatures . . . they had developed elaborate techniques of mass persuasion based upon portraying themselves as shallow and trivial. And obviously, they responded by rote to such stimuli, otherwise they would have ceased to practice it. It was yet another deception among them.

Humans, he knew now, were neither shallow nor trivial. They had minds the equal of those of the Cai . . . and in some ways superior, as a result of ages of compensation for limited senses. But the deception games they played were deeply rooted, and he had begun to understand why. By pretending simplicity, they could, for a moment, feel an understanding of one another as complete—within the bounds of the enforced simplicity—as their understanding of themselves. They needed—desperately needed—to feel that understanding.

They were so awesomely, terribly lonely.

With a start, he became aware of the omnipresent darkness of this world. In seven fives of days immersed among them, he had become numb to it. Sometimes he forgot to notice it at all. That, above all else, was frightening.

With the fright came a surge of yearning, of longing for his lost love. Nataea, he thought with a power that welled into his throat, please have leaped. We need you. I need you. I love you, my Nataea.

He concentrated now on the darkness. It had perceptible ebbs and flows. In the night, as people slept, it became less agonizing. He waited now for that gradual shift.

He had done what he could do now, to adapt, to acclimatize, to know this world that once had been Caiendon. He had put off as long as he could the thing he had set out to do. If he failed to find Nataea, he knew, Caidom was through. But if he failed to find her, he was not sure he would care.

Her physical self was dead. He would never again look upon that pretty, pixie-touched face, never again touch those soft, responsive hands, never hear the song of that lovely voice. But still, there was a thread of hope. Physically, Nataea was no more. But a person who was Nataea—just possibly—might be.

He tasted the ebbing darkness. It was time to begin.

He had prepared. He had learned. He had come to this place because the distractions were limited. And now the darkness was in its wane.

Aaelefein Fe-Ruast, last hope of Caidom, stood alone in a cubicle on Earth, bowed his head, and focused his mind and his resonance. At his throat the crystal senester came alive. Its seven clustered gems blazed and sparkled, reacting to his welling harmonies, magnifying them. Colors danced and resonances pitched and sang in seven rages of spectrum. Powerfully, the crystals pulsed, their facets radiating overlapping ranges of frequency, quelling the background of electromotive forces with corresponding but stronger opposite waves of atmospheric harmonics. He willed the pulses of the air be stilled. He sang the frequencies, and the senester blazed at his throat. Outward and outward raced the stillness of precisely countered harmonics. He pushed the stillness to the limits of the senester's vibrant power and held it there.

In the motel office, the ten o'clock news flickered out and the machine emitted only electronic snow and mindless buzz. North on Highway 59, a highway patrol dispatch went dead in mid-broadcast. In Marysville, Missouri, a gospel station's tower stood mute, its broadcast nullified. Pan American Flight 28 approaching Kansas City's airport found its radios dead and climbed for altitude. Citizens Band units on a hundred highways dropped their needles to the peg and went silent. Radio 540 Chicago, 50,000 watts, and satellite relays of BBC-TV to mid-America, suffered the same. They ceased. Ten thousand evening snacks sat cold in ten thousand micro-wave ovens as pulses from 30,000 meters to 0.3 centi-meters were counter-resonated. Military satellites, immune above the atmosphere, registered an unprece-dented phenomena; bedlam erupted on a startled conti-nent whose defense intelligence had just been compromised.

In the dark-pervaded quiet of a dome of silence past horizons, Aaelefein Fe-Ruast began the mindsong of search. From Ohio to Wyoming, in the pleasant silence of a suddenly arcane world, a medley of tender harmon-ies went out, touched with scintillance and couched in yearning.

In the quiet of night a lonely Caian called out to his lost love.

* * * * *

In a cove behind a croft high on the shoulder of a mountain peak, Sefraeonia the percept raised her head and poised, sensing. Winifraeda Feya stopped what she was doing, and Haralan Caharel-Ruast came from his castle.

"Aaelefein," Sefraeonia pointed eastward. "He searches."

Dr. Jacob Laurel, sitting beside the tiny Feya, shook his head, his eyes glistening. "My God," he said, "how beautiful."

* * * * *

Lieutenant Colonel Paul Davis, OD in the situation room at North American Air Defense Command Cheyenne Mountain, picked up his redline. "Sir," the voice told him, "we have another blackout. East. It's big, sir. Everything east is out."

"Everything?"

"Ten kilohertz into the infrared. Colorado Springs is right on the fringe. And something is happening inside, sir. People are . . . it's like some of them are listening, sir."

"Listening to what?"

"I don't know, sir." The voice was choked, muffled. "But sir, I . . . I think I'm crying."

*   *   *   *   *

Air traffic control at Wichita, with inbounds stacked for repairs on the VLS strobes, found itself mute. Jeff Burnes looked through wet eyes at the blank screens, the dead radios. He felt like doing the only thing he could do. He prayed.

*   *   *   *   *

Separately and independently, at Washington, Omaha, Leavenworth, Alta Loma, and a dozen other centers, commanders put their forces on Red Alert.

*   *   *   *   *

"Something's wrong with the TV," Henry O'Toole observed, but Hazel wasn't listening. She stood by the archway, cradling a dead long-distance call. They looked at each other. He stood up, and she replaced the phone.

They met halfway and put their arms around each other, unaware even of their daughter.

Margaret stood rigid, arms at her sides, fists clenched. Her pretty face was uptilted, eyes wide, mouth working, struggling with sounds. Over and over she murmured, "Ah-ay-eh-le-fane." It was a lyric, a refrain full of fantastic intonations, minor-key variations on a recurrent theme. It was a primitive, bleeding, pleading chord of heart-rending love, and she strove to sing it. "Ah-ay-eh-le-fane . . . A-a-e-le-fein."

From the great, dark eyes of Margaret O'Toole Harrison, the unrestrained tears of Nataea washed down shared pixie cheeks, and the lyric burst free.

"Aaelefein."

* * * * *

With burning will that made him tonemaster of the chord, Aaelefein pressed the mindsong outward and outward into the quiet of a vast bubble of silenced air. His empathy keen to the breaking point, the senester dazzling the room around him with dancing radiances, he pressed his song of search. Keening, pulsating, unearthly in its rending beauty, the soundless song went forth, driving even the darkness back.

Among the children of the haunted ones, lovers hugged and wept their joy. The ill and the whole, the young and the old, human and human-adopt, felt their souls rent, expanded, and mended with each pulse of the glorious, aching longing that barraged them.

Songs would be written, babies conceived, great works begun, and feuds ended because of this night. Churches would be built and covenants kept on the strength of it. Some could not respond, but many would. For the first

time in its history, the human race heard a lovesong of
the Cai.

Sapped and drained, Aaelefein collapsed to the floor.
The senester dulled. His song was done. With all his
senses, he followed the trailing, lingering echoes of it
and listened.

There, on the dimming, bittersweet keen of the final
pulse, wafting back to him, was a tiny additional thing,
a trace of highlight he had not put there—could never
put there. It was a lyric trill, notes of brilliance dancing
on the fabric of his song. It was a scintillance.

Moved beyond tears by the fragility of it, he concentrated. With his last energy, he fixed its direction in his
mind. There, out there, a person who was also Nataea
had heard the song. And from there, a tiny scintillant
trill riding the last echoes of his harmonics, she had
responded.

She was far away, but he knew the direction to go.

14

"Did you hear it?" Winifraeda Feya asked, great curious eyes on the man who sat beside her.

Jacob Laurel's septuagenarian eyes were moist in the starlight. "I felt . . . something. Something very sad, very beautiful. It was like music that grew within me, not from outside. It made me want to cry."

"Yes. You have empathy. Not very much, but a little. I had already sensed it. What you felt was mindsong, Jacob. Very powerful, very intense. The singer is Aaelefein. He willed the chord that brought us here. He seeks Nataea, who died when we arrived."

Laurel preferred, then, to have misunderstood. His capacity for wonder in recent hours had about reached its limit.

"Where is he?"

Winifraeda pursed perfect, ancient lips. "Out there. On this world." She paused, reckoning from the mindsong of Aaelefein. "He is more than a hundred fives of your miles from this place. Less than two hundred fives. His will is very strong."

"And he is another of you . . . like you?"

"Not like me, Jacob. I am Feya. In that way you are more like me than is Aaelefein. But he is of our race. Your race has never known us. Only your most ancient

ancestors lived when ours departed this world. And yet I
find it interesting that you do have, within your lore, a
perception of us. It is vague and confused, but it is there.
We are the people you call elves."

"Elves?" He stared at her, astonished. The wonders of
his past hours here, the mass impossibilities witnessed,
had left him numb to surprise . . . or so he had thought.

"It is a word I found in your pre-speech resonance.
You have almost said it more than once. Apparently
something in our appearance touches an image you have
that focuses best on that word. When Haralan first
brought you here, when I touched your mind to calm
you and learn your speech, I found it strong in your
vibrations. Elf. Elves. You knew us by forms of that
word."

"I suppose the word did come to mind," he admitted,
still staring, "but that is ridiculous. You people came
here . . . returned here, as you say . . . from another planet. Another solar system. But elves? Elves are part of
human mythology."

"Look at me, Jacob Laurel. Am I a myth?"

"No. Apparently not. But in our various mythologies,
elves range anywhere from little green people to demi-
gods. You are little, Winifraeda. But he isn't." He pointed to Haralan, then at Sefraeonia. "Nor is she. And
none of you is green."

"Niceties of folklore," the Feya suggested. "On some
residual memory of our race, yours has built a tapestry of
misconceptions. Humans cannot consciously remember
elves. We were gone before you were truly human. But
some of you, sometime, undoubtedly have seen pixies,
sprites, nymphs . . . those we call Cai-kindred—or, I
suppose, with your word, elvenkindred—and added to
racial memory some details from them. Sprites and their

various cousins are quite small as compared to Cai or
human stature. Woodnymphs, seen in shade, might
appear somewhat green to your eyes. It is their nature,
just as waternymphs can appear silver or blue."

"Those things are real, then? You are telling me there
are really leprechauns and . . . and trolls and gnomes and
dwarves, such creatures exist?"

"Take my hand, Jacob. I still have too few words."

Again he held her tiny hand and again felt the odd
awareness grow in him, as though a part of himself. He
had found he could locate its source through concentration. It was behind his forehead, just above his nose.

"Say those things again," she said.

"Trolls. Dwarves. Gnomes. Leprechauns. Imps. Fair-
ies. Vampires. Werewolves. Golems. Succubi. Tell me,
are you really reading my mind?"

"You mean do I know what you think? No. But when
you think a thing I know how you feel about it and I can
extrapolate. The Cai do not have telepathy, Jacob. Only
empathy. No intelligent race could survive telepathy.
But such strange images I perceive. Some seem . . . ah,
another good word—faerie . . . and some not. Vampires,
werewolves, and golems seem entirely human in their
essence. It is likely such have existed. The images bear
reality. But they must have been poor, twisted humans
inflicted in some terrible way. I cannot explain succubi.
You have no clear image of that, therefore I have no perception. But as to the others, yes. Your images of leprechauns and imps may be the same thing, possibly names
given to forest pixies. They are much smaller than true
pixies, who are nearly as tall as humans. The little forest
pixies are sweet, impractical folk who never achieved any
great degree of intelligence but are pleasant to have
around.

"Your impression of trolls and gnomes also has the feel of pixie, but very distorted. I don't like to think what might have happened to some of the poor pixies to make such things occur. It is very sad."

"You speak fondly of pixies," he said. "Tell me about them, please."

"The pixies were—still are, on Nendacaida and, perhaps, here, too—the sweetest race of beings ever to come to the light. They exist to comfort and to be loved. They are pretty, winsome folk, and always were quite caring toward both the Cai and your own ancestors, the Raporoi. It is possible for pixies to join with either Cai or human and produce progeny. Their seed seems to accept either race."

"You imply that humans and Cai could not join to procreate."

"No. I imply nothing. I simply do not know. Until now, Cai and humans have never met."

"And yet pixies could, with either."

"Of course. Our Nataea, the one who died, was part pixie. Some of her most endearing qualities undoubtedly came of her pixie blood. And there are some of your race, I suppose, who are part—," The Feya's eyes widened. "Haralan! Sefraeonia! Come here!"

When they came she said, "Children, I think Aaelefein's quest is more hopeful than we thought. Nataea was part pixie. If there were a human female who also is part pixie, and receptive, Nataea could have leaped. A true pixie was not her only chance. A *human* pixie might do."

Laurel stared dumbly at them. The little Feya had been talking to him, then suddenly lapsed into intricate song, which the others came to hear. The song—speech—whatever it was, dazzled his ears. He seemed to be hearing only part of it.

"What was that?" he asked when she finished.

"Our speech," she explained.

The other two turned away, and Laurel said, "Hey, wait!"

They turned back, puzzled—the tall, beautiful elf-man and the dazzling elf-woman. Laurel was appalled at how the latter affected him. You old goat, he kept telling himself, you're seventy-seven years old, not twenty-two. But he concentrated now on the thought in his mind.

He stood, went to Haralan, and said, "Lift your foot." The Caian looked puzzled. Winifraeda repeated the request in intricate song-speech. Obligingly, Haralan lifted a foot for Laurel to inspect. He pulled out a pocket tape and measured it. The big Caian's foot was nearly twelve inches long. He noted the fabric of the "shoe" Haralan wore. It was a soft, pliant material through which the features of the feet might impress in making a footprint.

Hesitantly, he approached Safraeonia. She smiled a heart-rending smile for him and raised a comely foot for his inspection. It measured six and one-half inches. He lingered over it for a moment. Narrow, shapely, high-arched, five toes as in a human, the same soft fabric of garment . . . and so damnably female! He turned abruptly, struggling to recapture his thoughts. "Thank you," he said over his shoulder.

He rejoined Winifraeda. She was gazing at him, a gentle, knowing smile on her tiny face, and he felt himself blushing clear to the top of his bald head. Abruptly, angrily, he asked, "When did your people leave Earth, then?"

She calculated it, drawing on the human speech symbols—his symbols—which still were so new to her.

"More than five millions years ago," she said finally. "Maybe as long ago as eight millions years."

"And how long had you been here before that?"

"Unknown, Jacob Laurel. Our lore, as yours, goes back only to the beginning of sentience. We believe we were brought forth by a harmonic blend, as your ancestors were. But I can tell you this. At the time of the fossiltracks that are so much on your mind—roughly one hundred million years ago—the Cai were full Cai and were the people of this world."

"Then the tracks . . . "

"Of course. A female was pursued by a lizard. Her male sought to save her."

He sat in silence for a time, trying and failing to digest the enormity of it. Finally, in a dazed voice of acceptance, he said, "I hope he did. I hope he saved her."

"I hope so, too, Jacob Laurel."

There was something in her voice that brought his gaze around. "Does it mean so much to you . . . something so long ago?"

"Of course, it means much. Do you think a Cai can tolerate misery? Don't you know what drove us from this world?"

"You called it darkness."

"Darkness, yes. The darkness of the Raporoi . . . poor creatures enslaved within themselves, seeking companionship and never finding it. Empathy is a terrible thing, Jacob. The loneliness of the Raporoi was more than the Cai could stand. My people wept for them, pitied them . . . finally had to escape from their sorrow. You understand that, Jacob. Just a moment ago you felt regret for the plight of lone-gone Cai on a world you never knew. It is strange and new to me, to think a descendant of the Raporoi could be concerned for Cai. By the lore, it was always the other way around."

A sadness like the weight of years came over Laurel.
He looked at the . . . *elves* . . . around him in this impossible roost. Disbelief was gone, along with the outrage of
being wrapped in a blanket and carried up here by what
seemed a maniac. There was too much evidence to brook
disbelief. It was late night, yet the luminosity of little
globes of pale light gave them what they needed. With
his own eyes he had watched Haralan extract the crystal
globes from the substance of the rock around them,
watched Winifraeda sing life into them. The altitude
. . . they must be at least nine thousand feet up. And yet
he was not cold. In this lair of strange beings, the
elements—the very air— complied with their desires.

He had heard/felt the rending forlorn song of a far-
off, searching elf. And even without other evidence, he
would have believed Winifraeda. She had touched his
mind. Strange, doll-like creature that she was, tiny and
resolute, he found her entrancing. And the others as
well. How could they be so alien, yet seem so very
human? He felt more strongly drawn to them than to
any human he had met in his seventy-seven years. He
felt a part of them, or that they were a part of him.

The hushed humming, hewing, and rock-fall sounds
from the shoulder of the croft came to him again, and he
looked around. "What is he doing over there?"

"Haralan? He is building a castle."

"Here? Why?"

Laurel would have sworn she shrugged. "Because he
has a need to build a castle."

"They'll be looking for me, you know. Down there."

"Of course they will. Those are your people."

"I don't know," he mused. "Sometimes I wonder."

"To be Feya is to be strange, Jacob. But to be Feya is to

be no less human—or no less Cai, or elf. Only more so."

"I'd like to meet a pixie, Winifraeda."

"Yes. You would like that."

He slept then, and his sleep was full of peace and beauty. He was comforted in a way he had never before known. Through the hours, he clasped the tiny hand of the Feya. The sun was over the croft when he awoke, refreshed as a child, as wise as any man could be. He looked at Winifraeda. They knew each other now. With waking, he found there was little about these strange and wonderful people he did not know.

Without thinking, he arose and went to where one of the little globes of elvenlight still pulsed, weak in the sunlight. He put out a hand and wished it to rest. It winked out and was gone.

Winifraeda's smile was radiance. "Welcome to the Feyadeen, human. Haralan selected well."

"I am aware of my own darkness, Winifraeda. I wonder if your blessing is indeed a blessing."

"Neither blessing nor curse, Jacob, but an act of life. Would you have preferred to continue to be less than you can be?"

He pondered that but found that there was no answer.

Haralan had brought food from down the mountain. Now he came with water from the snows. They refreshed themselves at leisure.

Finally, Winifraeda rose to her feet. "Now there is work to do. We must seek out the Corad-bane. Jacob Laurel, you can help us, I think. I hope you will."

The choice was his. "Will I live, do you think, to publish my knowledge?"

She smiled sadly. "How is it that people who can create lightnings and rearrange the substance of a world cannot foretell the future any better than the Cai?"

"Think of it, Winifraeda! My race is millions of years old. Yours may be hundreds of millions. Yet never before has there been a cooperative venture between human and elf."

"It is a shame," she said. "We should have known each other long ago."

15

In a subterranean vault below the Adirondacks, massed banks of quiet machines digested data. Electrons danced among microcircuits, sifting and collating data from fourteen source-programmed field banks in six states. Bits became bytes became megabytes, and the megabytes became a pattern to be transmitted. The machines fed.

Far in the inner recesses of a great brick structure thirty-six miles from the interior loop of Houston, similar machines hummed and sorted, collating the input from Texas and four states. The machines fed.

At a fenced compound within a military reservation in Wisconsin, banks of other, different machines mulled output from a system of orbiting satellites, comparing it with ground sources from SAC bases and DEW-line stations and from cooperating sources in Canada. Patterns were perceived. The machines fed.

Outside Akron, Ohio, and on a bluff above Vicksburg, Mississippi, at Leavenworth, Kansas, and in a secluded cove near Quantico, Virginia, other machines assimilated the findings of still other machines and fed their collations into the gathering pattern of numbers.

Intensities, locations, military and civil reports, all were reduced to tables of numbers and the numbers fed to the machines. The machines digested and, in turn, fed.

The U.S. Army Corps of Engineers' IBM-370 in Mississippi fed model-memory of the surface of the North American continent through open lines to the assimilating IBM-370 near Baltimore. The Baltimore computer overlayed the model with raw data collated at nine sources, allowed for ten percent single-point margin for un-debugged programming at field points, and busy analysts cross-referenced in Fortran against known phenomena. The whole—the pattern of it all—was fed across half a nation to the world's most-secured machine, big Cyber-205 resting in massive silence in the bowels of the earth outside Colorado Springs.

It was priority triple-one code red.

The programming had begun when the first authenticated blackout occurred, a multi-frequency blackout of wave phenomena in a circle of fourteen miles radius with its apparent epicenter located near Nederland, Colorado. The blackout followed by some days a similar but unauthenticated blackout centered in Wyoming. At NORAD command, it was noted that the relationship between blip and blackout was a line converging on the Pentagon's last-ditch outpost, Strike Command in the bowels of the mountain where Cyber 205 lived. When the third phenomenon occurred—the second authenticated—its apparent source was a peak near Denver. The silence was directly in line with the first two, and within a mile of the second. The blackouts were moving toward NORAD Command.

It was enough. The Secretary of Defense took the lid off. All the resources of the United States military defense system were unleashed. They were ready when it happened again—but unready for the magnitude of it.

No bubble of silence was this one. It blanketed the

entire midsection of the United States and into Canada.
From Ohio to Wyoming, airwaves ceased. The silence
lasted seven minutes and twenty-two seconds. The system was prepared, and it reacted.

At 0448 the secured line bleeped, and Major General
Stafford Clark himself picked it up.

"We have epicenter, sir," the voice told him.

"Exact?"

"Exact to within four miles."

"Where?"

"Ida Grove, sir. It's a little town on Highway 59 in
western Iowa."

Clark put down the telephone. "Ida Grove, Iowa," he
said. The most elaborate and most deadly condition-
reaction system in the Western World went into play.

*   *   *   *   *

Even before Greyhound Lines' number 440 reached
the roadblock outside Des Moines, Aaelefein Fe-Ruast
sensed the changes in the pulses of the air. Within an
hour's time, the general, muttering mesh of random
pulses which seemed normal background on this world
had changed, had toned. The very long waves and the
very short ones became few, supplanted by an intensity of
midrange waves, weaving an urgent pattern over the area.

Tight formations of fire-thrust craft raced by overhead, and some of the pulses came from them. Drawing
on his human knowledge, he placed them as SAC fighters out of Omaha, flying a tight grid centered over the
area he had just left. In the past hour, also, the only west-
bound traffic Greyhound 440 had passed was vehicles
full of nervous men, emitting pulses with their radio
apparatus. So it was no surprise to him when 440 topped

a hill and he saw in the distance vehicles ranged across the highway, blocking it.

The bus pulled over, stopped, and men came aboard. They began at the front, questioning each passenger, looking at identification, making notes, taking photographs. "Ladies and gentlemen," one apologized, "we are sorry to inconvenience you, but we have a state of national emergency. Please identify yourselves as you are asked. Following this, your bus will be escorted back to Ida Grove, where you will be detained for a short period of time. Arrangements have been made for your comfort, and you will be compensated for your inconvenience. Thank you."

As the passengers murmured among themselves, the men continued through the bus. When one of them came to Aaelefein, he gave his name—Alvin Frost—and a San Francisco street address. He had long since supplied himself with credentials. He had learned about credentials in Clover. Carrie Hummingbird had told him. Now he displayed credit cards and an insurance card as identification. "No, I'm sorry, I have no driver's license. I have no car."

The man made notes and went on past. Curiously, Alvin noted an increase in the sensory darkness about the bus. There were twenty-six passengers, including himself, plus the driver. He cautiously cracked the hard shields on his empathy. Fear, dread, anger, frustration, disgust—the emotions created a turmoil in the bus. The man's words had left all of them with various kinds and degrees of ire. They want so badly to communicate, he thought. And they work so hard not to. Why did the man frighten them? Why did he not just tell them what he was looking for? But the man's announcement had been couched to reveal nothing. In the miasma of darkness one passenger stood out. A young man, nearly at the front of the bus, emanated such dread that Aaelefein focused on him. The man was terribly afraid. He felt trapped, on the verge of panic. Aaelefein wondered what he had done.

As the interrogators reached the back of the bus, the Caian shifted in his seat. The movement caught the eyes of the two men standing in front, and he focused on them, holding their gaze. At the same time, he nudged the awareness of the frightened young man. Subtly, he fed the human's near-panic, turning it into panic. While the Caian diverted the attention of the two men, the young man bolted from his seat, dodged between them, and jumped through the open door. Aaelefein held the guards' minds distracted long enough for the man to run a hundred yards, then he shifted his gaze, and the two became aware that a passenger had escaped. At a shout, the two at the back ran forward. All four leaped from the bus, joined by more men from the roadblock.

Among gaping passengers in the bus, Aaelefein rose and walked forward, unnoticed.

Three cars blocked the road. A fourth was beyond them, a state cruiser with a uniformed officer standing beside it watching the chase beyond the far hedgerows. Aaelefein walked up behind the man and laid a hand on his shoulder. "Des Moines," he said, then went around and sat in the passenger seat.

It was eighteen miles into Des Moines. The urgency Trooper Jerry Evenson felt to get there prompted him to run with lights and siren. When the radio squawked, Aaelefein stilled the pulses immediately around the car and the sound cut off.

Not until they were well into the city did Evenson's determination begin to waver. He had seen a chase begin and had reacted, but now he began to wonder why he had driven into town. He pulled over at a street corner, his rooftop lights still running, and stopped. His passenger opened the car door, stepped out, and then stooped to look in at him. He said, "Thank you," and Evenson blinked. He hadn't really been aware that someone was with him until that moment. Confusion hit him. Flinging his door open, he jumped from the car and sprinted around to the curb. Midmorning crowds, drawn to the siren and lights, milled around, staring at him. The man who had left his car was gone.

The radio was squawking at him. "Forty-one. Come in Forty-one."

He got back in the car, killed siren and lights and responded. "Car Forty-one. Over."

"Forty-one, please report your Twenty."

He looked around, then reported dutifully, "Downtown, corner Eighteen and New Jersey."

There was a long pause. Then the dispatcher asked, "Des Moines?"

"Affirmative."

Another pause. "Forty-one, why are you in Des Moines?"

This time the long pause was his own. Finally he keyed the mike. "I don't know." Trooper Jerry Evenson had the sinking feeling that the world had gone bananas . . . or that he had. He fought down his confusion. With the discipline of his training, he ran a mental description of the man who had left his car. Tall, possibly six-four or six-five, whipcord slim, caucasian but vaguely . . . oriental? Brown hair, light (yellowish?) eyes, a strange, rather notable face, odd-seeming, all slanted planes and slanted lines, a . . . calm face? His discipline collapsed. The man had been right here, beside him, for . . . how long?

And he had somehow not really noticed him, nor quite been aware he was here.

He keyed the mike. "Dispatch. Car Forty-one to dispatch."

"Go ahead, Forty-one."

"Dispatch, can you patch me to Investigations Central?"

"Stand by, Forty-one." He waited. "Central. Code, please."

"Code five. Evenson, Gerald, Patrolman One, badge 6674182. Situation report."

A man's voice responded this time. "What is the situation, Trooper Evenson?"

"I was backup at the roadblock on Interstate 80 west of Des Moines. I . . . I think I picked up a passenger there and brought him to town. I cannot identify the man and do not, repeat do *not*, have him in custody. I . . . hell, sir, I don't know what happened, but I need to report to somebody."

He fidgeted as long seconds of silence passed. Then the authoritative voice was back. "Trooper Evenson, have you reported your exact location?"

"Affirmative."

"Then stay there, Trooper. Stay in your car, lock your doors, and remain exactly where you are."

The men who came for him, in three unmarked vehicles, were not state patrol. They were federal. With a precision that wasted neither words nor motions, he was escorted the two miles to the federal building, and into a third-floor suite marked only with a number. By the time he arrived there, he had sorted out, as best he could, a point-by-point report beginning at the roadblock when someone had jumped and run. And he had found a means of describing his "passenger's" features.

The man looked a lot like that character in Denver, the one they called the Centurion.

* * * * *

By two-fifty Central Daylight Savings Time, they had a backtrail on the man who called himself Alvin Frost, and teams of agents were tracking. In Washington, Baltimore, Omaha, and Denver, teams of theorists pulled off other projects were pooling their extrapolations for collation and probability curve. The entirety was fed into the massed memories of Cyber-205.

The United States was under military attack. The United States was under threat of attack. The United States had been infiltrated by agents of the USSR/People's Republic of China/Cuba/Etcetera for purposes of installing/testing/activating a device/system/sabotage network. None of the above had occurred, but rather a natural phenomenon previously unrecorded. Some combination of the above had been evidenced simultaneously. The United States had been invaded from outer space. Cyber-205 and armies of human servants processed each scenario for comparison with the data still flowing in.

Before midnight, they had found Carrie Hummingbird. By three a.m., they had located several bus drivers and a collection of recent passengers. By three-thirty, the town of Clover, Wyoming, was sealed. Mountain teams and chopper squadrons awaited first light to begin massive land-and-air search of the areas where the first blip and the two recorded blackouts had epicentered. The search was already going on at and around Ida Grove, Iowa, and in massive concentration at Denver and Des Moines.

16

Now Margaret found it hard to remember the old life.
She had stilled somehow in the two days following
that eerie, beautiful moment when her soul had
responded to a soundless lovesong. Somehow that new
part deep within her—she considered it now a sort of
alter ego—had at that moment become serene. The element of dread, of uncertainty, that had come with it on
that first morning was gone.

The overtones of her new element were surer now, less
wistful. The haunting melancholy remained, but now it
seemed more content. Slanting sunlight caught the first,
raw strokes of tone that would be the underlying flesh of
the face in the picture, and she peered at it, puzzled.
The color wasn't right. Why, she didn't know, but it was
wrong. Even blending it up to highlights and down to
shadows would not make it right. It looked sallow. Like
the two other new paintings she had done, those eldritch
landscapes that surprised her each time she looked at
them, she knew that even if what seemed right was obviously wrong, still, if it seemed right, it was right.

She thumbed through the welter of paint tubes,
selected a rich earth-tone in the sienna range and set it
aside. Then she scraped the canvas with a pallet knife,
squeezed sienna into her pallet mix, and worked it. She

brushed a daub of it onto the canvas, working down the
line of a cheek. Now it looked right. She held her hand
beside it in the sunlight. Flesh did not have such tones
. . . but his flesh did. And, strangely, hers had begun to.
It was a parallel-base—similar to but different from the
usual mix for fleshtone. It was right for him. Blended up
and down, worked and highlighted, it would be almost
. . . human? What a strange analogy. Its roses would be
coppers, its pales would be golds, its highlights would be
creams. Almost an Indian coloration, but not that
either. Fleshtones from the rich earth, brushed with the
clarity of sky.

Right or wrong, it was right. With growing skill, Meg
touched in the basic tone. The face she was painting was
the one she had dreamed. She had dreamed it since, fre-
quently. It was almost an obsession. She needed to capture it, to see it with her eyes.

She was painting full-face, but she could have done
profile or quarter view as well. She knew the face. To
paint was to analyze, and the face was amazing. There
was nothing right about it. Every plane, every angle,
every feature was just slightly . . . wrong. But they had to
be wrong to be right. A dozen times she had wanted to
lower the ears a bit, to square the temples, to widen the
jawline and straighten the eyes. But no, it would have
ruined him. Almost human? The thought intrigued her.
That was what she had here—a picture of someone
almost human, but distinctly not quite. Like her two
landscapes. She had never seen such places before. They
were unearthly. But they were beautiful. And it gave her
surprising comfort to look at them. Almost—another
odd thought—almost like going home.

In her mind, she turned the face to profile. It would
be the same story. To be right, the face would have to jut

too far forward from the neck, like the hook on a crochet needle. The forehead would be an angled bow, not a flat plane. The hairline . . . nobody really had a widow's peak like that, did they? And how could a mouth tip upward without suggesting a smile? But the smile was at the corners of it, not in the mouth itself.

Letting the sienna tint rest, she went to work on the eyes. Pupils slightly elongated, irises too large—and an impossible color—and each eye distinctly slanted under arched brows. Slanted, but with no epicanthic fold. No, this was not an oriental face. She didn't know what it was, but everything in it was wrong. And by being wrong, everything together would be right.

It was, she decided, a distinctly other way of building a face, as though different craftsmen had worked unknown from two sets of blueprints to achieve similar results.

The eyes must be yellowish, deepening to brown. But she had experimented with tone and found that the yellow of cat eyes was wrong. The yellow needed here was that of gold, deepening to oiled bronze. Metallic colors, not flesh colors.

As she worked, she hummed, and in the tune were the five syllables of that word: A-a-e-le-fein. It was a word, and it was music. The word and the face were the same.

Since the night of the . . . song, she had been preoccupied with completing this picture, but she went at it slowly, savoring each correct stroke, enjoying the doing of it. She worked each day at Mark's real estate office, and lately had been doing a new thing there. She sat in on interviews with him. She listened, and when it was done she told him exactly what the client wanted, how the client felt, and how he himself felt about the client. Mark was delighted. His business had never been so good.

But then, a lot of things were different since that strange night. By and large, it seemed the people around her liked each other better. She had no more explanation for what had happened than anyone else seemed to. The news media were turning cartwheels, alternately reporting theories, first, that the country had experienced a miracle and, then, that it had suffered an invasion. She didn't feel that either theory had much to do with how she felt. And how she felt, she knew, was the key to it. Somehow, the thing that had happened had happened for *her*. She wasn't about to tell anybody that, of course. But she knew.

Roy wouldn't come around today. Recently they had not seen much of each other, and in a way she was glad. His visits had become more and more painful to her. There was so much he just couldn't understand—and without his understanding, she couldn't explain—and his desperation hung about him like a darkness. She sensed it more strongly each time they met, and it hurt her. It was like . . . what must it have been to be the mother of young Helen Keller, to love a person blind and deaf and feel that person's entrapment, live that person's desperation? That was how it had become with Roy. Each day she was more aware of a terrible blindness that trapped him inside himself, and his loneliness there was a dark grief upon her.

He had felt nothing the night of the song. To him, it had been seven minutes of silence on his truck radio, and then fear when he read the reports of how widespread it had been. Roy had been relieved when they mobilized the National Guard two days later. He knew only what he heard and saw. She knew what she felt. And what she felt, in the past brief days, had become a truer sense to her than her sight or hearing. She could hardly remember what it had been to be . . . blind.

The colors on her glass pallet blended under her brush, and she pursed her lips. This time it was right. All wrong, but right. She began an eye. Hazel came out from the kitchen, watched her working for a moment. Then she asked, hesitantly, "May I see your picture, Meg?"

It occurred to her that, since she kept the canvas draped when she wasn't working on it, Hazel probably had never looked at it. "Sure, Mother. Come see what you think."

Hazel looked over her shoulder. "So that's who it is! Meg, that's a pretty good likeness. Why are you doing him?"

She was startled. Hazel seemed to know who she was painting. And with her quickening empathy, she also caught the undertone of "the picture's good, considering it isn't quite right." She had heard it since she was a child. But this was right. She looked around.

"You know who I'm painting?"

"My, yes. The likeness is . . . very close. Did you do it from a picture?"

Her newfound senses deserted her. Sometimes they did, with her mother. "A picture of whom?"

Now Hazel seemed perplexed. "Why, of him. Didn't you? Maybe you should get one and compare. The features don't seem just exactly right."

"Mother, who do you think this is?"

"Why, it's that 'Centurion,' of course. Who else could it be?"

Somewhere along the line, she had missed something.

Hazel went into the living room, rummaged through the stack under the lamp table, and came back with a magazine and two checkout counter pulps. The cover photographs on all three were of a man in exotic costume, and Margaret gasped. It was not the same face, but the similarities were remarkable. All the same slight oddities, the peculiarities of feature. They could be brothers. On the news magazine, the headline read: "Centurion—Enigma in the Mile-High City." One of the pulps said something about "Murder in Mountaintown . . . Professor Believed Dead." The other asked "Are Creatures from Space Kidnapping our Brains?" There was an inset of an elderly man with glasses.

"How long have we had these, Mother?"

"Oh, I don't know. They've come in." Hazel was taken aback at her daughter's interest. "I thought surely you'd seen them. There's been a lot about him on TV, too."

"I haven't been watching." She took them to the daybed and started reading. A perceived part of her observed what she read with fascination.

* * * * *

A strange serenity had prevailed for two days throughout the area encompassed by the "bubble of silence." From Appalachia to the Rocky Mountains, from Ontario to Louisiana, a lethargy of sorts gripped a stunned population unable to absorb either the seven minutes and twenty-two seconds of electromagnetic null that had been generally observed or the encompassed six minutes plus of unearthly splendor that more than one in four had witnessed. There were a thousand explanations of the first phenomenon, very few of the second. A miracle had occurred, and it was marred for those who sought its center by the quarantine imposed jointly by harried United States and Canadian officialdom. Both countries had declared a state of emergency. National Guard and Provincial Reserve units barricaded every major highway crossing the perimeter of the null zone. Nationalized state and local police prowled back roads and rivers. Air National Guard and Civil Air Patrol squadrons flew sweeps above. Nonessential air traffic was grounded. SAC, NORAD Command, NASA, and TAC held on red alert as scanners on roving satellites probed for any sign of hostile activity beyond the perimeters of two nations.

Until some better explanation was authenticated, it had to be assumed that North American intelligence and security had been compromised.

Quarantine. Those outside the null zone were stunned, as were three of four within. But for the one in four who had heard the song, it was a time of awe, a time of wonder. A miracle had occurred. It took time to digest. There had been a spate of odd news before it, some of which seemed to connect with it . . . Those small null zones along the spine of the Rockies, confirmation of a meteor-like sighting in upper Wyoming shortly before, which had registered in the negative on scanning devices. Defense against hostile powers was not the only scenario being viewed, either by the military or by their charges. Rapidly, the story spread that there had been a visitation from space, and panic was added to the blend. Dealing with Russians was one thing. Dealing with . . . who knew what . . . was terrifying.

Panic, lethargy, and euphoria. The country held its ground.

In large, quiet buildings at Omaha, Des Moines, and St. Paul, parades of people were herded one by one into rooms where they answered questions, submitted, in some cases, to hypnotic examination and, in most cases to the grueling task of dictating composite portraits of someone they had seen. When the evidence was in, it went by wire and courier to Omaha and from there to Denver and to Washington, D.C.

A sketch done by an Indian girl, Carrie Hummingbird, was characteristic of all the descriptions. It was the most elaborate and was corroborated by a photograph taken by a tourist at Beatrice, Nebraska, and another taken by an FBI agent at a roadblock outside Des Moines.

The resources of two nations went into a search for a man named Alvin Frost—a man who, according to continental computer searches, did not exist.

A parallel search, already underway at Denver, was intensified. This was another man. His only name, given him by a reporter for the *Denver Post*, was Centurion.

The two men looked alike, and they looked like no one else.

17

"It is an interesting hypothesis," Jacob Laurel mused. "I can expand upon it, I believe."

"If you must," the Feya said, busy with her floss. She glanced out across the great city, a vast maze of lights and sounds just starting to whisper now with the coming of dusk, not yet raucous with the coming of full night. From their perch atop City Center Four, Denver's tallest building, they could see for miles.

"Forgive me, Winifraeda, but to capture a discipline, I must commit it to words. For all you have given me I am still no Caian, only a human. To know is to verbalize and to verbalize is to understand."

"I begin to think the essence of humanity is that you have to understand in order to know. But go ahead."

Laurel perched atop a utility well hood, arms wrapped around his crossed legs. "Two races," he expanded. "Two separate races of beings, separately evolved and separated by hundreds of millions of years. And yet look at us. Some insignificant physical differences . . . the shape of a face, the capacity of a larynx. Look there at Haralan. Put him in a business suit, and he could pass for a human male in prime. Our two species, Winifraeda, are less different in general appearance than most of the varieties of human on this world. A Japanese would be far more noticeable among Norwegians than an elf is among humans. Do you mind if I use the word 'elf,' Winifraeda? There are a lot of concepts I'm still trying to get used to."

"I don't mind at all. It is your word for us."

"But your word for yourselves is, ah, Caian, or Cai."

"No. The way you say Cai is only an approximation of our name within the limits of your vocal range. And I say it that way to you because it is easy for you. You spoke lightly of the difference in capability of a larynx. In that respect, Jacob, we are quite a lot different."

"Well, yes, I have heard your speech. . . ."

"Very little of it, really. Your hearing can't encompass much of it."

"Well, then," he said a little crossly, "let me hear your name for yourselves—or what little of it I can—as you say it."

The syllable she uttered was brief, but immensely complex—a symphony condensed, collapsed upon itself. Laurel grinned. She was right. He knew he heard only a small part of it. "Fantastic," he said.

"It isn't really a name as you think of name, Jacob. It is a description. It describes us as we know ourselves in quite a lot of detail."

"Creatures of resonance," he told himself, "in a universe perceived as harmonics. And yet," he pointed out, "in most ways we could be the same race. I think you are as human as me."

"We are of the same world, Jacob. Elves and humans, both are products of the substance of this place."

"Yes, but we are separately evolved. Your people 'came to the light,' as you put it, at least a hundred million years before even the phylla from which humans evolved ever existed. You were gone from this world long before the earliest true human was born. And we did not come from you. But we are like two variations of the same song."

"Not the same, Jacob. Only similar. In some ways, we are opposites."

"Humans are vertebrates," he persisted. "So are elves. Humans are mammalian." He glanced at Sefraeonia, standing slim and curvaceous against the mountain dusk. "So, obviously, are elves. We walk erect, we are selectively omnivorous, the components of our bodies are essentially the same, we have fingers and feet very nearly alike, we have male and female and the functions are similar. . . ."

"You have five senses and we have seven," Winifraeda pointed out.

"Ah, yes, but at least one of the extra two is vestigial in us as well, as you certainly have discovered. We are separate as two alien races can be, yet we are alike. How can that be?"

"It simply is," the Feya said.

"Elfin acceptance," he snorted. "No, there is a reason. You speak of the 'essence' of the world—old Caiendon, Earth, it is the same place, is it not?"

"Not at all. When this was Caiendon, there was scarcely a trace of the world you now know as Earth. Now it is Earth and there are few traces of Caiendon."

"The difference is purely in the harmonic blend, I submit. The elements of it are the same. We come from the same seed, Winifraeda, and the seed is the living matrix of this planet, no matter how it is compounded. Therefore, the matrix is the key. We are culminant species, my little friend. Elves and humans, each may be the predictable end result of an evolutionary process that is not random after all. With a few minor variations, we are the same race, evolved twice.

"It might even be that, on this world, no matter how many species chains achieve culmination in the evolutionary process, they will all produce approximately the same creature. The 'essence' of the world might direct it, just as a creature's genetic makeup determines what it will become in maturity."

He pursed his lips, analyzing the thought, and the Feya glanced around at him. She was growing fond of this peculiar, rambling creature who found it necessary to catalog thoughts in order to comprehend them. She had decided that the process was a human adaptation, like their writing and recording—a learned compensation for their inability to retain lore.

Haralan, perched on the very edge of the great tower, looked up to watch a squadron of armed aircraft fly over. "They are agitated, Feya," he sang. "Their pulses are of urgency."

"I am sure we have aroused them," she said. "They can't know we mean them no harm."

Jacob Laurel was gazing across at Sefraeonia. "Most definitely mammalian," he murmured.

He wagged a finger. "Consider this, Winifraeda. You elves are mammals, but at the time your race came to being there were no mammals on this world. Lord, there weren't even birds then."

"All of the elvenkindred are mammalian, Jacob."

"Yes, but only the elvenkindred. And you have said yourself that you are all related—cousins, as it were. Do you know, your few species must have achieved a straight-line evolution entirely within a phyllum. What an idea! Linear evolution within a single strain. Like breeding a racehorse from an emergent hippodon without affecting the environment around it."

"That seems quite reasonable," the Feya agreed.

"But the test is in the culminants," Laurel warmed to his subject. "Your nearest cousins are pixies. Ours probably are apes of some variety—certainly a more distant relation. Yet we didn't come from the true apes, apparently. We are simultaneous evolutions."

"We came from the pixies," Winifraeda said.

Laurel stared at her. "I thought you didn't know where you came from."

"I do now. You just told me. I pursue your reasoning a step further, and it says that the Cai descended—or ascended—from pixies. Therefore they are our ancestors. Or rather their ancestors were our ancestors. But pixies have not changed since the beginning of elvenkind, Jacob. They have always been pixies, just as we are elves."

"Then maybe you achieved culmination while they settled for only completion." He pointed a pedantic finger at her.

"Hold this, please."

He spread his hand and the Feya deposited in it what appeared to be nothing, but he held it dutifully. Only with her help could he perceive the floss.

"You prove my point," he said. "The matrix—the fabric of the living world—fosters evolution of species until a true culminant is reached. Then the process is complete, and the entire phyllum stops where it is. Do you know what I mean by culminant?"

He felt a sensory touch at his mind, but she shook her head, "No," she said. "It seems an entirely human concept, though. I don't think we would need it."

"I am theorizing that the impetus of the world's matrix dictates evolution to the point where sentience is achieved—where a race can truly think—and then one step beyond. A sentient species is complete—"

"Like pixies."

"Yes, like pixies, I suppose. But a culminant species has one thing more—a conscious need to evolve further. And when that need appears, the natural process stops."

"That seems unreasonable, Jacob."

"Yes," he muttered, suddenly baffled. "It does, doesn't it?"

"Then what makes you think we have this need?"

"I really don't know. But I know we humans do. We . . . we ache to be something more than we are."

"We are the same, Jacob. To be Cai is to be dissatisfied. We are drawn, but we know not to what."

Safraeonia had wandered off across the roof. Now she returned with withes for the floss. They were long, thin pieces of metal. Winifraeda glanced at them and agreed. They would do.

"Linear evolution," Laurel mused. "A strain takes off on its own and produces culminants, eons ahead of any other strain progressing beyond the early vertebrates. And then a half a hundred million years later, a thousand strains take off simultaneously in a race for culminants, and one succeeds. And not so far ahead of some of the others."

"Are there other sentients here, then?" Winifraeda worked her aluminum withes.

"There were. An early variant, *Homo suprens*, could think as well as us, but he was no culminant."

"How do you know?"

"Because *Homo sapiens* defeated him. He's gone."

"You killed your pixies?" She stopped, aghast.

"*Suprens* was no pixie, Winifraeda. He was an aggressive, implacable being. Between him and *sapiens* only one could survive."

"He was no pixie." The Feya nodded. "And humans are not elves."

"It may have been *suprens* your ancestors encountered."

"The Raporoi were not implacable, only frightened and lonely."

"Maybe," he muttered, "they are the same thing."

A helicopter, drawn by some movement atop the tower, hovered above them and a harsh glare bathed them. It flicked back and forth, from the Feya and Jacob Laurel to Haralan at the edge of the roof. Haralan raised a hand in casual salute. The light held for a moment, then flicked out. The copter spun away.

"That's done it," Laurel said. "Now we'll have the police on us."

"Be careful with the floss," the Feya said.

"We'd better get away from here, Winifraeda. No telling who will come to see what we're up to."

"We will go, Jacob. But first we must seek the Coradbane."

It was almost full dark. Laurel watched big Haralan's silhouette against the fading sky as Winifraeda draped her floss. In a moment, she spoke to the warrior-elf, and he drew his sword, raised it and set it humming. In the darkness, the crystal blade sang eerie green. Sefraeonia came close and took the Feya's hand. Silence hung about City Center Four.

A door banged open, revealing a lighted stairwell. There were men among them then, armed men with beams of white light. In the sudden glare, Jacob Laurel bolted upright. A policeman, his young eyes wide in the dancing light, pointed a drawn pistol at Haralan where he stood holding his sword.

"No!" Laurel's shout was lost in the roar of the gun.

Its flame stabbed at the caped silhouette, and Haralan slumped to the roof, his sword going dark. Laurel grabbed the policeman's arm, clung to it. "No! They've done nothing!"

The burly young man shrugged him off, flashed a beam at him as he fell, and flicked it away. It fell on the Feya, and the man froze. Tiny and silver in the white light, she regarded him with great, wise eyes that saw past the beam. Laurel rolled half upright and launched his bony frame at the man's knees, which buckled when he hit them. The gun spat bright flame into the sky as the policeman crashed backward to the graveled rooftop. Wildly, Jacob Laurel looked around. Another policeman raced past him, his flashlight waving. Its beam fell on Sefraeonia and held there. The man paused, stunned. Involuntarily, his light played upward to her round breasts, down to her slim legs—the beam piercing the diaphanous stuff of her gown—and back up to her dazzling elfin face.

"Oh . . ." he breathed. "Jesus!"

Then there was a rush, a thud, and the light was gone, spinning away into the abyss. Floundering in half-light from the open stairwell, Laurel saw the policeman bent backward, half over the roof-rail, a large, raging elf atop him. Haralan pressed him back, and the crystal blade raised high, screaming now in its resonance, blinding bright against the dark sky. Laurel didn't hear what the Feya sang, but he felt it. A brief command. The sword stopped, stood motionless. Then Haralan rose to his feet, pulled the uniformed man away from the roof edge, and flung him aside. With a long stride, he reached the other policeman, just coming to his knees, and kicked the gun out of his hand. Laurel heard the muted snap of bone breaking.

Again the Feya sang, instructing. Haralan responded. Then he spun and snatched up Laurel, folding him in his cape. Wildly, Laurel saw the shadows of Sefraeonia and the Feya, receding, merging. Then with an impossible leap, Haralan cleared the edge of the roof, he and his burden, and they were falling, falling away, as blinding light washed the roof above them, roaring with a thunder of descending rotors. Jacob Laurel closed his eyes.

18

"Elves?"

In utter silence, the word hung as if displayed, a tangible impossibilty waiting to be explored. Winifraeda Feya perched in the high chair that had been found for her, tiny and lustrous in the cone of bright light falling on her and the blanket-shrouded Sefraeonia. They were at ground center of a bowl-shaped room deep in the recesses of a fortresslike building. The tiers of men and recording devices around and above them were a welter of intentness outside the cone of light. She could see them perfectly well, but of course they didn't know that. She knew from Jacob Laurel that their sight was in a narrow range below the ultraviolet.

She felt sorry for them. Even in their eyes, they were blind.

"That is your word for us," she repeated. "You call us elves. We came to the light on this world, but longer ago than you."

The man who asked most of the questions was a handsome, sturdy individual in uniform, his trimmed hair graying at the temples. "But you said you came here from another world," he pressed.

"We did." The Feya was patient. It was another element of their racial darkness that these creatures could not know truth in one another and must forever search blindly for it. "We came from Nendacaida. But our ancestors came from here. They left here before yours . . . evolved."

"You speak English like a native."

"I learned it from a native. Doctor Jacob Laurel shared his speech with me."

"You say 'elf' is our word for you. What is your word?"

Obligingly, she sang it for them. High in the dark arena a sensitive sonic device destroyed itself. Needles on other devices around the room clicked on their pegs. Men muttered and scurried about. The interrogation had gone on quite a long time, but the Feya was patient with them. They were, after all, trying to learn truth. At one point, early on, she had shared the truth with two of the men through the touch-sense. But those two were not here now. They had been locked away somewhere. The others suspected they had been mind-manipulated.

Since the Feya and Sefraeonia had surrendered, quite a number of humans had been either confined or relieved of service. Those who had seen the Feya or knew of her were under tight surveillance while security clearances were reviewed. On the other hand, most of the males who had seen Sefraeonia before they got a shroud over her—particularly the younger ones—were simply unfit for duty.

Winifraeda found it interesting, the immediate physical attraction between Cai and humans, and she was startled at the intensity of it. Those young men had simply looked at Sefraeonia and . . . become disoriented.

"Where is Doctor Laurel now?" The iron-templed man resumed his questioning.

"He is with Haralan. They will wait for us somewhere."

"And Haralan is the Centurion?"

"I don't know that word. Haralan is, within your
speech range, Haralan Caharel-Ruast. He is our companion, the continuity of the chord of five. He is Eldretten, a
refugee from the south of Nendacaida where the Corad
touched. He is an armsman."

"Is he the one who took Doctor Laurel from his
home?"

"Yes. That was Haralan. I sent him."

"There are two injured policemen in the hospital
right now. One has compound fractures of his right arm,
the other has a dislocated shoulder. Did Haralan do
that?"

"Of course. One of those men wounded him with a
weapon. The other threatened Sefraeonia."

The interrogator mopped his forehead with a handkerchief. "How did you interrupt the electromagnetic
sequences? What device did you use?"

"Haralan used his blade. I asked him to. The air on
your world is very busy."

"Do you mean the sword he was seen carrying?"

"Yes. He resonated it to calm the pulses so my floss
would work."

"And how, exactly, did he cause it to so resonate?"

"He sang to it. We have not your race's tonal limitations, you see." She knew the man did not see at all, and
she was sorry. She wished him well.

"Then was it Haralan who caused the massive disruption of the electromagnetic spectrum that occurred on
July the seventh at approximately twenty-two hundred
hours?"

The strange usages were unfamiliar to the Feya, but

she knew the meaning. "No, that was Aaelefein. He was calling to Nataea."

"Aaelefein. Another elf, I presume?"

"Yes. Another elf."

"And Nataea?"

"She died when we arrived here. Aaelefein is looking for her."

"Winifraeda . . ."

"Win-if-ra-e-da. That is how my name sounds within your tonal range. Five syllables.

"Winifraeda, do you realize that in addition to the North American Defense System having been hopelessly compromised, those seven minutes of disruption resulted in psychotraumatic experience for an estimated nine and one-half million people in this country? Are you saying an elf did that?"

"I am sure most of them enjoyed it. Aaelefein's song is lovely. Did you hear it?"

The officer blinked. "I did not." With a shake of the head, like a lion tormented, he stood and turned. "That will be all for tonight, gentlemen. Staff will assemble reports at o-eight-hundred. And I want every scan, every reading, and every instrument effect fed into the CYCOM system by o-four-hundred, program override code one one nine. Place our . . . guests . . . under maximum security. Further interrogation at o-eight-thirty." Then he added, "Elves? My Lord in Heaven."

Winifraeda and the blanketed Sefraeonia were escorted down into the bowels of levels far below the fortress building. The apartment they were secured in was clean, the air was fresh, and the locks were multiple and secure. From a dozen hidey-holes, machine eyes and ears spied on them. Winifraeda made note of them.

"Winifraeda," Sefraeonia asked, "may I remove this

thing now? It is very uncomfortable."

"Of course, child. They required that you wear it because you distracted the young males so much. It was difficult for them to remain objective."

"I know. They are so . . . sweet, Winifraeda. And so terribly afraid. I understand why our ancestors left this place. The loneliness of these people is almost more than I can stand, and it grows worse here among so many."

"We have work to do, child. Concentrate on it. Can you find withes in this place? Some of those bed supports there might do. I will make the floss."

Almost as an afterthought, she sang a few trills for the watching machines, so they would watch only one another. She felt she needed privacy for the exacting task of extracting floss from the air.

Atop the building last night, the floss had reacted. It had streamed upward. Therefore the Corad-bane had been below. Now they were in an underground place. Even before the test, she suspected the results. When finally the Corad-floss flowed away from its bane, it pulled down on the spring-metal withes. The bane was above. Whatever it was, it was mostly at the level of the ground. And whatever it was, the Corad-resonated floss shunned it violently.

The Feya pursed her lovely lips. "Sefraeonia, we have learned all we can learn from the floss. It is time we consider other means. We had best go and find Haralan and Jacob Laurel so we can think together. Jacob's human mind might be of help to us now."

"I think the people here want us to stay, Feya. They have bolted all the doors."

"Perhaps we can come back another time." Winifraeda retrieved her diadem from its hiding place in her robe. She resonated the locked door, testing up and down the scale, until the lock slid free. Beyond were three armed men in an anteroom. Focusing with the diadem, the Feya resonated soothing infrasonics to them. When their eyelids drooped, she and Sefraeonia passed by them unobserved.

In all, there were eleven locks between them and the street. By the time the eleventh had been opened, two full squads of armed guards were glancing around in mild confusion and an entire system of surveillance machines had been co-opted. The machines continued to spy, but they spied only on one another. They would go on doing so until some human set them straight.

In the late hours, away from the building, Sefraeonia stood slim in moonlight and breathed deeply. "Somewhat better," she said. "The darkness was terrible in there. There is so much fear."

Some miles away, in a laboratory ringed with security, technicians completed tests under the supervision of technologists. Every possible analysis had been run on the blood samples brought from the roof of a downtown building. Computers verified the findings. The blood was almost human. Almost, but not quite. It was not quite the blood of any known creature on Earth.

This, with everything else, was fed into the banks of slave computers that were the continent-wide retinue of Cyber-205. In its top-security location beneath a mountain, the big machine received, collated, and digested the findings. A billion bytes of data on the electromagnetic force phenomenon were at Cyber-205's disposal. This information was simply a few more bits.

Nothing in the master machine's immense programming equipped it to be incredulous. Its human keepers had no such protection. Elves or not, the subjects of scrutiny were not of this planet. Arcanists provided their lore for comparison. Cyber-205 responded. Those not of this planet, by a probability of 872 to the ninth power, were elves. Definition . . . corollary . . . semantic override . . . redundancy factors . . . Cyber-205 clarified. Elves.

They scrapped the multiple scenarios. There were elves running loose on American soil. They had the ability and the equipment to compromise national security at will, to nullify national defense. They were a threat. Among the billions of sentient creatures who were masters of this world, some few had continued to accept the existence of elves. To a race matured in blindness, acceptance of the unseen is normal. But no elf ever was equipped to understand the results of such acceptance. Humans steeped in constant fear had made of their fear an awesome strength. Faced with a perceived danger, they would react with fire and iron. As Cyber-205 issued its judgments, the dark heritage of organized humanity coalesced into fierce determination. The word rippled outward, rings of fear on dark water, and the ripples became a tide.

The lonely darkness that was humanity became a deadly darkness.

Moon-dappled in the quiet of a sleeping suburban street the Feya sensed it. It rode the pulses of the air.

"We must use care, Sefraeonia." She felt a pity beyond any she had known before. "They do not know how to love us as we love them. So they will kill us if they can."

"That way," Sefraeonia indicated. "Haralan calls us."

"More precisely," the Feya corrected, toying with the odd, pedantic mindset she had learned from the human Jacob Laurel, "he calls you, Sefraeonia. His wound pains him, and he wants you by his side."

*   *   *   *   *

Far away and on the move, Aaelefein also sensed the sinister change in the patterns of the pulses and understood that there had been a shift in intent. He had known that people sought him. Now he knew their search was deadly.

19

To a generation of young disenchants exposed to university life, he was "the troll of the stacks." To the researchers, librarians, and superintendents who encountered him trundling boxes of books from one place to another, he was simply Willy, part of the furniture. He saw himself as William Herschel Marsh. Those technically in charge and those using the library's resources came and went, brief shadowy impressions against the reality of the books. But William remained. It was his library, and he took care of it. Rarely did he venture beyond its walls. The world out there was strange and hostile to one unfortunate in both appearance and mentality. It was even more rare for someone to venture into his private domain, the little space he had appropriated for himself behind the nether stacks, where he kept the necessities of existence—a cot, a hotplate, and a toilet.

But now William had company. One was Jacob Laurel. The other was injured.

"By chance delivered to my door the refugee lies bleeding," William muttered as he soaked a cloth at the tap. "Without the hunting lions roar, the clash of chase receding. But in my house, alone and poor, a guest lies needing . . . needing."

"What is that, William?" Jacob Laurel didn't raise his eyes from the still figure on the cot. With his body armor and trappings removed, Haralan looked even more human. He lay flat on his back, eyes closed, not unconscious but oblivious, concentrating on the wound in his side where active flesh pinched together to seal the bullet hole. He had bled, but not too much. The crystal sword lying on his chest hummed with the resonances of his concentration.

"I don't know," William said. "Something somebody wrote." He brought the towel and damped the elf's brow with it. Neither of them had the slightest idea how to help Haralan cure himself. Every few minutes, the elf's lips, jaw, and throat moved, always in the same pattern. Each time the crystal blade iridesced briefly from dull gray to milky and back, dim shimmers dancing on it. Laurel discerned it.

"He's calling," he said. "So the others can find him."

"Then they'll be coming here?"

"I suppose so." Laurel frowned at the thought that something might have happened to them. Staring at Haralan in his pain, he wished there were some way he could apologize for the human race.

"Are the others like him?"

"They are elves, too. One is a girl, the other a . . ." How could one explain the Feya? "I'm afraid they're in trouble, William. They're looking for something, and they don't even know what it is. And I don't know how to help them find it."

"The mighty seek abroad for truth," William said, "and carry chains to bind it. I watch the hopeless quest depart, then turn a page and find it."

"What's that?"

"Something somebody wrote." William shrugged.

"I've never found a question that can't be answered right here." He swept an arm at the wall of books that was the library's lowest stack.

"I'm afraid this one can't be," Laurel mused. "It's older than any book . . . or the race that produced the books."

"So are some of the things in these books." William placed a studious finger to his lips. "Seems like every time you ever came, and I helped you find things, you sought something that was older than books."

The elf's lips moved again. Iridescence danced on the sword. William looked at him curiously. "He looks odd enough, but what makes you think he's an elf? He looks human."

"There are some physical differences, William. For instance, he has an extraordinary vocal ability. I have no idea of the extent of it. His orbs are larger—for seeing in the infrared, is my guess—and the pupils are elongated. He has thirty-six teeth—an extra set of canines. But the primary differences are sensory. He has seven functioning senses. He has acute empathy—the organ for it seems analogous to our pineal gland—and some sort of tactile awareness beyond ours. He is aware of harmonics between the ranges of our hearing and sight, and possibly into the higher wave spectrums. The receptivity seems to be in his hair. His follicles have sensory nerves. And he can do more than . . . listen, in those ranges. He can communicate in them. Something odd about his vertebral structure, too, that I can't fathom. It's almost like ours. The 'almost' bothers me.

"Also, he has some aptitudes we don't have. He uses harmonics the way we use heat and light. His science is based on resonance as ours is based on fire. I suspect that right now he's directing the molecular vibration of his body to heal that wound. He has remarkable control in that field, William. I know for a fact"—Laurel shuddered—"that he can control impact."

"How do you know?"

"When he was hurt, we—he and I—fell fifty-four stories straight down from the top of a building. Six hundred feet! But we landed softly. Then, before he moved, he . . . did something and the sidewalk under us just disintegrated into little pieces. It pulverized."

"A man described to me an angel," William quoted, "it was a wondrous sight. But if it was so hard to see, then how'd he get it right?"

"I know," Laurel snapped. "Somebody wrote it." He paced from wall to rack of the cubbyhole. "Do you mind if I look around?"

"It's after hours." William glanced at the clock on his wall. It was almost four-thirty in the morning. "But go ahead. You know where everything is. Watch for security, but don't worry. They never come past the second stack."

"Keep an eye on him. Let me know if anything changes."

For an hour Laurel prowled the dim, tight corridors of the library's sub-basements, not knowing exactly what he was looking for. When he returned to the cubbyhole, the Feya and Sefraeonia were there. The elf-girl hovered over Haralan, holding his hand. Winifraeda sat on the cot beside him. William stood in a corner, dazed.

"The floss has told me all it can, Jacob," the Feya said. "We must search now by other means. This is your world. Do you have any ideas?"

He just looked at her. She might as well have asked him to pinpoint Atlantis. Come to think of it, though, he admitted, she could probably do that herself.

Haralan had begun to respond to Sefraeonia's touch.

She knelt beside him, holding his hand, and lay her head atop the crystal sword on his chest. Laurel knew she was singing in some wavelength beyond his senses. After a moment, Haralan's lids fluttered. His free hand came up and caressed her head, strong fingers gentle on the smooth contours of her face.

The Feya stood up.

"Come with me, Jacob. And you, too, William. Let Sefraeonia tend to Haralan. Let us go somewhere else and talk."

"Talk about what, Winifraeda?"

"You talk to me, Jacob. I will listen. Maybe you will give me a clue."

They sat around a scarred table in dim light, and Laurel talked . . . about the Earth, about the human race, about the arts and sciences. William prompted him occasionally, bridging a gap. Winifraeda, a smudge of silver in the dimness, simply absorbed it. But when his talk came around to his own particular interests, she responded. "Tell me more of these anachronisms, Jacob."

He shrugged. "There are thousands recorded, Feya. Evidences out of time, things that couldn't be where they were found. They are the puzzles that keep archeologists from being smug. Tunnels in South America where no tunnels should be, stone structures from times when no method of building them existed, a thing that seems to be a metal rod running through the core of the planet, an iron pillar that does not rust, an ancient bison skull with a bullet hole in it . . . humanlike footprints in middle Cretaceous chalk." He grinned at her. Her great eyes regarded him, waiting. He went on.

Eventually William got up and went away. He returned with three aged, dusty books and plunked them before Laurel. Laurel inspected them, nodded, and selected one. Expertly, he thumbed through it until he came to a catalog. He began reading from it. Shaped shards imbedded in dinosaur bone. Woven reeds mingled with an ichthyosaur fossil. Dig oddities such as the Viking stone in central Oklahoma, the Leyden jar in a Sumerian tomb, the eccentricities of Mount Ararat, the eye-fooling Ramapur Stone, the . . .

"How does it fool the eye, Jacob?"

He pondered. "It is a large piece of what appears to be quartz crystal, Feya. About two feet by ten inches at most. It has the appearance of having been shaped in the form of a teardrop, and its prismatic qualities are puzzling. It bends the light in odd ways. Oh, and it photographs black. From any angle, in any light, it photographs as though it were solid black. They didn't know that when it was unearthed in Turkey back in the nineteenth century, but it was an oddity even then. It has been quite thoroughly researched, but it remains just that—an archeological oddity."

"Where is it now, Jacob?"

"I haven't the faintest idea. William, can you find a glossary on it?"

"My eye's deceived," William muttered, staring at the bright little Feya, "what stands revealed before me's better hid. Better for one never to have learned that what one could not see, one did. Somebody wrote that." With a shake of his head, he shambled off into the darkness.

"Are many humans like him, Jacob?"

"A few. Not nearly enough."

William was back in a few minutes. "The Ramapur Stone is in Chicago. It is on loan from the British Museum to the University of Chicago. It has been there since 1932, and no one has ever asked that it be returned. It has been shown at the Museum of Science and Industry, but it was returned to the university."

Jacob Laurel chewed his lip. He had not shaved in . . . how long was it? A week? Two? The bristles on his face were becoming a beard. He had not worn a beard in forty years. "I suppose," he told the Feya, "that now you want to go to Chicago. Could you explain to me what your interest is?"

With tiny fingers, she leafed the pages of the open book. "You keep your lore in this."

"In a manner of speaking, yes."

"It has the taste of earth and fire about it. Very human. What you described, Jacob, was a testament—a record grown in crystal so that some particular bit of lore may be preserved. But I am sure my ancestors left no testaments behind when they transferred to Nendacaida, so how could a testament exist on this world? Humans have not the capability to grow such things."

"Supposing it is an elf book," Laurel pressed. "How can you be sure none were left here? Surely, when an entire race migrated, something was left behind."

"Something was. Many things. The Cai-kindred who stayed to comfort this sad place, the very essence—you would call it matrix—of Caidom that still clings in some hidden places here. But no testaments. The lore is clear. They were all taken . . . except one, of course, but you see it all the time."

"A testament?"

"More or less. When the Cai prepared to leave, they took from this world a mass of its substance from which to extract enough life-substance to seed the new world, to begin its mantle. They left the remains of that mass circling above old Caiendon, a symbolic gesture. That mass is a testament with only one message: It is a light in the darkness . . . It means we once were here."

They sat in silence for a time. Then the Feya said, "When Haralan is well enough, we will go to this Chicago. Will you come with us?" Jacob Laurel knew she knew the answer.

In the wee hours, careful to avoid security, Laurel climbed alone through the subterranean floors of the library until he found a room with a west window. Beyond, in silvered darkness, slept a campus of students.

For a long time, Jacob Laurel looked at the moon. He knew of only one place on Earth where there was a hole that might account for the extraction of the mass the Feya spoke of. The Pacific Trench. Abruptly, he realized that he had learned the answer to the puzzles regarding continental drift.

20

A deep dread haunted Roy Holloway now. The thing he had feared most, feared with a sick abhorrence magnified by past experience, was before him, and he was powerless to stop it. The one he loved was changing, and he was losing her because of it.

He hadn't seen Meg lately. How long had it been? Several days? A week . . . maybe more? It had come to the point that he dreaded being around her. Although he desperately needed her presence, the only light in a world gone murky, the changes in her were beyond his comprehension, and they hurt him.

Ever since his trip, when he had returned to find drug freaks at the fairgrounds, she had not been the same.

The knowledge tore at him. Strangely, he was more drawn to her than ever before. There was a radiance about her, a vibrance that was simply incredible. But they could not communicate. Each time he tried to discuss his concerns and the matters that were important to him, she seemed to withdraw. And the things she talked about mystified him. More and more, she dwelt on exotic subjects that repelled and worried him. She spoke in concepts, not subjects . . . colors and sounds, sensory perceptions, awarenesses. She seemed obsessed with awareness.

There was a tight, hard knot in his gut. He had read of "expanded awareness," and knew it was a concept at the very root of the drug culture and its related freak philosophies.

The days passed, and his one-time closeness with Meg deteriorated. He knew she was aware of his hurt. Hell, she seemed aware of everything these days. But it seemed to hurt her, too, and the gap widened because of the hurt.

He had asked her what was happening. Repeatedly. But she rattled on about some marvelous change that had come into her life . . . something wonderful or awful that she couldn't seem to tell him about. She said she saw things differently. What things? Everything. She said her senses had expanded, that her eyes had changed, that there was something in her that was improving her. He listened . . . for as long as he could stand it.

Bullshit! he told himself again, mulling his confusion. What was she talking about? She spoke analogy, obviously, but what? People didn't change. Not in that way, anyway. But what she meant by the things she said mystified him.

Finally, one evening when they sat together on the sunporch at her parents' house, she shook her head in exasperation. Reaching across to take his hand, she held it between hers and pressed it warmly. She cocked her head and gazed at him, waiting for some reaction. He didn't know what she expected.

And she realized that he didn't know, and something between them died. It was as though the taking-of-hands thing was a . . . a final attempt to prove something, but what? Why wouldn't she just tell him, in plain language, what was bothering her?

And she was always working on that damned paint-ing, adding to it little by little, and then just looking at it. He had looked at it, too, and didn't like it. It was a male face, but it represented something more than that. It was an abnormal face, like a caricature . . . a smooth, oddly tapered mask of a face . . . a smiling, catlike face that seemed to know too much. It wasn't a normal face. He wasn't even sure it was human.

And then there had been the oddest thing of all. They were at his house for coffee after a movie. She had tried to hide it, but the movie seemed to bore her, as though it meant nothing whatever, and the only light was in the kitchen where they sat. After a while she had gone to the bathroom, which was at the end of the hall. He had stacked map racks and spec-bins in the hall. She had gone and returned before it dawned on him that she hadn't turned on any lights. She had traversed a littered and cluttered hall in complete darkness and never bumped anything.

Meg had always suffered from night-blindness.

Lately Roy had buried himself in his work and tried to stay away from her. But when he slept, he dreamed of her smile, her eyes, her soft hands, the pretty pixie face that seemed more pixyish each day, and he needed her. He loved her and he needed her, and something was ter-ribly wrong.

It was early morning when Roy Holloway drove out to the old fairgrounds. His eyes were red-rimmed from lack of sleep, and a hard certainty twisted at his gut. He had paced throughout the night, sleepless, struggling against a knowledge that he didn't want to think about. But he had finally admitted it to himself. He knew what was wrong with Meg. He supposed he had known it all along, deep down.

The fairgrounds were empty, but he sat in his pickup, thinking. Never again, he had promised himself, would he be blind to those he loved. And never again would he turn away from the awful truth when it was right there in front of him.

The nut cults were good at what they did. They made fortunes from the conversion of innocents. They were pushers and drainers. They sucked the souls from decent people and destroyed them. His rage clawed at him, blinding him. Teddy . . . poor, altered little kid. And Dorothy.

And now Meg. The plastic casing of the steering wheel strained in the grip of his big hands. The plastic broke, and a shard of it gouged his thumb.

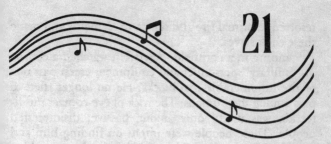

21

Aaelefein knew they sought him. The busy air of this world had thrummed with pulsations that made his scalp tingle ever since the night of his song. He had disturbed them, and they reacted with massive organization and a deadly determination that puzzled him.

More and more as he pursued his lonely quest, Aaelefein was absorbed with these strange, beautiful, aching creatures that had sprung from the Raporoi of legend. The haunted ones, lore called them, and they were indeed haunted. The terrible darkness that hung over them was not so much their sensory blindness, it seemed, as it was their awareness of how blind they were and their awful need to overcome it. Keenly pitched personalities trapped in unending aloneness, they strove mightily for the comfort, the revelation, the satisfaction their excellent minds told them was possible but their narrow senses forever denied them. Lacking all except the most primitive communication abilities, they compensated by creating marvels of arcane machinery, mystic things that spoke and listened to one another within the ranges of the Cai's parsing-sense, then translated their messages into the brief ranges of sound and sight their masters could comprehend. Lacking the vocal ability to control harmonics and thus to activate resonance, they

resorted to primal fire and the earth elements and made
these their slaves.

Standing in a cornfield, Aaelefein watched a convoy
of "military" personnel and equipment creep past one
of the innumerable roadblocks. He no longer tried to
pass among the humans. The trick of eye-contact misdi-
rection was useful only among passive, disinterested
people. These people were intent on finding him and
would not be deceived. Nor could he blend among them
safely. They knew him too well. A hundred times in the
past two days he had seen reproductions of his own face,
heard and read descriptions of his physical appearance.
For people who did not communicate easily, the children
of the haunted ones communicated awesomely when
they were aroused. In their blindness they did prodi-
gious magics against which the Caian had no defenses.
They were frightened, he knew. They had no understanding of him . . . not even the ability to understand
what it was to be Cai. And in their fright, they were formidable. He had not thought of humans as dangerous.
He knew now that they were.

Strangely, even as he suffered for them, he yearned for
their company; he found he had come to love these miserable creatures. Yet he knew they were deadly to him
when aroused, and now they were aroused.

Military . . . he had learned the word and the concept,
but could only guess at the enduring agony that brought
a race of sentient creatures to formalize and honor the
arts of killing their own kind. Such a concept was
unknown among the Cai. Fully sensed and empathic,
the competitive urges of the Caian folk tended in other
directions. Even Haralan, stout armsman of the robust
Eldretten people, had surely never harmed another
Caian—or any thinking thing. In any clan it was the task

of the armsman to defend the folk and their kindred against the mindless lizards and primitive carnivores that sometimes got out of hand; not to threaten or to harm people. Through all the ages of Caidom, it had always been so.

But then, among humans the existence of warriors served the arts of ruling. Such arts were needed among the blind.

Curious, he touched the feelings of some of the green-clad soldiers in the convoy. The predominant emotion, sharp above the omnipresent darkness of known mortality, was fear. Young males, armed and conditioned to use their fire-in-metal devices without hesitation upon command, still they were afraid. They were afraid of him, of his presence on their world, and they would kill him blindly rather than face the evidence of their blindness. His heart went out to them. He wished them solace and a warm place to hide their loneliness.

Aaelefein blended with the cornfield as a squadron of fighter craft howled overhead, electronic sensing devices sweeping the land. He kept his silence, though the hair on his head resonated with their scanning impulses. Humans, he knew, had lost—or never had—the wide-ranging parsing-sense. The hair on their bodies was purely ornamental. Their follicles, while retaining the organic shape to transmit resonance to the clusters of sensory fiber touching them, did nothing more than support the mute hair growing from them. In the vast range of sensory experience between their limited hearing and their even more limited sight, they perceived nothing. That was why they had the machines to do it for them.

Aaelefein could not read the messages in the resonance of the machines. It was mindless resonance, coded for interpretation within human sensory range. But he felt it and knew its insistence.

He wondered how long he could elude them. There were too many of them, too intent and too organized, for him to hide indefinitely. He would have to use the senester again to find Nataea, and when he used it, they would close in with their machines. They knew his direction of travel, and their cordon was closing massively around him. Yet he had no choice. He must find Nataea for the chord, for the last hope of elvenkind. And most of all, he knew, he must find her for himself. That tiny trill of response, fragile out of the vast darkness of a hostile world, was what he lived for now. Nataea was out there, and he would go to her.

It was amber dusk. Billowing spires of cloud stood overhead, roiling in the red of vanished sunlight. Distant lightnings laced the horizon, and the air was sweet with the music of summer storm. He waited. When the first fat drops of rain splatted dark upon gray dust, he knew it was time to move.

Once more he let his senses sweep outward, around him, reading the presences there. Many of them were fatigued, most of them were frightened, and all of them were lonely.

He tasted them and knew their feelings as he knew his own. He was tired, frightened, and lonely, just as they were. For too long, he had been immersed in a world of darkness, a lonely world without comfort. He knew fatigue, and a harsh overtone of desperation had been with him since he had left his companions of the chord. The desperation of search had replaced that first, blinding grief when Nataea had gone, and it had been a better thing than that. But it was taking a toll on him.

Had his song not brought a response, it would have

become despair. But Nataea was there. She had leaped, and she waited for him now.

The response—the song in it—concerned him. Nataea had found a host person, but the response had been awkward, as though two who were not blended tried to sing for one. Two distinct and separate people . . . not the single, more-perfect person a leap should have produced. Yet, on this world, how much could be the same? She had found a host. She was there. For now, it was enough.

He sensed the men out there, and their loneliness was akin to his own. Yet lately there had been a subtle change. In their dark persons now—at least in a few of them—there was a hint of something more. As though his call-song itself might have impressed something upon them. Maybe some of them had heard it. He knew that some had a trace of empathy. And now some had just the barest touch of Cai-essence.

A stealthy hundred yards put him out of sight of the roadblock below, beyond a terraced rise. Head-high rows ran parallel. He sprinted the half-mile to the next fence row and sank silently into brush as his ambience-sense detected clustered movement on the back road beyond. A group of men, armed with various weapons, approached.

". . . more sweep and we'll check in," one of them was saying. Of the group, only he wore a uniform. He scowled into the intensifying rain. "He's prob'ly holed up someplace by now anyhow, this rain comin' on like it is."

"George, how you gonna know whether aliens like rain or not?" another asked. "Hell, we don't know how that thing thinks."

"We don't know what it can do, either," George cautioned. "So you all keep your eyes open. Remember, this is a creature from outer space we're after, not a human bein'."

"You believe what you want to," another snorted. "I seen the pictures, too, and I say it's a Russian spy. You don't think the Army's going to tell a bunch of civilians the truth, do you?"

"Looks kind of like an Iranian to me. I saw a bunch of them up at Northwestern when Bobby started school there. Years ago."

"Nothin' says an Iranian can't be a Russian spy. I imagine some of 'em are."

"You're chattering like a bunch of idiots," George said. He pulled a handgun from its holster. "All right, spread out like before. We'll go in here. Come the other side, we'll call it a night."

"George, I'm gettin' awful wet, an' it's too dark to see anyhow. Why not quit now?"

"Because we still have to walk back to the cars anyway, and we might as well sweep the field while we're doin' it. Come on now."

They spread on the road, stepped across the ditch, and spread fence wires. The nearest one to Aaelefein was a boy, barely out of childhood. He cradled a heavy shotgun, and his mind was dim with exhaustion. Crawling through the fence, he passed within several feet of the still Caian. Along the line, men straightened, glanced from side to side, and then stepped out into the cornfield. After they had gone several yards, Aaelefein got to his feet, puzzled. In the taste of several of them was that slight Caian echo . . . something oddly serene lurking among the phantoms of fear and darkness that were their predominant emanations. He had felt it in the boy, a faint touch of psychic resonance that was more than human, almost a shadow of resonated empathy.

Even as he hesitated, his senses told him someone had altered pace. He glanced back. The boy had stopped, turned, and stared at him, eyes wide with wonder. For an instant, the eyes of the boy and those of the Caian locked across dim yards, then the boy shouted, "Hey!" The shotgun swung up, and the Caian leaped the fence, the explosion racketing behind him. The shot went wide. Aaelefein ducked and darted across the road into brushy woods beyond. Behind him was melee. "Hey, that was him." "Did you see that jump? That's no Iranian." "Don't stand there, dammit! Come on!"

Before they reached the road, the Caian was far away across the wooded lot, field, and another road, running in the rain, long legs pacing freely in tremendous strides. Why had the boy sensed him? he wondered. Where did he get the ability?

The missed shot, he knew, was intentional. The boy had aimed to miss. The young human had given him a gift.

With the rain came swift night darkness, and Aaelefein Fe-Ruast raced on, easily outdistancing men. But he knew he could not long outdistance their seeking machines. He maintained the lizard-hunting pace for three miles before his muscles began to tire, his breath to falter. He had not put enough distance between them yet. He knew their tactics; they would converge from all sides, form a circle of massed manpower, and close in. He must be beyond the circle before it formed.

Reluctantly he lowered his chin and sang resonance-chords to the senester. He felt its quick vibration as it picked up his harmonies and built upon them. He sang pulsing subsonics into it, with a blend of resonances in the parsing ranges, a running song to himself. The senester amplified the vibrances and bathed him in them.

Instantly he was made stronger, his nerves and muscles soothed and stimulated by the resonance. His pace picked up as he entered a shelf of dark hills, stepping up and away from the tilled flats. Full night was on the land, but he had left the rain behind. Where he passed now, pale moonlight washed the land in silver, shadowed beneath stands of forest, bright on the little meadows among the hills. With the healing senester to help him, he ran on, up swale after swale, and then down and down in a long grade.

He came to a river and crossed it, his human clothes sealed in the bundle of his cape, his body rejoicing at the ambient coolness through which he swam. Second to air, water was his natural element. Even the darkness of the humans was muted in its depths. Beyond were more forests. He recalled the charts he had studied, the maps. He had left Illinois. He was in Indiana, and his senses quickened. Near now, very near, was the locale from which his song had been answered.

He would have to use the senester again soon, call again to pinpoint where she was, and he dreaded it. They would know the silence when it began, know its cause and close in on him. He would get as close as he could, find a hiding place, and risk his call. Possibly he would find a place remote enough, even in the closing mass of questers about him, to call and then escape before they reached him. He could not evade the sensing machines, but maybe he could escape the men who used them one more time.

Why had some of those who passed him had about them the taste of Caiansong? Why had the boy? Had some among them really heard his song?

* * * * *

In stationary orbit, a scanning satellite recorded nineteen minutes of unusual, low-power harmonics from a ground source progressing along a line of movement, a peculiar blend of subsonics and several VHF-UHF frequencies, nondirectional. As it recorded, the machine fed data to its ground control stations, which poured it into the thickening web of electronic data flowing westward toward Cheyenne Mountain. Other strands fed the details of a sighting of the alien in eastern Illinois, grade two confirmation, verified.

Deep in its subterranean lair, Cyber-205 assimilated these and myriad other inputs, and its readouts blinked attention.

The moving pulse of harmonics and the alien were one and the same, probability .991. Seek and target. Time allowances were read into the equation with reasonable variants. Pace sensors in grid, coordinates follow. Implacable and uncaring, Cyber-205 continued to do what it did better than any entity on Earth— digest data and produce trends.

22

It was 0400 precisely when the dark chopper touched down at Offutt Field. Those waiting in ranks, coated against the drizzle, saluted as aides stepped down followed by the husky figure of Major General Stafford Clark, who chopped a brisk return and then strode toward the command center, the receiving group falling in behind him.

In the briefing room, they took their places with quiet precision. Clark slipped out of his coat, accepted a cup of coffee, and turned. "Well?"

"We have the situation as of 0350, sir," a subordinate officer said. "But Mr. Tracy from the Secretary's staff is on his way in. He should be landing any minute. Would you prefer to wait for him, sir?"

"Hell, no. Let him pick up the pieces when he gets here. Report the situation."

"Yes, sir," the officer said. He turned to a man with birds on his shoulders.

"Colonel Mayo, sir," the officer said. "SAC Third Wing detached, liaison to NASA Houston. We have a confirmed sighting of a lone elf—"

"Alien," Clark corrected.

"Sir?"

"I said *alien*, Colonel. Those aliens in custody identified themselves as elves. They are aliens." A hard, humorless irony rasped in his voice.

"Ah . . . yes, sir." Mayo glanced around at the faces circling the long table. "Aliens. We have a confirmed sighting of a lone, uh . . . alien just before 2100 hours at the edge of a cornfield south of Danville, Illinois. We have a report from EMSAT of scanner readings on a multiple resonance source moving in a direct line from that point toward the Wabash River, bearing approximately 96 degrees local. NORAD's bank confirms hypothesis that the resonance source is the same, uh, alien. Assuming retained speed and direction, the subject crossed the Wabash a little after 2200 hours and is now approaching Shelbyville, southeast of Indianapolis."

Clark peered at the chart where an aide wielded a pointer. "On foot?"

"When sighted, yes, sir."

Clark glanced at his watch. "You assume the alien has been traveling at more or less fifty miles an hour for the past seven hours. On foot."

Mayo frowned. "Yes, sir, I know how it sounds, but it is a possibility that he can move that fast."

"I don't question the speed, Colonel. Based on what we've learned, I'm not surprised at that. But I do question the endurance factor. Gentlemen, this is Dr. Steinbrenner of Southwest Research Institute. He is cleared under provisions of the National Emergency Defense Act. Doctor, let's hear about the red cells . . . in plain English, please."

One of the men who had arrived with Clark, a sallow, bespectacled man with whiskers, opened a case and leafed through files. "Yes. Ah, here it is." He spread out a sheaf of papers, squinting through thick lenses. "Yes. We obtained a sample of the elf . . . uh, alien blood taken from a building in Denver. Analysis shows it to be structurally similar to human blood with a few interesting exceptions. The coagulant factor, for instance, is—"

"Red cells, doctor," Clark prompted.

"Yes. Red cells. The red cells of the elf blood are platelets similar to human and other terrestrial blood. But we are struck by a certain, uh, plasticity in their nature. Among the tests made was a subjection to various electromagnetic wave ranges. We found—not at first, of course, but after some exhaustive procedures—that certain composites of resonance—certain harmonics, if you will—cause changes in the cells. They grow."

In the silence, Steinbrenner looked around, staring through his glasses. "That is," he continued, "the individual cells become larger, fully functional, and capable of carrying substantially more oxygen. We were able to induce growth of slightly more than forty per cent in mass of a single cell."

"But other than that, Doctor," Clark asked, "it is like human blood?"

"Well, no, sir, not exactly. The coagulant factor, as I said, is—"

"I mean in its function of carrying oxygen to the body organs."

"No, sir, not in that respect. I mean, except for the expandable platelets, their bloodstream fuel function is similar to ours."

"May I see the harmonics you used to make them grow, please?" Clark received the paper and handed it across to Mayo. The colonel looked at it, then thumbed through telex sheets before him. He pulled one out and compared the information. "Roughly the same, sir. These parameters are approximately the blend registered by EMSAT's scanner."

"Very well," Clark said. He took the pointer. "Here was the sighting, here the impulses began, and here they ended: at the river. The alien had gone approximately eight miles before he started enlarging his blood cells— and whatever else he did to keep himself going. Then from here to the river, he ran with the assistance of whatever he was using to induce the phenomenon. But from there on, no impulses were recorded. Therefore he did not continue at the same speed and direction for these additional hours, but either stopped some place or slowed to a pace requiring no, uh, harmonic assistance. If we assume half-speed same direction, or less, then he is somewhere in this area now." The colonel traced a long ovoid on the chart that extended from the Wabash River near Cayuga to a point near the southwest edge of Indianapolis. "Concentrate the search midway through here, gentlemen. That's where our alien is."

Colonel Mayo raised a hand. "General, are there any leads on the other ones? The other aliens?"

Clark frowned. "Not a clue. Not a damned clue. Let's concentrate on getting this one first, though. He's the 'singer.'"

Guards opened the briefing-room door to admit a wedge of civilians. The two trailing had the appearance of Secret Service. The lead man, bland and handsome in a dark coat and tie, presented a hand. "General Clark? I'm Tracy, from the Secretary's office." His mild, glancing eyes devoured the room, missing nothing. "Care to fill me in?"

Clark nodded. "Briefly, we have concluded that our singer is in this area here, between the Wabash River and Indianapolis. We have troops in cordon at present from about here"—he tapped central Illinois— "to here." He scratched an arc from Fort Wayne to Louisville. "I have just given the order to close in at all possible speed and concentrate here, where he is."

Trace nodded. His voice was mild. "And when you find him, General?"

"When we find him, he will be . . . reduced."

"That seems a bit impetuous, don't you think? After all, he has hurt no one."

The general squared his shoulders. "For more than seven minutes on a recent evening, sir, our continental security system was completely nullified. Seven minutes! That's long enough for the USSR to put every bird it has right through our window."

"But they didn't."

"No, they didn't. They weren't prepared for a 'sudden silence,' as the TV people are calling it. But they will assume if it happened once, it can happen again. They might not hesitate a second time."

"Assuming they desire to put birds in our windows."

"We can assume nothing else, Mr. Tracy. The National Emergency Defense Act and its subsequent orders are quite clear."

"The Act was invoked three days ago, General, when we had to assume we were dealing with hostile terrestrial powers. Now, it seems, the situation is quite something else. The President's order is being rescinded at this moment. You will proceed to locate the elf, General, but there is to be no 'reducing.' I want to be perfectly clear on that point. Good Lord, the National Academy of Sciences wants to talk to the creature, not autopsy him."

Clark's cheeks had gone pale. "Do you know what you're saying, Mr. Tracy? Hostile or not, that creature has the capability of exposing us to attack without warning or retaliation. Nuclear attack, Mr. Tracy. He has to be stopped before he . . . does that again. And since we don't even know how he does it, there is only one way. Hell, man, the scientists can have the others when we find them."

"It isn't just the scientists," Tracy said, steel in his level voice. "During the past day and a half, there has been a concerted citizen plea the like of which Washington has not seen in its history. I don't know what that creature did, General, any more than you do. But several million people in the mid-continent have decided they've experienced some kind of miracle, and they want him spared. We have to listen to that, General. After all, we work for them."

"Then do you want them dead?"

Tracy's mild eyes glinted. "The issue is decided, General. You will receive new and amended orders by morning."

"Well, I haven't received them yet!" Clark stormed. "And until I see a Presidential decree that the Act is no longer in effect, by God, I'll assume it is." Livid, he whirled on the uniformed crowd. "You have your orders, gentlemen. And until I personally countermand them, they stand."

Without another glance at the bureaucrat, Stafford Clark turned on his heel and strode from the room, his staff scurrying to follow him. Out on the gray-dark tarmac, a wing of fightercraft waited, their wicks lit. By full daylight the general would be in Indiana.

In the briefing room behind him, Colonel Mayo spoke to the silence. "He has a point, you know. Friendly or not, that thing out there—elf or alien or whatever—is perfectly capable of getting us dusted."

"You can call off SAC," one of the others suggested helpfully to the suddenly deflated Tracy.

"Sure he can, but this is a ground operation. The general is calling the shots."

A lean officer in the rear, liaison to the Attorney General's office, muttered, "I expect the Secretary is acquainted with the provisions of *posse comitatis*."

Tracy looked around, a faint, sad smile pulling at his lips. "Thank you, sir, but it will do no good. Without NEDA, the military has no authority to pursue fugitives on American soil, of course, but it would require an act by a state legislature to invoke the clause. I'm afraid there just isn't time."

There were no more suggestions. Colonel Mayo shrugged helplessly and stood. "Gentlemen, we are under explicit orders. I suggest we get our butts in gear."

As they filed out past him, Tracy turned and stared at the chart on the wall. Idly his finger traced a long ovoid extending from the Wabash River eastward to a point near Indianapolis.

Somewhere in there, in that tiny space, a lonely, exhausted elf was being hounded to ground by a massive military machine. Tracy blinked his eyes rapidly, fighting down the sick feeling of impending tragedy that had ridden him for the past two days.

He wished General Clark could have been with him in Denver. He wished the general could have spoken with . . . could even have just seen . . . the lovely creatures he had met there.

He wished the general could have seen the Feya.

23

"It is more than just two extra senses, then?" Jacob
Laurel pursued. "Of the five senses I have, you have
them to a greater degree?"

The Feya looked away, watched the night-time coun-
tryside flowing by—banked fields sharply delineated as
bright radiances between the more somber, heat-
trapping hedgerows, the shades of overlapping, flowing
air masses, the little brightnesses of sleeping creatures.
She found the infrared a restful range, recuperative
between the rigors of their mission. The paved highway
running away behind them, releasing its trapped heat in
the night, was brilliant red. The surface on which they
rested was blue-cool, the top of a semi-trailer, the sides
of which were stenciled: Dartmoor Packing Co. One of
the things Winifraeda craved rest from was the constant
probing, analyzing, searching of the human mind of
Jacob Laurel. Patience, she told herself. If I had been
blind all my life and now learned about sight, I would
ask questions, too.

"Not all five," she said. "Your senses of taste and
smell are very similar to ours, though I suspect we might
perceive the messages differently. But in terms of audible sound and visible light, our ranges are far greater
than human. Consider the kind of world this was when

the first Cai ascended. We could not have survived with
limited hearing and limited sight."

"But how much different are your senses, Feya? What
do you see out there right now . . . I mean with your
eyes?"

"Fields, roads, houses, various structures, creatures,
wooden poles, metal skeletons, air masses, patterns of
energy dancing in all directions. . . . I see life and the
matrix that supports and serves it."

"That's what I mean," Laurel said. "Except for where
there are electric lights, I don't see a damned thing. I
expect my eyes are gathering all that, but it doesn't
record on my brain."

"As to sound," the Feya continued, "my ears tell me
about twice what yours tell you. They respond to sounds
too low for you to hear, and too high. Are you trying to
classify sensory ranges?"

"Of course I am. That's what we're talking about."

The Feya shrugged. It was a human communicative
symbol that delighted her. "If you say so, Jacob. In that
case, take my hand so I have the words . . . there. Now,
can you form an impression in your mind of a . . . yes, a
spectrum? The electromagnetic spectrum, I see. Very
well. We have touch-sense into what you consider the
infrasonic range. I am using it right now. The skin of our
hands is in contact. The vibrations carry feeling and
intent. From there, we can hear up to and including your
audible range . . . do you realize that what you visualize
as audible range is much wider than what you actually
hear, Jacob?"

"That's because I'm getting old."

"We'll have to do something about that some time.
Anyway, I can hear sounds into what you consider ultrasonics and long-wave radio range."

"You hear radio broadcasts?"

"Not really, I only hear the pulses. The meanings they carry are coded for re-translation into your sonics. I can't sort them out. I also hear, but rather vaguely, those wavelengths you perceive as chemical smells in the acrid range. You smell them. I hear them as wave phenomena."

"Interesting," he muttered.

"From about the upper limit of my hearing, I parse. The two senses somewhat overlap at that point."

"Parse. We don't do that at all."

"Oh, you do, but you have never learned to perceive it. Your race didn't have to. The planet was tame long before you came along. Your hair is mostly just to warm your head . . ." She glanced at his baldness in the dark. "I am sorry, Jacob. I didn't realize you were sensitive about that."

"I'm not. My brain has been cold for thirty years."

"You are. Never lie to an elf when you're holding her hand. I told you about infrasonics."

"You parse. And parsing is what?"

"Simply an extension of receptivity on up the spectrum. But the sensory organs are the hair . . . follicles? Yes. I parse from the limit of my hearing to the lower limit of my sight, which is your infrared. From there, my eyes see into the ultraviolet range."

"You make me feel terribly short-changed."

"Parsing is rarely a pleasant sense, Jacob. The harmonics are too vast."

"So much for parsing," Laurel grumbled. "Still, I'd like to try it."

"Later," the Feya said. "You really aren't equipped for it right now."

He turned to her in the dark. "Are you serious, Feya?

You mean I can experience another sense?"

"I don't know. Maybe one day we can . . . shape you up. The capabilities are vestigial, apparently. You've just never used them."

Behind them, Haralan and Sefraeonia lay close together on the trailer roof, talking in a range Winifraeda knew was not audible to Laurel. Curiously, she let her senses carry their song from hearing through subsonics to the tactile infrasonics. Her hand grew vibrant in his. Laurel looked up, his eyes wide, then turned to look back—toward the front of the vehicle—at the other elves. Suddenly he had . . . heard? . . . their voices.

"I think there is a possibility," the Feya said.

"Ergo: six senses. And the seventh?"

"You have it, but you've only just begun to use it. Call it . . . relating is as good a word as any. It is a perception of ambience, of changes in relationship within the ranges of resonance. It is the basis of empathy. The sensory organ is inside your skull."

"Ah." Laurel breathed. "Yes, I have felt it, right behind the brow. The pineal gland."

"That tastes like a misnomer, that word 'gland,' but yes. That organ. You have related. The ability will grow as you use it. I suppose most humans can do that. They just don't know how, or don't know what is happening when they do it. The night Haralan came for you, to bring you to us. You were relating then. He would not have found you otherwise."

"Creativity?" he mused. "The alpha phenomenon?"

The truck rolled on through night-touched miles, headlights in front for the eyes of its driver, bright heatlight rolling away behind for the eyes of Cai.

Jacob Laurel was asleep, shielded by Haralan's cloak, when Sefraeonia told them there was another roadblock

ahead. This one had truck-mounted towers and search-
lights.

Haralan grumbled at having to leave the vehicle
again. His wound still troubled him. But Sefraeonia
pressed his hand and smiled for him, and the pain lessened.

With Laurel wrapped in his cape, the Feya clinging to
his back, Haralan leaped from the slowing truck, caught
his balance, and faded into the night-shadows of a roadside culvert. He deposited his charges and rose to his
knees, waiting for Sefraeonia. He heard her startled,
querulous cry. Seeking lights had found her, still standing atop the high trailer, and the roadblock came alive.
Bathed in the brilliance against earth-night, she could
not deflect notice. Men shouted, jolted awake by the
vision. They had guns. Well he knew, from the building
in Denver, the reactions of armed humans to those
caught in their lights. Again he sensed the presence of
panic.

"Be still, Haralan—" the Feya said. But Haralan was
gone.

"What's happening?" Jacob Laurel muttered, staring
around. The Feya found his hand and pressed it. From
the dark culvert, they watched with combining senses.

For a moment Sefraeonia poised atop the trailer, confused in sudden brilliance that smote her eyes, a white
sylph bathed in splendor. Men moved, their bulging
eyes fixed on her, blind to the darkness. Nine wore military green, two the garb of state police. Unthinking,
their guns sought the target of their eyes. Then there was
a rage among them.

Screaming diamond crystal sliced the base of a light
tower, and it fell, crashing, onto a jeep. Sefraeonia
leaped into darkness as guns thundered over her. The

remaining light gyrated and fell, its beam askew, side-lighting chaos on the road. A machine pistol moved in an arc of radiance, severing what it touched. Two more guns clattered to the pavement. A soldier buckled and flew backward, propelled by a large Caian foot. Haralan was among and through them, his blade a dancing swirl of bright resonance, cloak streaming crimson, armor lustrous, his lizard-keen an alarm in the shattered night air. And through it came the singing call, "Sefraeonia, run! Go far! Go far . . ."

Then the sword's radiance dimmed as the Caian was hit again and again by tough young humans and borne over and down under their weight. Flailing, singing his distress, he was buried beneath them.

The truck driver, his vehicle barely stopped, stared at the chaos on the road in wonder. Then, with an oath, he shifted gears and hit the gas. Great wheels barely missed the mass of straining bodies on the road as the driver sought the darkness beyond. Past fallen towers, crushed vehicles, and shouting men, the semi crept, picking up speed. A police car was nudged aside, and he had open road in his beams. Behind him were shouts . . . one gunshot or two, he couldn't tell. Massed gears sang as he fought for distance. Dartmoor Packing Number Nineteen, its driver frantic, hit the road.

He had gone three miles before he became aware that he was not alone. When he turned to look, he nearly went off the road.

"Our apologies," the silver doll beside him said. The old man next to her stared back at him in the cablight with eyes as huge as his own. Tortured rubber sang, and the truck swerved. A tiny, lucent hand touched his as he wrestled the wheel, and he knew angels singing. She said no more, but he knew. They were distressed. They would be grateful to ride with him a way.

An intervening hill blanked the glow of chaos far behind. Awed, dazzled, he honed the big machine's harmonies and lined it out eastward along serene night highway. The tiny hand remained on his. In the flood of awful sweetness that surged through him, there was also a sadness, a bitter longing that was not his own.

They . . . you have friends, he thought. They are back there.

The answer came as knowledge sensed. Yes. There are friends. But we must go on.

24

The Air Force and its missions had been called off. With revocation of the National Emergency Defense Act, countermanding orders had gone out. But the Army remained in the field, closing a cordon on western Indiana, mobilized and unstoppable except through its commanding officer. The orders had not caught up with General Clark.

With the end of NEDA, the workings of civilian society jumped back into play. News media swarmed over the land and fed confusing masses of information to the world.

Extraterrestrial creatures were at large. They had landed in the Rockies and were now at various places around the country. Two had been captured and interviewed at Denver, but had escaped. Clips of that interview escaped security and were broadcast, co-opting everything else. The "night of the song," the "miracle night," had been the work of the aliens. Awe spread like fire through nations . . . awe that was fear to some, hope to others. As newspapers fought deadlines and networks fought incredulity, what would become the clearest account was assembled by staff newsmen at BBC-Canada. They found and interviewed Robert Tracy, Deputy Secretary of Defense.

The creatures claimed to be, and probably were, elves.
There had been five of them. Now there were four. One
was known as the "Centurion," the Denver legend. One
was a girl—even BBC lacked the words to describe her.
And one was a Feya, ". . . something quite beyond what
we are accustomed to defining; you'll have to simply rely
on pictures and the following recorded excerpts." The
fourth also remained at large, but there were pictures . . .
a tall, striking . . . man? Almost human but not quite.
Reminiscent of the Centurion but not quite.

To some, the creatures were fearsome; to some, they
were captivating. There still was no word from the
elderly academician who had been abducted by one of
them, but the—Feya?—spoke of him and assured that
he was safe and acting of his own volition. Those who
believed her at all believed her fully.

Then there was news. One had been captured. At a
roadblock in Illinois, combined Army and local police
had apprehended the one called Centurion. According
to the Feya, his name—confined to human range—was
Haralan. Word was, he was in tight custody and being
flown to Washington. The thing he carried, a crystalline
shortsword that had devastated vehicles and equipment
at the roadblock, was on its way separately to the
Georgetown laboratories of the National Science Foundation.

*   *   *   *   *

Margaret Harrison, alone in her parents' home in
Rockville, watched the news and wept. Stout Haralan,
loyal Haralan—the name sang rainbows in her mind, its
full harmonics known to her.

Chained like a beast, threatened by ready guns, livid

cloak drooping from broad shoulders, his beloved blade taken from him, he was watched by the dull eye of television as he stepped aboard a sleek jet transport with military insignia. To the limited senses the camera could capture, he disappeared into darkness beyond. She felt deprived. She should have seen more of him. The machines showed too little. She could only imagine the harmonics of regret pulsing through him, soft tear-song of a proud warrior humbled.

Consciously, in a mind that had accepted dichotomy as a way of life, she did not know Haralan. But the silent side of her, that roseate, sparkling aliveness that had come to her in a dream of elven features, knew it all and wept, and Meg wept with it.

Sometimes it seemed she could hardly remember the Margaret of before that awakening—that singular, blind, dull person who had been her. Her moments now were moments of music, of brilliance, of sweet-sad beauty that dulled the memory of life as she had known it. From the moment she had accepted the brilliant otherness that was now within her, it had grown, become more strong and serene, a life-essence so vital, so aware, that what it shared with her was a glory that caught in her throat. She knew it shared as much as she could accept, but that was still only a little. It was open to her as a true friend is open. But they both—and the plurality was real—stopped there. They knew each other, were each other in every physical sense, but still they were two separate souls, and the barrier seemed absolute. She wished often, and knew that it—its name was Nataea—wished too that they might simply become one.

The early fear was gone. Now there was a powerful, pleading need in both of them to somehow blend, to become what they together could be. But the barrier was

there. Nataea, the other self, could not stand full min-
gling with the humanness of Margaret. Nor could Margaret stand the full otherness of her . . . guest? No, more
than that. Nataea—a song of many colors she could
think but not yet sing—was so much a part of her now
that they were intertwined. But only as dear, close
friends. The barrier was unbreakable. Gone was that terrified time when she had come so close to rejecting the
tiny, vulnerable spark that clung in her. She knew
Nataea now, and she loved her as a blind person loves
the companion with clear sight who might share the
wonders of color and form. And she knew Nataea loved
her as well, but differently—a deep, ancient love of one
who stands above the Earth for one who stands upon it.

It was curious that such concepts were no longer puzzling. The act was there, and she found with Nataea's
help that she did not have to understand in order to
know. On the muttering screen a metal bird raced past
the camera, dwindled, and took to the air. Inside its ali-
en skin, a loyal, defeated Caian slumped in bondage.
Nataea wept with Margaret's flooding eyes, and Margaret shared her sorrow. Stout heart, beloved Haralan.
Bright harmonies comfort you and carry you to a gentle
roost.

What would they do to him, those blind ones who
awaited? *Help him, please,* her otherness begged. *This is
your world. Do something.*

Is this my world? The thought puzzled Meg. If this
were my world, I could affect it, couldn't I? But what can
I do? Yet, you have given me so much.

There was so much. So many little, odd things that
came with the glory. There was the morning she had cut
her hair short. An impulse? A suggestion. And now each
hour it seemed she found new musics in the world

around her. Her scalp had tingled strangely for a time. Now she revelled in it. Bright pulses sang to her where none had ever been before. Her senses had expanded, had quickened.

For a time her throat had ached each morning, and now she found she could respond to birdcall, to the trill of insects, to the rustle of bright leaves. She could sing, and the world sang with her. And there was the precious, painful thing, the awareness behind her brow. She knew so much she had never known, in ways she could never have imagined, and it hurt her. Never had she felt such love for those around her . . . or such intense sadness that they must be as they were.

Do something. She turned off the depressing dullness of the TV and went to the phone. It remained, like all its electronic kindred, a dull, lusterless function, small and cramped in a bright, expanded world. It had no song, just noise.

She dialed assistance, then began the gamut of transfer and retransfer to some person of authority she did not know and had no idea how to reach. Crank call, her human self thought. I'm about to become a statistic someplace—one of how many thousand crank calls received today? *Please*, the presence begged, *cynicism hurts me. I do not know the feeling. Please try.*

She heard the front door open and close, felt the confused suffering presence of Roy Holloway approaching. "My name is Margaret Harrison," she told another voice. "I must speak with someone in authority about the alien who was captured last night. I know him. Please, who can I talk to?"

Two more voices came and went. Roy stood behind her now, hurting, a presence of anguish. Then, on the phone came a man's voice, crisp with discipline. "Mister

Tracy's office."

Tracy. Yes. She had seen him on television. He seemed sympathetic. "This is Margaret Harrison. I need to speak to Mister Tracy."

"The Deputy Secretary is not available at present, Ms. Harrison. May I help you?" The voice was insistent, persuasive. Someone had told him the subject.

"Well, maybe you can. It's about Haralan. I want to help him. I want to . . . intercede somehow. He—"

"By Haralan, do you mean the alien captured last night?"

"Please, he's no alien. He is a decent, gentle person. You see, I know him. He is a good friend. Please don't let him be hurt. Please—"

"Where are you calling from, Ms. Harrison?"

She ignored the question. "Can you or Mister Tracy protect Haralan? And Aaelefein? I know they are looking for him, too—the Army, that is. But he's looking for me, that's all. He isn't harming anyone. Please don't let any of them be hurt."

There was a pause. The darkness behind her was an agony. She sensed other presences at the far end of the telephone connection. Oh, Roy, she pleaded silently. Why can't you understand? Why are you so human?

"Ms. Harrison," the voice was gentle now, but strained, "do you know the Feya?"

"Yes . . . yes, I do."

"Then can you tell me the Feya's name?"

"Winifraeda."

Another pause, more presences. Then, "No, I mean her name in her own tongue . . . as she would say it."

The otherness surged forth, desperately. Her throat ached. Without knowing how, she sang the name. The instrument at her ear quivered with massed resonances.

There was a sputtering on the line, electromagnetic distress, then the phone went dead. Defeated, she replaced the receiver.

The hurting, confused darkness behind her was overwhelming. She whispered, "Hello, Roy," and turned.

He towered above her, his face gone white, anguish in his eyes. He tried to speak, but his voice failed him. In her, the Nataea presence dwindled far down, battered by the emanations of his presence.

"Roy," Margaret steeled herself. "I tried to tell you. I wanted you to know."

His mouth worked. Waves of hard anger lashed out at her, waves black with pain. "Know what?" he managed. "That you're in with them? You of all people, Meg, mixed up with the nuts . . . the crazies? You even know their names?"

"Roy." She closed her eyes tight, shook her head to clear the confusion and the pain. "You don't understand. Why don't you understand? It isn't what you think . . . not at all. They're real, Roy. They are real, wonderful people. They aren't at all what you've made yourself believe. I know. I . . . I don't know how to explain it so you can understand, Roy. I am one of them. Roy, I am. I really am!"

His face went whiter still. She knew it was hopeless. He had no rapport. He could not understand even if he wanted to. He was only human. He was blind, hopeless, stubborn, and violent. His raging loneliness was his whole essence. She felt battered by it, wave after crashing wave. The otherness in her whimpered its pain.

"I knew it!" he shouted, his voice trailing into the ranges beyond his own hearing . . . but not beyond hers. "From the first day, I knew they had you. God help you, Meg, I loved you! I loved you so!"

In the darkness was great, unbearable loss, and a resolving intent for vengeance. Big shoulders hunched, his arms great knots of screaming muscle, he strode past her toward the sunroom. She followed, pleading in voices he could not even hear. At the table, he stopped and grasped the painting, stared at it with blind hatred.

"It's him, isn't it, Meg? He's the one. And now he's looking for you again? Well, by God, he won't have you. I guess I won't have you, but I promise you he never will, either. I'll kill him first, Meg. So help me God, I'll kill him!"

She sagged against the doorway, tortured by his violence. She heard the painting tear as he pulled it apart with knotted hands, heard its pieces fall to the floor, heard his footsteps thunder as he swept past her, heard the front door slam. Inside her the lovely otherness wept, battered and abused.

Aaelefein . . . the name sang in her mind. Aaelefein, be careful. All your strength, all your gentleness, is no match for that. You're out of your world, Aaelefein. This is his world, and it is deadly to you.

It wasn't the Nataea side that thought this, Meg noticed. That side was bruised and hiding, deep inside her. The plea-song in her mind was her own.

25

"So far, all we've got is tacit insubordination. Until he is physically handed his orders, we can't assume he knows what they are." General Morey Flanders squinted through the haze of his cigar smoke at the four across from him. "Sure, he knows the orders are out, but a guy with an army around him can duck the 'process server' for quite a while."

"The man's a maniac," Peter Kistotten snapped. "Doesn't he know what he's risking?"

"As he sees it, Pete, the rest of us are jeopardizing the nation, not him. I've known Stafford Clark for a long time. He was the toughest, most volatile, stubbornest son of a bitch on the team at the Point. And he hasn't changed a bit. He's one-way all the way and to hell with obfuscation. He's the kind of general officer a country has to have in emergencies and can't stomach the rest of the time."

Cyrus Wingo, his long face gray and shrewd in its halo of white air, drummed thin fingers on the vinyl arm of his chair. "In short, he thinks he's Patton."

Flanders chuckled. "Something like that."

"I have senators from nine states breathing down my neck," Kistotten said. "Their constituents are up in arms. They want assurances from us that those creatures won't be harmed, and they want them now. So how do we give them that assurance?"

"Hell, Pete, nobody here wants to hurt them. But we do want to know how they do what they do, before somebody else gets hold of the technology. You saw the charts. For seven minutes and twenty-two seconds, the mid-continent was as vulnerable as a john in a strange whorehouse. Lord, son, we had our pants on the floor and no place to run. The eastern bloc could have unloaded on us right then, and we'd never have known what hit us. That's what Stafford Clark sees, and he's out to make sure it doesn't happen again. From that perspective, I can't say I blame him. What do you want to do, bring him up on treason charges for defending his country?"

"Nobody's suggesting that, Morey." Cyrus Wingo slipped into the judicious role that had captivated two generations of voters and their elected representatives. "The suggestion is that it might be expected of General Clark that he follow orders—delivered or implicit. He knows the president has rescinded NEDA. He knows the Air Force and NASA have been called off. Bob Tracy told him as much when they met. But he is deliberately evading his orders. He has four brigades in the field out there, and if their orders aren't specifically to shoot on sight, that's the tenor of the campaign. The instant that alien is spotted, he's going to be dead. And we'll have a morale collapse in this country like you haven't seen since the Civil War."

"I didn't see the Civil War," Flanders reminded him gently. "Besides, I think Clark has some degree of discretion. He isn't going to dump national chaos on us."

"Isn't he, though?" Kistotten leaned forward earnestly. "General, maybe you don't know the trend of thinking out there. A lot of people are scared to death

because aliens have landed. But a lot more have made
. . . I don't know, heroes or something, out of them.
That . . . emotional event eight days ago, that 'psychotraumatic experience' as the shrinks call it, was profound. I believe the estimate is that one out of every four
people exposed to it experienced a . . . some say revelation, some call it a miracle, an awakening, call it what
you will. We're being bombarded, General. Those people are telling us we're wrong to eliminate the aliens.
And if we don't respond, I dread to think what will happen to this country's military. Like it or not, sir, we work
for them, all of us."

"That psychotraumatic experience was an open window for a few thousand nuclear warheads to fly through,
Pete. Consider that."

"Are you defending Clark's action?"

"I'm saying let's be very careful. Sure, I could overrule
him. I could draft an order right now to his seconds, taking them out of the field. I could also fire him. Either
one would take a couple of days to implement fully, you
realize. And either action would result in a crumbling of
regular army morale and destroy a good soldier. Do you
want to do that?"

"I want him to receive his orders and obey them.
Then we won't have a dilemma."

"Unfortunately, what you want him to do and what
he sees fit to do are two different things. Gentlemen, let
me explain this. The National Emergency Defense Act is
more than seventy years old. This is only the second time
in its history that a president has invoked it. The first
time was World War II. You don't drop a thing like that
into place in this nation and then just wipe it off without
traces when you're through with it. By the nature of the
Act itself, field commanders have a great deal of discre-

tion in how they respond to field situations. That discretion can be seen as even covering response to the Act itself."

"If any of those elves are hurt, General, we are going to have a revolution on our hands." Kistotten said it flatly, finally.

In the silence that followed, General Flanders shook his head. "I can understand how people feel," he admitted. "I've reviewed the clips. That little Feya . . . marvelous! Absolutely beautiful! And what I'd give to see that . . . girl without a blanket draped over her. From what I've heard, just looking at her would take thirty years off me. I look forward to meeting the big one . . . Haralan? . . . this afternoon. No, gentlemen, I have no lack of awe for this occasion . . . the first landing of extraterrestrial beings. But at this moment, I'm not ready to wreck my army over it. I just can't see the odds." The words pained him. He was not a man to pass the buck. But this was his best judgment, and he would hang with it.

All three turned then to face the fourth man in the big room, the final authority.

The President of the United States looked from one to another, the weight of the world in his tired eyes. Then he lowered his head, rested his chin on cupped hands, and studied the red leather cover of his desk.

*   *   *   *   *

In Georgetown, deep within a big, old house set back on manicured lawns, people gathered in silence to look at the device on display on a covered laboratory table. It was a double-edged shortsword of black crystal, carved-gold guard and pommel bracing a grip of resilient stuff that looked like swirls of emerald and chocolate.

Stacks of empirical data told them some of what the blade could do, and the theorists were in concurrence that it was, in fact, a broad-spectrum resonator capable of harmonic variance. Some among them hypothesized on the basis of evidence that they would find that the blade was in fact a bundle of crystalline fibers feathering outward to form the edges. Others suspected a single, unvariegated crystal of infinite molecular variation.

But learning what it was would not be the first task. They knew what it could do, and the priority at hand was to find out how it did it.

*   *   *   *   *

High in a building whose walls shielded much of the parsing sense and all of the other senses, Haralan stood straight and grim as strong, gentle hands removed the iron bonds from his wrists and ankles. He touched those around him with a gentle probe. Unlike the ones who had brought him, he sensed no real hostility in these, no great fear, only a determination to duty. He could respect that, and he wished them well. But his concern rested with his companions. Where were the Feya and Sefraeonia now? Had they, too, been captured? He hoped not. If they remained free, they could make their way to Aaelefein. Aaelefein could protect them.

He thought how vulnerable Sefraeonia would be, alone on a strange world, weaponless and defenseless. Her percept skills would help her very little. She could find a place to hide, but for how long? She was no warrior. She had no instinct for self-preservation, only a warm trust that those around her would care for her. She was not meant to be alone. What could she do? His great, gold eyes misted at the thought of her sweet vulnerability.

The intent ones about him had all stepped back, leaving him alone in the center of the room. He looked around. It was a large cubicle, ten or twelve paces across, with sparse furnishings and no adornments. What they needed, these people, was a taste of the Eldretten crafts. A structure did not have to be only useful. A little beauty would not spoil its usefulness. He thought of his castle on this alien world, his partly done roost hidden on its peak. He would like to finish it, he decided. Somehow he would like to overcome the awful darkness of this place so that it could sing as did Nendacaida . . . then complete the carving of his roost and— His thinking turned aside. He had almost visualized the emblems on its completed arch. He did not want to think now of vine-conjoined clansigns. Almost, he had seen the twin spires of clan Canenden adjoined to the seven petals of clan Cos. It was too much to consider. Even in the thinking of it he had gone too far. Neither Canenden nor Cos was his to portray, and he was ashamed at his thoughts. Only through loneliness would he have—sought for— Sefraeonia in his mind. He adored her . . . but didn't love her.

A door opened and more people entered, both men and women. He sensed again no hostility, only determination and a great curiosity. One of the men stepped forward and spoke to him in the curious, foreshortened sounds he had heard from other humans. He wished now that he had taken the trouble to learn something of humanspeech from Jacob Laurel, as the Feya had. He recalled a gesture. He shrugged and spread his hands. It was the best he could do.

The man tried again. There was frustration in his aura. Haralan shook his head as he had seen Laurel do, and shrugged again. The man tried again. At a loss,

Haralan held out a hand for touch-thought, and the man backed away a half step. Surprised, the Caian realized they were afraid of him, afraid of what he might do should they touch. But how could he learn if he could not feel their intents? Looking around, he felt for someone receptive, and found her.

She was a thin female with lenses before her eyes. She seemed shy, reticent, but there was no fear of him there, only wonder. Smiling, he walked carefully around the man, past the alert guards and directly to her. He held out his hand. She was startled, her eyes magnified huge behind their lenses. She caught her breath, dropped the pad in her hand. Then, hesitantly, she joined hands with him, and he saw her eyes clear, felt the comfort flooding her as their harmonies conjoined. Holding gently to her fingers, he led her back to the center of the room, seated her in a chair and knelt beside her. She gazed into his eyes, then looked around at the man. "He doesn't understand our language, sir. He thinks I can help."

The man had gone pale. "Miss Simmons? Is he . . . in any way hurting you? Are you all right?"

"Oh, yes!" She felt flustered, and Haralan soothed her. "Yes, I . . . I don't know what is happening, sir, but I'm just fine. It's as though he and I are—" She blushed furiously. Haralan had inadvertently touched some rather deep desires. He withdrew with an apology. Nothing had warned him that this female's private feelings could be so easily accessed. Still, he held her hand.

"Mister Rogers," she bit her lip, "I don't know if I can handle this, sir, but I'll try. Tell me what you want to ask, and maybe we can . . . sort it out between us. I . . . oh, my God, sir, I think I love him!"

26

Sefraeonia was near to exhaustion. She had run and she had hidden. She had found food in the fields and water in the streams. She had made her way afar from the battlefield on the highway, but now she was lost and confused. Without crystals, with only her own senses, she had no hope of finding the others. She did not even know if they still lived.

Everywhere she perceived humans, all around her, at every step. So far, she had avoided them, and she seemed to have gotten beyond the troop concentrations. Throughout one day, she had followed the sun westward where Haralan had pointed, using the inertia balances natural to her as she flew across varying lands on narrow feet that bounded and rebounded with the momentum of past hills to give them speed. Once or twice she might have been seen, but she thought not. She had come far and fast. Westward, toward a place she knew. But now it was dark again, and she shivered with exhaustion as she huddled in dusk at the edge of a village. She needed help.

No patrols caught her senses around this place, no searching warriors, just people coming and going in the night-sweet air, and animals in the fields.

Most of the village was quiet. The clusters of people

had broken up and dissipated to their homes. Only at one place did there appear still to be a group. It was a stone building with vehicles resting outside and people in. Frightened and lonely, the elf-girl watched the place. There was warmth there, the warmth of companionship. In her loneliness, even human companionship, even the darkness, seemed desirable. She was not used to being alone. It frightened and confused her. There were men there, and she sensed none of the intent so prevalent about the patrols. These were men relaxing, at peace. Desperately she craved them, craved their nearness. She feared for the Feya, even for the odd little Jacob Laurel, but mostly she feared for Haralan. The big, devoted Caian had saved her life, she knew. She had heard the bullets sing, heard his lizard-call, sensed his violence as he went among the men at the roadblock. Had he died there? She couldn't know. She was too far away now to know.

Huddled and shivering, her breath came in great gasps as she tried to concentrate on healing the damage she had done herself by coming so far, so fast. Had she a crystal she would have used its curative powers. But she had none. She had only herself, and she was frightened and terribly lonely. For a long time she lay still, until she had traces of her strength back. She could go no farther as she had come. It would take days, she knew, just to recover from this day's exertions.

She was away. But she had no idea where she was.

"Run far," Haralan had told her, and so she had done . . . as far as she could. But now her lostness came to haunt her. She could rest the night here, but with daylight the people would find her, and she knew the human reaction to hidden or fleeing game. They were a young race, still strong in the instincts of the carnivore.

She would be dragged down.

Could she somehow find the others? Only the Feya and Jacob Laurel had understood where they were going. Aaelefein? No, he was off somewhere on his quest, far in the other direction. He had the skills to evade them for a time. Haralan, if still he lived, had the skills to defend himself up to a point. The Feya had the skills to pursue a search. Sefraeonia had no such skills, nor the tools to do them.

Again and again, as her mind searched for possibilities, she pictured the mountain roost and the beautiful castle Haralan had begun there. She knew he was not aware she had crept in while he was gone, and seen on the arch the seven petals of clan Cos. It had pleased her more than she could express. He had done that for her, even though he lacked the temerity to show it to her.

The roost. It was to the west. It was the only place on this world she knew. If she could make her way there, maybe they could find her. Maybe Haralan would come for her.

In her resolve she knew she needed help. Frightened and lost, her great eyes dark with dread, she gathered resolution about her and got to her feet. The place where the men gathered had a little electric light in front, a curlique thing of red and purple. It seemed to her a beacon, a thing of hope.

Through the night-dark, littered street she walked toward it.

*   *   *   *   *

Star City wasn't much of a town, Buddy Chance knew, but it was his town. He was king here. All the others went about their business, but when he felt like intervening, they all stood aside for him. He was big and he was mean, and he knew they all feared him. He relished it. King of the mountain, that was old Buddy Chance. He took pretty much what he wanted, and they all stood back and let him do it. He didn't own a damned thing except his old house and some worthless land, but that didn't matter. Part of what the others owned came his way. It was his due, for letting them be.

He glanced around him in the smoke-hazed neon of Charley's Bar and Grill. The crowd tonight was mostly the towners. His buddies. Buddy's buddies . . . the idea appealed to him. He guessed he could hold off Comanches with this bunch, and if he said jump, they would jump. He was the king of Star City. Three beers under his belt glowed in the warmth of his status. He was reaching for another one when the room went silent. It was as though a switch had been kicked off. Scowling, he looked around and his eyes bulged. There in the door stood the most gorgeous female he had ever set his eyes on. A vision . . . hell, a gawdam miracle! His heart beat faster at sight of her. His breath became clipped, and he felt his neck swell in his collar. His nostrils picked up an odor in the room, which he instinctively traced to the other men there and which enraged him. It was the smell of rutting.

Sam Maxwell had come half out of his booth at sight of her. Now he came the rest of the way, his shoulders straightening, eyes abnormally bright. He strode toward her, edging between her and the open door. "Well, well, well," he said, his voice hoarse. "Look what Heaven done sent my way. And who might you be, chickie?"

From the stunned silence that clung to the room, a voice came from the end of the bar. "Gawdalmighty, Sam, take a look at her, will ya? Hell, man, that's one of them elves the TV's been talkin' about."

"Hey, Jenk's right," another said. "Jeez gawd, she's one of 'em!"

Sam Maxwell had pulled up with a start. Now he peered at her more closely, the thrust of fine face, the slanted curves of cheek, the huge, slanted eyes, and his voice grew ragged. "I'm a son of a bitch! Hey, you're right. This is no chickie, this is a real, honest-to-God elf we got here. An' a girl one at that."

"You ain't just woofin' about that," one said. More of them were on their feet now, crowding in on her. She backed along the wall, obviously confused. Someone closed the door.

"What's that she's got on?" one asked.

"I don't know," another snorted, "but there ain't much of it, is there?"

"Back off!" Sam Maxwell's voice was threatening. "I got first dibs on this one . . . unless somebody here wants to argue about it. Back off and wait your turn. Lord," he turned back to face her, "I've had me some women, but never no elf."

Maxwell was big, whipcord strong, and as mean as a snake. Buddy Chance knew this was not the time for reason or for show. Slipping from his stool, he strode across, came up behind Maxwell, raised a ham-sized fist, and pole-axed him where he stood.

That would hold the rest of them for a while. No good letting them forget whose town this was. He scanned startled eyes, nodded in satisfaction, and turned to the frightened girl. "I do believe you boys are right," he proclaimed. "This is a sure enough elf and I never seen one of these flat out, either."

She had sidled as far back as she could go. Her back was against the bar. Without hesitation, Buddy Chance reached out big hands and caught the folds of her garment. Slowly, deliciously, he pulled them apart. Beneath was the most perfect pair of breasts he had ever seen. Gasping, his swollen neck bulging his collar, he reached and touched.

Tactile infrasonics laden with terror and desperation hit him with a force that bowed his knees. Suddenly the game was over. Fear washed through him, near-panic, a terrible, frightened loneliness hammering deep into his mind. His eyes glazed, his mouth hung open, and his senses reeled. Beneath his rough hand was tenderness . . . fragile, vulnerable, lost and afraid. It hit him like a plea from a deathbed, and the remorse that flooded in upon him—his own—was unbearable. For a moment he stood frozen, shaken to his core by the unutterable beauty, the terrible sadness of the creature he touched. It was a tidal wave of longing, pleading . . . She needed help. She needed him.

With a ferocity beyond anything he had known, he whirled to face the others. "Get back!" he roared. "All of you, back across the room. Now!" When they hesitated, stunned, he pulled a skinning knife from his pocket and flicked the blade open. "Get back there now! By God in Heaven, I'm gonna kill the last man that moves!"

They bolted. Shocked and shaken, they raced across the room to huddle there in a wide-eyed mass.

"Now turn around and face the wall!" he thundered.

Obediently, blindly, they turned away. With a roundhouse heave, Chance hurled the knife. It thudded half-blade deep in the pine panel above them. "The first man as looks this way had best grab up that knife, because I'm goin' to kill him with my bare hands!" The fear in them all was tangible. Not one turned from the wall.

After a moment to assure himself, Buddy Chance turned again to face the elf-girl. Then the king of Star City did a thing he had never done before. With pooling eyes, with overwhelming sorrow, he knelt before her and saw his own tears splash on the dirty floor. He was himself no longer, he knew. The Buddy Chance of a moment ago was dead and gone. The king had become a slave.

A soft hand touched his balding head, and he knew somehow. She forgave him. She accepted him as the help she needed. The gratitude he felt then was an emotion he would never lose. He had been forgiven. He looked up at her, his cheeks wet with unashamed tears. With an effort he got to his feet.

"If you can let me know what it is you need, Missy, I'll do it or die tryin'."

27

Her name was Rose. She told him that, and he pronounced the human syllable with a delighted twitch of upturned mouth. The afternoon had not gone well for the humans. Many had come and looked at him, argued over him, spoken to him as he held Rose Simmons's small hand in his own. She had responded for him as she could, still flustered at the sensual arousal of sharing the deep infrasonics with a healthy male elf.

But Haralan had neither the Feya's skill at extrapolating meaning from emotion, nor Aaelefein's skill at subspectral communication. So, in the evening, they had all gone and left her to teach him human speech.

They had shared food and shared resonance. There was little they didn't know about each other now. The touch-senses left nothing hidden. She was startled at the depths of unabashed emotion in the elf, the power of the love, dread, humor and devotion so readily reachable in the big almost-man. He, in turn, was disturbed at the implacability, the determination, the barely shielded violence couched deep in her spirit. These humans were strong, he realized, tough and viable, unyielding in odd ways. He also discovered the two people who were Rose Simmons—the austere, efficient person she presented to the world and the warm, seeking person beneath. He was delighted. He wasted no time introducing the halves of her to each other.

Full night rested beyond the single window now. He was progressing well. If his human speech was hesitant, still it could convey a wide range of thoughts.

They practiced now without the touching of hands, letting him perfect his vocabulary.

"What will you tell them when they come tomorrow, Haralan?"

"Whatever they want to know," he said matter-of-factly.

"Well, they're going to want to know all about you, your people, your own world . . . Nendacaida? I expect they are going to wear you out with questions. Do you mind?"

"No. Then will they let me go?"

She was saddened. "I don't know, Haralan. I don't think they know what to do with you. But you really are an honored guest, you know . . . not a prisoner."

"I am not free to leave."

"Well, no, I suppose not. But it's for your own protection. A lot of people are afraid of you. Because you're different . . . because you come from another place.

"I mean them no harm. Will they give back my blade?"

"I don't think so. Not now. They want to learn how it works."

"Don't they know? I will tell them. It is a crystal. I grew it myself, a long time ago. Its song is my song. When I sing it, it responds to me."

"You say you 'sing.' Oh, you mean your language?"

He was puzzled. She took his hand and asked it again.

"Language is small," he explained. "Sing is large. Sing means . . . all the kinds of knowing, said in all the harmonies."

She nodded after a pause. "I can grasp that, sort of. But the blade . . . it responds to you? Is that through resonance?"

"It pulses to song. That is what crystals do. They make the song stronger so it can be used."

"All crystals?" Impulsively she removed her glasses. "These?"

He took them. Through them her eyes had been large and bright. Without them they were large and soft. He knew that what little sight she had was lessened by their removal.

He held the glasses, touched the crystals with his fingers, peered through them. They were not very good crystals. Something interrupted his thoughts. Outside, beyond the shielding walls, had been a faint echo of terror-tone, a spark going out. Senses extended, he listened. Again there was a terror-trill, abruptly ended. He could not trace its meaning.

He held the glasses before his face. Rose saw his mouth open, his throat work, and suddenly a feeling of warmth flowed over her, a feeling of security and trust as though someone she loved had wished her well. Eyes widening, she asked, "Did you . . . did the glasses do that?"

"It is a simple song," he said. "It is a hunting song for warriors. I like it."

"Oh . . ." she was flustered again. "I do, too."

"That is how my blade works. I want it back. It is my . . ." He took her hand again, seeking a figure of speech. "It is my rusty blade."

She giggled. "I think you mean your 'trusty' blade, Haralan."

He stood abruptly, strode to the single window, her

glasses still in his hand. "People are dying out there, Rose."

The comment puzzled her. Just what senses did the elf have? "This is a big city, Haralan. People die all the time."

"Yes." Still he stood at the window. The trills he had heard bothered him. There had been four, now, the last one very clear. His scalp tingled, seeking messages from the window. His high ears were keenly pitched, his nostrils dilated. Below was a night-lit street, almost deserted, beyond a hedged fence. It seemed peaceful enough, but his warrior's lizard-sense was at full.

Rose saw none of it. To her near-sighted eyes, he was a red-gold blur at the window. "Come sit down, Haralan, and let's try some more ranges of word and meaning."

There was a sound at the door. Haralan turned quickly as the bolts gave way and the door slammed back on its hinges. Men scurried into the room, bent low, weapons in their hands. He heard Rose scream, "Haralan!" and then one of the men triggered his weapon. The elf saw Rose come to her feet, heard the dull chatter, saw the stabbing tongues of flame, saw her eyes go huge as a row of holes laced across her body. The other men were advancing on him. One raised his weapon in a peremptory gesture. Haralan knew the meaning. They wanted him to go with them. He looked at Rose, sprawled in blood on the polished floor. They were five. They were stronger than him, and each armed. Yet . . . the lizard-alert song rose in his throat, and he bellowed it, full-volume and full-range. They froze, the dread harmonics slamming into their limited senses. The instant was enough. With a lunge Haralan hit the window, crashed through and plummeted eight floors to the ground.

Arms spread, toes sensing, he touched . . . and stood.

His feet ached with the absorbed momentum of his fall, but he restrained them. He felt the charge flow up his legs, through torso and shoulders, and out his arms, every cell of his body accepting a part of the potential energy. He was a battery on full charge inertial storage, for the moment a walking bomb. Carefully, restraining the terrible urge to release the pent energies he had absorbed, he turned and raced toward the front of the building. A dead guard lay sprawled by the outer door, another just inside, their throats cut. At the stairs he found another, and three floors up still another. Using part of his withheld momentum, he flew up the succeeding stairs, still retaining most of it.

They were just coming out the door. As the first turned, Haralan demolished his face. The second he hit from behind, feeling the man's spine snap between his shoulders. A chop to the throat killed the third, and power-surging fingers crushed the neck of the fourth. The last was the one whose weapon had barked at Rose. Even as this one was turning, Haralan grasped him by arm and leg, raised him high . . . and released all the remaining fall-momentum in a swing.

The far wall buckled, crashed through, and the floor beyond was a wide trail of blood and tissue as the spewing thing that had been a man thudded against another wall in the distance.

Stepping over the bodies around him, Haralan strode to Rose and knelt beside her. She lay on her back. Even glazed in death, her wide eyes still looked soft. Carefully, he replaced the glasses on her face, then held her still hand for a moment.

He stood then and looked around him, red cloak streaming as he turned. Never before in his warrior life had he killed sentient beings. He wondered why he felt no remorse, and then he knew. One by one he looked at the four sprawled in the doorway, the mashed thing in darkness in the next room.

Lizards.

Through midnight and moonset, Haralan sat in shadow atop the same building and watched excited people come and go below him. Their frenzy hounded the air. Finally, in the time before dawn, there was calm. The Feya had taught him the art of seeing Feyadeen. He stood on a cornice and turned slowly, wide senses ranging. After a time he found the taste he wanted, fixed its location in mind, and set out. It was not very far away.

* * * * *

High in the Pentagon, in that cloistered interior region known to some as "Eagle turf" and to others as "Angel territory," General Morey Flanders set aside his latest cigar and rubbed knuckles into his eyes. The men standing across the desk from him, he knew, were just as tired as he was. It had been a long night, and tomorrow was going to be one hell of a day.

Tomorrow? It had been tomorrow for hours. "Just brief it for me, Fred," he said. "I'm past reading the fine print."

"They were Boris Fodorin's men, General. At least two of them were, and we can assume the others pending a fix. One was a U.N. courier, the other a known plant. Details are in the box if you want them. The one with the . . . collapsed throat may have been a Pentagon staffer, semi-top clearance—a hell of a note, sir, beg your pardon, but it looks like we've harbored a sleeper in internal security. If he's who we think he is, he has a perfect record going back twenty-three years. A tough one."

"How about the splattered one?"

The man shuddered. "I saw it . . . him . . . myself, sir. What's left of him. Right now they're picking through the mess looking for teeth or prosthetics or something to identify. General, we don't know what did that. . . ."

Flanders turned mild eyes toward the ceiling. "Offhand, I would say he irritated an elf."

"Well, the elf's gone. Not a trace. We have everything available on tight search, and three squads of special forces people on the NSF building, in case he wants his sword—"

"Which, I assume, is no longer there."

"No, sir. We retrieved that, just in case. It's my guess, sir, that our visitor headed for the hills hours ago. No telling where he is by now. We're feeding everything through CYCOM, but there's really nothing to feed. We just don't have a clue."

"Anything new on the others?" Flanders cocked a gray brow at the other man.

"General Clark is still in the field, sir. Somebody isn't trying too hard to get his orders to him, seems like, but we're doing all we can. CYCOM says the singer is in that same little strip in Indiana, and Clark has pulled everything he can lay hands on in there around him. He has a cordon of solid manpower a half mile deep. Unconfirmed elf sightings from here to yonder, as you'd expect. Maybe one that looks promising. A farmer in Illinois says he saw the girl one, going west." He looked sheepish, glanced aside at his counterpart. "The confirmation is that he was stuttering and his wife says he never stutters. Not much, but it's all we have. No sign at all of the little one."

Flanders rubbed his eyes. "Okay, get on with it. Keep a line open here and feed me anything you get. A bunch of us are going to be playing Congress games in the next few hours."

When they were gone, he breathed deeply several times, found his extinguished cigar and relit it, thinking it might be worth the hassle to put a severe presence in Cuba.

The door opened softly and closed. Flanders looked up, cocked a brow, and forgot his cigar. After a long moment, he exhaled and crossed his arms on the desk. "It's you, is it?"

Haralan stood spread-legged before the closed door, his arms folded, elven face hard and expressionless.

"I want my blade," he said.

28

Aaelefein rested through the day, tasting the presence of hostile men amassed around him. He had hoped they would pass by him. He did not trust the humans to adjudge his course, with their poor senses, but he did trust their machines. Consequently, he had never homed directly on the place where he knew Nataea to be, but had gone slightly off-course, feeling the presence of armed and organized men closing on his flanks. He had kept to a straight line, guiding by the place the morning sun would appear at equinox.

In this manner he had come to a place he knew was directly north of his goal, and now he waited. The pursuit should pass. Then he could bear right from his course and flank the trailing masses of it, signal once more for exact bearings, and thus go directly to her.

But as the day wore on, he knew they would not pass. Instead, they surrounded him still, many more humans than he had imagined, deployed in miles-long columns of searching clusters on both sides of his route, closing in.

He was awed. The sensing machines they created in their blindness were more formidable than full senses ever could have been, and he could find no fault with the minds of those to whom the machines spoke. No

blind pursuit was this, but a reasoned, disciplined scouring of where he might be, given various alternatives.
They were thoughtful, these sad, haunted creatures.
And more and more, even as they pressed him, he found
them beautiful.

They were industrious beyond the ken of Caidom—
determined, inventive, and prolific, a boisterous young
race resolute in the face of their weaknesses, keen wills
reaching beyond their limitations for the impossible and
attaining it. Given their iron and their fire, given a concept to muse upon, an idea to pursue, there was little
they could not accomplish, Aaelefein decided. They
fought their blindness and, in doing so, they overcame
every other obstacle.

They carried their darkness like a sword. He felt it
strongly, all around him, these young warriors of Earth.
He considered simply hiding, letting the chase disperse.
In the place where he was now, a state park, a span of forest and stream among lazy hills, it would be easy for him
to go unnoticed, at least for several days. Their patience
might wear thin, their drive turn elsewhere. But he
thought of the Feya, with pretty Sefraeonia and sturdy
Haralan, pursuing their quest for the Corad-bane, rely-
ing on him to provide completion of the chord for their
return. He thought of Corad-ravaged Nendacaida,
beautiful refuge-world, facing annihilation. And he
thought of his Nataea, lost and lonely, frightened guest
of an alien being, whose faith was in his finding her. She
waited. No, he must proceed.

He fingered the senester thoughtfully. He knew that
its music—his music—was known now and that ears
were listening for it. The range of his harmonics was not
greater than the capacity of the machines to hear.

The original strategy was ruled out. The humans were

not in chase now, but in cordon. He might escape the cordon, but at first pulse of the senester they would know his new route, and their machines would tell them, with infallible logic, his destination. No, he must keep them on the path they were on. He must call first and then change course. And that meant he must somehow reach her again with mindsong—must use the senester—right here among the searching hordes.

Silently he roamed the woodlands, sometimes within eyesight of armed patrols seeking him. He crisscrossed the park. There were many good places to hide but no places to hide and sing. With finality, he selected a spot, a large rock overhanging a stream. It was not better than any other place, but its aesthetics appealed to him. It was a pretty place, secluded yet open. It reminded him of Nataea's clanhome among the Brightwaters. It would be a pleasant place from which to call to her. It also, if it came to that, would be a restful place to die.

So through the waning day he rested, watching, listening, parsing, tasting the scouring groups that came and went around him. He hoped for a clouded sky, but it remained blue-clear into the evening. At dusk he removed his human clothing and donned his own. The blue-silver cape, clan colors of a Fe of Ruast, in silhouette against a night sky would be more eye-deceiving than the garb of men. And more than that, he sensed other darkness closing in. The darkness of humanity was a stew about him. But the darkness of something else hung heavily in his mind. Doom or destiny? Whichever, it was dark in nature. With widened eyes, he drank the colors of the night. Pitched ears cherished the sounds of the evening in their hushing tones, and he knelt to spread his hands on the succulent turf of a rich world. A deep, sad longing came. Would these eyes, these ears, these hands ever again taste the resonances of Nendacaida?

The will-master Aaelefein had never been given to premonition, but suddenly it was there, and he wept deep down at the longing of it. How bitter . . . to die outcast on a strange, uncaring world, to die at the hands of people as wise as he, in their way as gentle. To die . . . at least, then, he told himself, to die trying. The supple corselet, beyans, and placet of his own garb were a relief after more than nine fives of days in human dress. Blue and silver rippled cool in the light of a rising moon.

He blended in foliage as a file of dark, creeping soldiers passed within a stride of him, their eyes roving the night, weapons ready. Then for a time he followed them, curious. Their emanations were harsh. All of them were young, superbly tuned individuals, keyed to a fine pitch. And they were nervous. His nostrils would have told him that if his follicles had not. The smell of fear was about them.

They feared him, and they were out to destroy him. They did not understand. Would he understand . . . if he were one of them and blind? Probably not. He pitied them. Even more, he wished he could remain with them.

They made a circling sweep of a quarter-mile of pathway. Where paths crossed they stopped to converse quietly with another patrol, then went on their way. Aaelefein faded into the night, back toward the stream.

When the moon was a handspan above the hill beyond, the elf opened broad senses and tasted for proximity. For the moment, there were none near him that he could sense. A hundred yards behind him was a cluster of men fanning through underbrush, but he thought none closer. They were so thick about him he could not be sure.

It was the time of stilling, when day was gone and night not yet in full harmony. He could wait no longer.

Keeping to the deepest shadows, he made his way to the open verge behind the rock. He sensed once more. All remained still. Only the busy pulses of the air persisted. Steeling himself, he strode out to the rock and climbed atop it. Full moonlight bathed him, rippled in the stirring waters just a leap below. Night sounds lullabyed. He touched the senester at his throat, parsed keen the throbbing pulses and pitched harmonies to still them. Up and down the register of resonance he ranged, building a leaping bubble of counterharmonics that pulsed out and out, countering and cancelling the flowing waves. Not so far this time. He needed only to reach a few long miles. The senester glowed with resonance, broadcasting an utter silence. It was far enough. Then with soul doom-shadowed, heart bursting with longing, Aaelefein lifted his voice in mindsong, pouring all the love he had into the lonely call. Oblivious to all around him, eyes tight-closed in concentration, the Caian stood tall on moonlit rock and sang his heart to his lost love.

Behind, the foliage rustled. Then flame spat white, a crash of thunder split the silence, and pain erupted inside him.

* * * * *

A few miles south, Margaret Harrison sat bolt upright in her bed as the sweet aliveness that lived in her strove to answer the first harmonies of a song that had no sound. Almost, her throat returned it. Hope and confusion welled within her. Without reluctance, she raised her head, opened her throat . . . and the harmonies ceased. As though a light had gone out, the splendor of

resonances in the air was cut off. It was so clear, so near.
But it was gone. The companion within her whimpered,
began to cry deep down. And Margaret found herself
crying with it.

The song had been couched in silence, but there was
no silence now. Her scalp tingled with the vibrations that
were the stuttering music of ordinary air. Through her
open window, she could hear a television set blaring
across the street. The silence and the song were gone.

*   *   *   *   *

Silver moved in night shadows. Beside a shuttered fac-
tory on a silent street in Cicero, the Feya abruptly turned
her head and played the air with bright senses. The silent
pulses caught her parsing notice, and her scalp tingled as
the first low harmonics of Aaelefein's mindsong entered
the void. He was to the south—and not so awfully far
away. Happiness swam through Winifraeda as she heard
the notes, the weaving strains of soft lovecall.

Her eyes went moist at the plaintive, pleading tone of
it, the desperation of a strong-willed Caian devastated
by the loss of his one love, striving now with all that was
in him to find the tiny spirit of her.

Silver in shadows, she listened as the strain built . . .
and stopped. Abruptly, without warning, Aaelefein was
gone. As though he had never been. The air of this sad
planet thrummed busily again, and the mind-darkness
was a dull ache.

Beside her, Jacob Laurel, barely sensing the sweet-sad
harmonics of the moment, twitched when the call ended. "What was that, Winifraeda? What happened?"

"It was Aaelefein," she said simply. "He called, and
his call stopped."

"Do you want to go to him, then?"

She considered it. From his touch she knew the old man was very tired. Days of adventure had strained his resources.

"No, Jacob. We must trust Aaelefein. Only he can do what he must do. We should go on to Chicago. I must see the Ramapur Stone you spoke of. If it is a testament, I can read it. It may tell us of the Corad-bane."

29

Alone in his inner office, General Flanders took the report and his face, already drawn with exhaustion, went gray.

"Well, that tears it all," he told the scrambler. "What kind of security is on it?"

"A-one," the voice said. "Clark called in his cordon and turned command over to our people as soon as the singer was eliminated. He's placed himself under quarters arrest. We have special forces in the area and no leaks, at least so far."

"Death is confirmed?"

"We're still looking for the body. He fell in the creek. But it was a dead shot."

"Okay, then. Keep looking, keep your boys around the area, and keep your lip zipped. I've got an elf on my hands here that has already killed five men . . . fortunately, they were bogeys. But I don't want the word out about the singer. Tight security on the whole affair until I say otherwise, okay?"

"Yes, sir."

Flanders cradled the instrument, wagged a finger at his exec. "Johnny, this report is A-one security. Not even 'need to know' without my authorization. Personal. Now, who beyond the site knows about it?"

"Three of us. The general, myself, and Colonel Sommervel in PenCom, ready to back you."

"Okay, let's keep it that way for the moment. God only knows how Haralan's going to take this. You go see Sommervel personally. Explain the situation to him. Then you and he take a trip someplace . . . fly out to Ellington and inspect the civilian layout or something. Don't come back here until I tell you."

When the exec was gone, Flanders steeled himself. Three floors down, in a room ringed by Special Forces people and packed with select scientists, Haralan was explaining how his "sword" worked. Out in the dawn streets and in three other cities, FBI teams and Military Intelligence were harvesting suspects for screening. Haralan had touched all five of the men who tried to take him. Flanders shook his head at memory of the results of those "touches." But according to Haralan, he knew the "taste" of their kind and could identify others. Flanders wondered what the courts would make of that, but for the moment he was satisfied that a screening by the elf could set Soviet infiltration back five years. In return, the elf would have his sword and his freedom. And the President might have Flanders's neck on a block. But it was his best deal, and he would hang with it.

"Get me Tracy at the White House," he told the telephone. "If he isn't there, find him. I'll code and scramble personally when he's on the line."

He held through a two-minute pause. Then the line clicked. "Sir, Mister Tracy is on his way here."

"All right, put two of my own staff on the gate. As soon as Tracy shows, bring him to me." It was the longest ten minutes he had ever waited.

"I need your help," Flanders told the deputy when he arrived.

"What in hell's going on, Morey? This town is about to jump out of its skin."

"Quite a bit is going on . . . sit down, dammit . . . that's better. The whole package is on your desk. Or will be in the morning. At least all that I can tell you now. We caught an elf. He calls himself Haralan when he is talking to us. We have him here, and I've made a deal with him. More than fifty people will be herded into our general staff briefing room at noon today. It'll be quite a crowd . . . a dozen or so U.N. people, several high-level military personnel—our own—a federal judge, some Congressional committee staffers, a few immigrants, a couple of D.C. cops, a few key lobbyists, several people from Central Processing . . . a real mixed bag. Every one of them is in MI's 'maybe' file."

Tracy looked aghast. "A federal judge?"

"You're going to see several familiar faces today. This is the scenario . . . by the way, have you heard anything from Indiana?"

"No. Should I have?"

"No. I'll explain later. The scenario: You will be in that briefing room with Haralan and one staff officer, as well as a squad of Special Forces people I've personally selected. When our suspects are brought in, Haralan will meet them. He will touch hands with each of them. Each time he says something like, 'lizard' or 'lizard taste' or such . . . don't worry about it, he knows what to do . . . that person will be arrested and charged with espionage, sabotage, treason, or whatever our files say we might make stick."

Tracy digested it. "And what will I be doing?"

"I want you to put the secretary's stamp on every arrest we make . . . and if Haralan gives any of them a clean bill, you can apologize to them."

"On what grounds am I going to agree to do this, Morey?"

"On the grounds that I'm telling you it is the correct thing to do, and you know damn well if I say it is, it is. Hell, dream up your own grounds. By fourteen hundred hours today, my friend, we will have busted into matchsticks the best domestic organization Ivan ever had."

"With an elf."

"Precisely. One of these days, with a lot of luck, we'll understand how that creature down there does what he does. Right now, let's just use him. When it's done, you can release the story to the press . . . or the Secretary can, or the President if he wants to. With one exception. For the time being, this is a straight spy-ring breakup. Facts and figures from the files, MI and FBI cooperative effort, any trimmings you like. But no mention of elves. There are more reasons than just our credibility, take my word for it. A lot more."

"You haven't mentioned yourself, Morey."

"I won't be there. For the . . . duration, I have to stay away from Haralan."

"Why?"

"Did you ever try to keep a secret from an elf?"

"You know something."

"Just don't try."

"Has this got anything to do with Indiana, Morey?"

"Drop it. Just don't try. I've got other fish to fry, anyhow. I'll be in touch with you."

"So how about the elf? Where do we keep him?"

"Oh, we don't. After he does his bit today, he is to be given his blade and taken wherever he wants to go and set free."

"Free? You mean just . . . turned loose?"

"Do you think I'm a damned fool, Tracy? We'll be

looking after him every step. But he can go where he pleases."

"You want to find the others."

"I'd like to know where they are, yes."

Tracy suddenly looked cat-pleased. "In that case, Morey, I'm one-up on you. At about 6:30 this morning a caravan of an estimated three hundred and twenty civilian vehicles busted one of our roadblocks in western Missouri. Citizens, Morey. Station wagons and pickup trucks, farm trucks and limos, sport cars, yes, and a few television news teams with them. They just pulled up, stared down the guards, and drove on through. And the elf girl—Sefraeonia?—she's with them."

It was Flanders's turn to boggle. "They have her?"

"You mean do we have her? Lord, no. Neither do those people. It's more like she has them. They're her . . . escort, Morey. And they're spreading the word and more are joining them all the time. It's a pilgrimage of some kind . . . a crusade. I don't know what it is."

"What are your people doing?"

"What can they do? They're just following along to see what happens."

"Do you know where they're going?"

"Someplace the TV people are calling 'Elvenroost.' West, somewhere."

Flanders drummed his fingers. "Then I suggest you tell Haralan that when you meet him. It will make him feel better."

Tracy was thoughtful for a time. "You know what you're doing to me, don't you? By your deal, I will be the one who turned the elf loose. Under the law, I won't have a leg to stand on. No matter what happens next, there will be hell raised. As an example, just what is it I will turn loose? An illegal alien? If he's human, what's his nationality? The law demands nationality, but it doesn't cover nationality beyond this planet. Or maybe we stand on the fact that he isn't human. Then is he an endangered species? By the Feya's . . . testimony in Denver, their species definitely is endangered. That's why they're here, looking for . . . for something. My God, Morey, we don't have the body of law to address this situation."

Flanders held his gaze. "Military law has its advantages. It takes contingency into account and places authority beyond the accepted norm. It doesn't matter whether Haralan is a person, an extraterrestrial creature, a living fossil, or a dangerous animal. We're dealing with situations, not technicalities. But the fact is this: I have given Haralan my word, and we will stand by it."

"Where do you think he wants to go?"

"I haven't the foggiest notion. I think it will be interesting for all of us to find out."

* * * * *

Group tours were rare at the campus museum, particularly in summer. The tourists and conventioneers usually homed on S-and-I across the street. But this was a gaggle of teachers on campus for a week of seminars, and when security opened the doors at nine they filed in, a squeaky-voiced matron acting as guide. There were nearly thirty of them, mostly women, mostly of young to middle years. But there was one elderly man with a little girl clinging to his hand. The child was bundled oddly for the season, wrapped from head to toe in a low-pulled stocking cap and bright plaid coat.

Winifraeda was decidedly uncomfortable in the enclosing garb, and her hand in Laurel's let him know that. But he had no better idea. He had rejected her idea of resonating the locks and gaining entry during the night. It just didn't seem necessary to him to break and enter when they could simply walk in.

They followed the tour for several minutes, until they reached a turn beyond sight of the sleepy-looking guard at the door. Then they parted company with their temporary companions.

"Do you know your way here?" the Feya asked.

"No. Never been here before. But museums are all alike. The oldest displays—and usually the best—are set back in some alcove somewhere so they're hard to find. And the real good stuff is probably boxed up in a cellar."

"Then let us find a cellar."

It was after noon, the tour had long since departed, and the building echoed silence when the two conspirators found a storage vault deep down, a basement ceiling-deep with dusty cartons, forgotten oddities, broken furniture. Laurel looked around, dismayed. The Feya fingered her diadem, hummed to it in silent harmonies. She shook her head, removed the fusty stocking cap, shook out silver hair, and tried again. Tone after tone, medley after medley she tried, then turned suddenly and pointed. Beyond a solid wall of boxes, something had responded to her resonance.

"We had better start digging, Jacob," she said.

30

Elvenroost.

The word was magic. And the stunning, unbelievable face that voiced it in soft, carefully human tones for a million television receivers was magic as well. Never had a concept, a word, a face and form, had such effect on so many people. No blanket-shrouded creature of mystery was this, as in the ferreted footage from official interviews in the federal building in Denver. This was Sefraeonia unveiled, tall and slim, striking in a way no human had ever quite been, soft elven features aslant and vital as almond-dark eyes found the vulnerable souls of the millions who gawked at her broadcast image.

Elvenroost. She spoke but little to the outthrust microphones, the prying cameras that ringed her in the sunlight of Missouri ridge-country. She had too few words yet that they would understand. But she told them, as a glowering cadre of tough and weathered men stood ready to defend her from the slightest inconvenience, where she wanted to go. She had no description of the location, except that it was west. The media dubbed it Elvenroost. There was no doubt she would find it, and the mass of people following her would find it, too.

"Do you mind if we come, too?" a woman with a microphone asked, her professional cynicism weakening.

Sefraeonia seemed confused for a moment. She reached out to take the hand of a hulking, heavy-shouldered man next to her. The newsperson repeated her question. Dazzling eyes lighted with understanding. "Yes. Come. Come to Elvenroost. Come and see what Haralan has made."

The invitation sang through millions of sets, a personal invitation to each of those who sat breathless, their eyes riveted on this stunning creature. The cameras swept. Already there were nearly a thousand various vehicles in the caravan which paused in central Missouri. In the lead were the farm trucks, jeeps, and motorcycles of a phalanx of unlikely guardians who had named themselves escort and protectorate to the elf-girl. Their leader was the burly Buddy Chance, whose eyes now were visionary's eyes, though set in the face of a brute. Like a knight of ancient chivalry, he worshipped and protected Sefraeonia.

They were on a pilgrimage. A pilgrimage to Elvenroost, where some bright temple held answers to questions people did not even know how to ask. Among those one in four who had been touched by alien song in recent days the magics melded. The eerie, inspiring lyric of that night had become their Holy Grail. Now there was a vision, and a promise. The vision was the startling, unearthly beauty of Sefraeonia. The promise was Elvenroost.

Across twenty states cars were loaded, gasoline supplies stretched, food stores mobbed, and the untouched gathered to watch with awe as their neighbors sped away to find their touchstone.

By the time the mounting caravan reached Chillicothe, its numbers had swelled to two thousand . . . and more on other roads which would converge. A double stream of vehicles nearly eight miles long crept past St.

Joseph, while lesser caravans spearheaded up through
Joplin and down through Bedord, and others blended at
Kansas City to move on west.

When the "Seffy Convoy" paused at Norton, its line
stretching back now almost to Marysville, converging
traffic on other roads clogged Omaha, Lincoln, Topeka,
Salina, Wichita, Tulsa, Oklahoma City, Dallas, Fort
Worth, and Waco.

On half a hundred roads the leaders came up against
the remains of the military's "silence quarantine," piled
up at roadblocks for long moments, then dismantled the
roadblocks and moved on. In some places, whole units of
National Guard went with them for lack of contrary
orders. Regular army still held main roads at Rapid City,
North Platte, Goodland, Syracuse, and Dalhart, but
hasty orders from Washington through unit channels
pulled them back. Confrontation now would be disas-
trous. By lowest estimates, nearly a million people were
on the roads now, seeking Elvenroost, and more were
packing to follow.

That evening, Buddy Chance backed up sixty miles of
cars in little St. Francis while he found a telephone to call
his mother. In the magic of the moment, of finding his
new self and leaving Star City with Sefraeonia, he had
forgotten about Ada Chance waiting for his visit at the
nursing home. He needn't have worried. The old lady
had seen him on television, knew where he was, and she
was content.

"But, Arthur," she warned him, her voice cold and
stern, "if you harm one hair of that sweet little thing's
head . . . or if you let anybody else bother her . . . by
Heaven, Arthur, I'll put the dogs on you. You hear me,
now!"

At first dawn of a sparkling morning, Sefraeonia sat

secure on the humming hood of a wending Chevy
Blazer, her percept-senses ranging ahead. There, far off,
was a faerie hint of Caidom, far brighter than when she
had first seen the peak, brighter and stronger for the little time the Cai had been there. To the south of it was the
west extremity of the great city. Beyond were higher,
more noble peaks, but they were just peaks. Only the
spire with the shouldering croft had comforted lonely
Cai in a strange world. Only there had the Feya draped
her vaporfloss, had Haralan crafted his castle. Only there
did the seven petals of clan Cos shine new on living rock.

Her spirits lifting, she pointed the way, and Buddy
Chance got on the CB. Elvenroost was in sight.

Interstate 70 to Aurora was a solid double row of vehicles waiting for them to pass and lead. People gawked
from their windows as the Blazer passed. The image of
the elf-girl had been stunning. Her actual presence was
devastating. They lined the road by the thousands, and
she gazed at them, feeling their soul-darkness, aching
for them, wishing them well. But as she passed and they
knew her, she sensed a subtle change in the overbearing
grief that was humankind—a lifting of hearts, a perceptible ebb to the terrible darkness. In her they saw a
chance to be more, a chance to be better. In her presence, in the myriad things she meant to the multitude of
them—divine revelation, extraterrestrial visitor, singer
of songs, beauty from beyond the stars—was hope. They
sensed it powerfully, and she sensed their longing. They
hoped . . . for something better, something the song of
Aaelefein had told them was there to be hoped for. In
their blindness they hoped for light and followed
Sefraeonia to find it.

The realization saddened her. She wanted to help
them. She wanted them to see. But hers was not the gift

of Aaelefein, the strong of will, the singer of harmonies in tapestry, nor even of lost Nataea whose scintillance of lyric brought radiance to all who heard. Sefraeonia had one abiding skill. She was a percept. Where trace of Caikind lingered, she could find it. She perceived its harmonies. Still, here were people trusting in her to give them something they could not even conceive but that they knew they lacked.

Snaking Highway 119 toward Tolland was solid machines flowing in the wake of Buddy Chance's Blazer, the spigot of a funnel that meshed at Denver. Light planes and helicopters flew convoy overhead, as jet fighters from three bases ranged the fringes of the great convoy, feeding back reports.

Vectors were fed to computers. The winding direction confirmed what CB radio and national news had told officialdom. The destination, Elvenroost, was on Cassion Peak just east of Rollins Pass. The spearhead funneled tighter onto a winding mountain road toward East Portal. A military helicopter touched down and waited at a roadside park. A rank of motorcycles reached it first and hove alongside, the blue Blazer following.

As uniformed men stepped out on the highway, Buddy Chance pulled over, stopped, and stepped out of the car. He strode to the ranking officer, a black man with stars on his shoulders. "Now look here, mister, you get that thing out of the way. Sefraeonia wants to go up there, and we're takin' her."

The man smiled, raised a hand. "A moment, please, Mister Chance. We won't stop you. But I need to talk with her if I may."

Sefraeonia had come forward, and the men stared at her. God in Heaven, the officer thought, she makes me want to pray. He bit his lip, straightened out his emotions, and bowed to the elf. "Ah, can you speak English well enough for us to talk?"

"I can say a little," she responded, taking Buddy Chance's hand. "You are . . . army. Do you know where Haralan is? And Aaelefein, and our Feya?"

"No, ma'am, I don't," the officer apologized. "But I'm sure they are safe. But, ma'am . . . miss . . . we have a problem. All those people back there—" He gestured behind him to where a solid line of vehicles crowded the road. "I guess you know they all expect a . . . miracle or something. Can you do anything for them?"

Sefraeonia frowned, sifting the words through Chance's understanding, picking up the intent from the empathy. She shook her head. "I can do nothing except show them the roost."

"But, miss, when they've seen it . . ." He took a deep breath and turned to Chance. "Look, Mr. Chance, we've got a real serious problem here. You see those people back there. You may not have any idea how many there are, but they've come here expecting . . . hell, I don't know what. You know people, Mr. Chance. If they wind up disappointed, God help us all. She's going to have to do something. Can you help?"

They stood there in the cool mountain sun for a long time. Chance held both of Sefraeonia's slim hands, and a deep bond of meaning flowed between them. He understood people, all right. He knew what the man meant, and he made her know. In turn, he tried to understand what she knew, and pieces of it came together. Finally he turned again to the officer.

"She says she can sing to 'em. She says she can sing . . . hell, I can't find a word for it, but it's like, uh, comfort or something. But she says she isn't a good singer. She says she has no . . . some kind of sort of, like a tool, only it's more like a rock or a diamond or something."

The officer pursed his lips in thought. He had all the briefing. What his command knew of elves, he knew. "Crystal," he said. Chance nodded.

"Can she activate a crystal in the mountain?"

Chance absorbed for a time, then shook his head. "Her skill is not that good."

"Well, how about a crystal diode?" They both looked at him, blankly. "Look, can I . . . talk to her directly, do you suppose?"

Reluctantly, Chance released one of her hands. The officer took it. He almost went to his knees. He wished his wife were here. Now, for once, he could tell her . . . He pulled himself together. He thought of a crystal diode. He thought of germanium ore, of resonar imbedments in plastic . . . In desperation he called, "Pete, get the panel off that ILS, and bring me a diode. Hurry!" A minute later, his pilot came with a dark, wrapped crystal. He handed it to Sefraeonia. She held it, and her eyes brightened. Yes. She could sing this.

The officer expelled a breath he felt had been held for an hour. "Mister Chance, can you stall things for a few hours, maybe call a rest here or something? We've got some equipment to rig. I don't know, maybe it will work. If we don't give it a shot—" He looked away at the gathering miles of humanity, waiting. "If we don't make this work, we've got some real trouble."

Back in the helicopter, General James Edgar closed his eyes as tight as he could for a moment. He had things to do and no extra time. But once they were done, come hell or high water, he was going to take some time off. He would go home to Sally, tell her how he loved her . . . and hold her hand.

31

"The quartz is exposed in a wide shelf about two thousand feet above base. Sonar says it runs well into the mountain, and they've made a stratum up in the spire reverberate by pulsing the shelf. The people here with NSF say technically the whole thing can serve as a resonator if they just knew how to trigger the pitches." Brigadier General James Edgar squinted tired eyes and recradled the receiver on his shoulder as he watched white-coated teams and uniformed men scurrying about the vast cavern beyond his plexi-glass wall. In the distance, under arc-lights, was the side corridor leading to the cushioned lair of Cyber-205. No one worked with 205 directly. Instead they worked with the great machine's slave banks.

He thought General Morey Flanders' patched-through voice sounded just as tired as he was, but Flanders was staying on top of it. "Theoretically," Edgar continued, "if Sefraeonia can resonate that crystal spire up there, the sensors can feed through CYCOM's system to Cyber-205, which can then feed translated electromagnetic impulses to a whole bank of receptors to be bounced back right into the crystal base of the mountain. And when she sings, that mountain should sing with her. Sort of a world-class amplifying system. NSF's wave-theory people are going nuts."

"Can you dry-run it in any way?" Flanders asked from a thousand miles away.

"Negative. All we can do is get 205 to 'thrum' the quartz a bit. We've tested that. But we can't generate the kind of harmonics these elves generate. All we've got is electromagnetics, and what they do is a vocal thing . . . like sonics stretched clear across the spectrum."

"So the machines will translate."

"That's what we hope, yes."

"You call it singing, Jim, but I gather it really is just talking. As they talk, there is no difference between talk and song."

"There must be some corollary for song, though, General. If they're people, like we are, there must be . . . ritual codings of vocalized ideas or emotions. They have babies. They must have lullabies."

"That's a good thought, Jim. See if you can get her to sing them a lullabye. Something to soothe the savage beast. How many people do you have out there now?"

"SAC guessed forty thousand this morning, but USCGS flew pictures of the region and counted the bumps. They're saying now there are nearly a million people within forty miles' radius of the base of Cassion, all trying to crowd in. A lot of them have tried to go to the top, but we've held them back so far. I don't think the stampede will start until the girl gets there. That fellow Chance . . . God, what a thug! He's cooperating, though. He'll keep her away until morning. Or maybe I should say, she's cooperating. I don't think he gives the orders."

"One thing, Jim. We've still got plenty of Stafford Clarks breathing down our necks. There is to be no interruption of essential wave patterns for intelligence and security. Let everything else go to hell for a few minutes if you have to, but keep those satellite and NORAD channels clear."

"Can do, General. We've backed all our stuff into the EHF range for the time being—some of the SAC people are having a hemorrhage about that, but they're going along—and CY-205 won't remit anything in that range. I think—I hope—that it won't make any difference here. I'm more worried about a million disappointed Americans than I am about Ivan right now."

"We don't have to worry about Ivan internally for a while, Jim. His domestic organization is a shambles, thanks to our friend Haralan."

"The elf? I heard about the sweep, General, but not that your elf had anything to do with it."

"That's good. It's absolutely QT. If we can keep the media happy with your operation there and our sweep here, it'll give us a chance to get some other things cleared up. By the way, Haralan will be with you in a few hours. He is a free agent. He's earned it. He's on his way out to see about Sefraeonia."

"I thought you had him under wraps."

"Not any more. But Tracy's with him. You'll give Tracy full cooperation short of endangering your operation. Anything else, Jim?"

"Well, yes, sir, there is." He paused, then plunged ahead. "General, we've got aerial and satellite photos of Cassion Peak, we've got climbers' reports and quadrangles, USCGS topicals and the works, and we've had scoutcraft ranging the mountain for hours. But, sir, we can't find Elvenroost!"

"You said you had the spire reverberated. If you have the spire, why don't you have Elvenroost? Three separate elves have told us precisely where it is. It's behind the 'croft' and the croft is the spire—where your quartz lode is."

"We've looked, General. That spire is just a flake on the side of the mountain, nothing behind it but a crack . . . it doesn't appear to be more than twenty feet across."

"Jim, can you delegate what you're doing at Cheyenne and get back up there immediately? Meet Haralan when he arrives—quietly. You can't very well whisk Sefraeonia away with a million people watching, but Haralan has been there. Get him to show you. Twenty feet, you say?"

"Affirmative. About that."

"Puzzling. Haralan and the Feya both described it as a cove maybe two hundred yards wide. You get up there, Jim." The chuckle that followed was dry and tired. "And when you find it, and get plugged in, have a nice singalong, Jim. And keep me posted."

* * * * *

The big chopper from Lowry Air Force Base settled on a flat four miles off 119, and James Edgar stepped forward with his exec to meet it. Two crewmen were first out, followed by a rumpled John Tracy, who was followed by an elf. Edgar took a long look at the latter. Haralan was even bigger than he had expected, tall and lithe, with broad shoulders flaring his crimson cloak. Hesitantly, Edgar stepped forward and held out a hand. The impact was not as stunning as with Sefraeonia, but it was deep. At contact, he felt he and Haralan knew each other better than brothers ever could. He grasped the big hand as he said, "Haralan, we need your help. Please take me to Elvenroost." He was very glad there was only sincerity in him.

The elf studied him. "Where is Sefraeonia?"

"She's there." Edgar pointed. "She's safe. Can we reach Elvenroost in this?"

Haralan glanced back at the helicopter. "If we must."

Tracy stepped forward. "General Edgar? John Tracy, Deputy Secretary. What's the problem?"

"The problem is, sir, we have to rig up a resonating system on that mountain by morning. The girl says she will sing for those people out there . . . do you understand about that? Good. But she can't do it alone. We have CYCOM and NSF trying to juryrig some kind of amplification system into a quartz lode up there, to translate her vocals into electromagnetic force for resonance." He still clasped Haralan's hand as he spoke.

The elf nodded. "Sefraeonia will comfort them. I can show you how."

When they were aboard, the helicopter lifted off and Haralan hovered in the cockpit hatch, pointing the way. They climbed, and in the evening light saw the snaking lines of pilgrims clotting roads to the east horizon. Cassion loomed before them. Haralan pointed, and they veered southward along its face. Edgar, watching past him, saw the reality of hundreds of charts and photos unfold. They rounded a shoulder and the spire was before them, a huge, tilted flake of broken-off mountain leaning back toward its mother.

Haralan pointed at the crack. "Go in there," he said. The pilot looked up at him.

"Sorry, sir, but there ain't no way this thing is goin' through that crack."

Haralan said again, "Go in there."

"Haralan." Edgar was beside him. "There isn't enough space. You can see the blades . . . the wings on this ship. We have to have at least a hundred feet of clear air to drop through safely."

Impatiently Haralan reached around and took his hand. "This place is Caian. Look now. What do you see?"

Edgar gasped. The "crack" was an optical illusion, a matter of mindset, of perspective. Looking now, he saw its lip jutting well out from the mountain, far out to reveal a wide pocket behind the croft. Last sunlight glinted on sparkling quartz. Below was granite and blue dusk. With his other hand he touched the pilot's shoulder. "Can you see it now, Captain? Good. Take us down."

"Humans have only one way of looking at things," Haralan muttered. The comment sounded ironically human.

Pilots and passengers were wide-eyed as they stepped down on the cool tuft of Elvenroost. Under purpling sky the hidden cove was a splendor of blues and gray-greens among deep red walls. They looked around, walked around. There was a feel to the place, a slight, tingling arcanity that was at once pleasant and disturbing.

"Cai-essence," Haralan said. "Here is presence of Caian-kind. It is very old. When this world was Caiendon, this song was everywhere."

At first their human eyes could not discern the "castle" they had heard about. But when Haralan pointed it out to them, suddenly it stood clear. Edgar was awed by the illusory nature of it. He had stared at this wonder and not seen it. Now that he saw it, he couldn't imagine how he had failed to perceive it.

They wandered through it, dazzled. Finally Edgar brought them back to reality. "We don't have much time. Haralan, you know what needs to be done. Can you show us how?"

The Caian strode to the middle of the cove floor, followed by humans. He turned, pointed up to the spire shouldering the croft above them. "Crystal. It runs deep, but it must be . . . tuned so that Sefraeonia can use it. It must sing for her. It is simple. You listen to Sefraeonia's voice, you shape that crystal to her nature, it will sing as she sings."

Shape . . . the crystal? They stared at one another. Haralan indicated his blade. "You show me the shape. I will cut it for you." The finality of it told them. If they would do their part, he would do his.

"I think we need CYCOM," Edgar told Tracy.

"I think you need a goddamned miracle." Tracy said.

Late in the evening, at a roadside park that had become both a military research base and a waystop for thousands of travelers, people clustered about in awe as Sefraeonia sang simple trills up and down the spectrum for banked receptors. Most of them heard some of what she sang and were deeply moved. Few of them heard much of it, though their scalps tingled and the place behind their brows throbbed with enticing promise of beauty just beyond reach. Their groping awareness of their own blindness made the elf-girl sad for them, and that too she sang into the faceless machines. Vocal tones the range of the middle spectrum were captured by diaphragms, diodes, resonators, and ranked forks and translated into electromagnetic impulse. Spectra beyond were fed as imprint to carrier waves in vast ranges.

Under Cheyenne Mountain, Cyber-205 digested the total with a part of itself and displayed turning line diagrams on cathode screens. Endless columns of numbers rolled from printers. One full bank of terminals with their generators and lights now stood in the place of

Elvenroost, and the people there divided their time between readout duties and cautious glances at the tall, dour alien, the elf, who strode impatiently among them. In the shadows of the castle John Tracy sat and watched the bright tableau. With sudden wisdom, he saw Haralan's problem. Why did they do all this? Why so many people, so many machines, so much frenzy? Surely it would be simpler just to bring Sefraeonia up here and let her sing while he carved the crystal to receive her song.

Tracy shook his head. He would not try to explain that there was another matter that had to be considered. CYCOM had its orders. The diagram must be true to the elf-girl's resonance—with one exception. The EHF ranges must be silent. Tracy doubted whether the elves would understand . . . could even conceive . . . the idea of organized enemies. He didn't want to try to teach them right now. He liked them better untaught.

The plans, recorded resonances, came through, and Haralan scurried up the sheer face of the pinnacle of quartz. Hoists brought supervisors up to join him. From the floor of Elvenroost they watched, and felt the song of Haralan's blade as he began shaving the spire.

Far below, beyond the shoulder of Cassion, a Colorado National Guardsman raised his rifle to bar the approach of an unauthorized person. Then he blinked, looked around in confusion, and resumed his position. He wasn't sure why he had done that. He wasn't even sure he had.

It was after three in the morning. Bundled and tiny in her old patchwork robe, Margaret sat on the front steps watching the neon cats make their rounds on the blue lawn.

She felt numb. For two days she had fought the terrible dread that welled inside her, fed by the hard grief of Nataea. She had tried to soothe the weeping spark of sweet life there, to reassure and maintain a measure of hope. But it was a tenuous hope. They had both heard the song of Aaelefein—so near, this time—and both felt the awful abruptness of its ending.

She was glad her parents had been so preoccupied. It would have been difficult to keep her fears from them, and she didn't want to dim the joy they had found, first from what she and Nataea had shared with them, and then from the beautiful first song, when Aaelefein had first called to her. They had been different since then . . . so richly alive, seeking and eager for beauties they had never known before.

A lot of people had been different since that evening. Many thought a miracle had occurred. Not everyone, unfortunately—Roy was one of those who had felt nothing, heard nothing at all—but many had been profoundly moved by that powerful, silent music that was like stars singing for them.

And the past day or so they had followed in fascination the news of elves and Elvenroost and the migrations of believers moving westward to see for themselves. Their decision to go had been spontaneous and abrupt. They had packed the car just hours ago and were trying to get a little sleep now before starting out. Margaret could sense them, strongly, eager and excited, like two children facing a marvelous adventure. She was glad they were going. It would be a wonderful experience for them.

And she wanted to be alone now . . . alone with that grieving, beautiful spirit that was so much a part of her, yet was not her. She needed all her strength to calm and sooth Nataea. She needed all her concentration to cling to a tenuous hope.

We don't know what happened, her human mind reasoned. It could have been any number of things. We don't know that he is gone.

Please . . . the tiny response from inside was so bleak, so devastated, that it shook her and brought tears to her eyes. *Please, leave me alone. I want to die.*

The sheer agony of the little life-spark tore at her throat. Once—so recently—it had begged her to let it remain. Now in its misery it begged her to let it die. Her response was totally human, the tough, resilient determination of her race—qualities derived from eons of blind uncertainty. Faced with defeat, the human side of her rejected it and clung to hope.

We don't know he's gone, she thought fiercely, willing the Nataea essence to consider it. He might still be out there, still looking for you. For us. How can we give up hope?

The grieving scintillance wavered for an instant, and

the human mind of Meg pressed its advantage. When you died, a stranger on this world, you had no hope of leaping. Yet you tried . . . and somehow you did. Could he have known that?

He knew I would try.

Could he have known that you succeeded?

Negative . . . a bleak acceptance.

So he had no reason to hope. Still, he came looking for you.

He was Aaelefein. He did what he must do.

Duty? Nonsense. I heard his call. It was my ears . . . my senses . . . that received it for both of us. Those were not the harmonies of duty. It was a song of love.

And I loved him, as well, the scintillance seemed to say. *Please, this is cruel. It hurts me. Aaelefein is . . .*

He is not dead! What's the matter with you? How can you accept a thing you can't be sure of? I don't accept it, not for one minute!

His song ended.

But we don't know why! There could be other reasons.

I loved him so.

Then how can you give up so easily? Have you no faith in the one you love? Can't you accept that he might still live . . . at least until we are sure?

Your thoughts are hard . . . they hurt. Please . . .

What kind of people are you? They say your race is thirty times as old as mine . . . and I know from you that it is. Yet you don't have the fortitude to hope?

We have always hoped.

For what?

We have never known. We have only lived . . . and longed for something.

Well, I'd be ashamed to have lived hundreds of millions of years and still not know what I wanted.

You are no better. Your race does not know what it wants, either.

Maybe not, but we get out and try to find it. Or at the very least we try to give it a chance to happen. We don't just . . . surrender.

Our races are different. That is why we—you and I—have never been able to complete our blending. You have your harmonies and we have ours, and they are discordant.

Yes. They are discordant. And I'm beginning to understand why. For all your beauty, you give up too easily.

Unfair. You judge only me. Strength of will is not my greatest virtue. I have given you all I have. You know my limits. Aaelefein's will is . . . was . . . very strong.

Then have faith in his will. I love him, too . . . with your love, and maybe with my own as well. And I'm not giving up on him!

They had achieved a sort of truce, an accord that did nothing to alleviate the melancholy dread they both felt, but that recognized the value of Margaret's stubborn, human determination and used it to shelter them both.

One of the neon cats had found an indigo frog and was playing with it while the other watched. Two blocks away, a car turned the corner and rolled along the silent street. Idly she noted the orbs of its headlights, the shimmering crimson glow of its hood, magenta aura of its driver, the elaborate song of its humming engine, the myriad harmonies of its tires rolling on the pavement.

Inside the house, the telephone rang. Margaret started to stand, then sensed her mother in the upper hall. Lights went on, and she heard-felt Hazel coming downstairs to answer. Henry was awake, too. They wouldn't wait for morning to begin their journey.

Inside, Hazel lifted the receiver. "Hello?" A pause. "Who? Oh. No, I'm her mother." Pause. "Who? Well, I suppose so. Just a minute . . . Meg? Are you awake? Meg?"

She stood, glanced back at the lovely night-glows, and went to the door. "I'm here, Mother. Who is it?"

"Somebody from Washington, Dear. From a Mister Tracy's office. Do you know him? Heavens—" she glanced at the clock—"they keep strange hours, don't they?"

"I'll take it," Meg went inside.

Hazel handed her the phone. "Speaking of strange hours," she muttered. "We're all keeping them."

She lifted the phone to her ear. "Yes?"

"Margaret Harrison?" The man's voice was tinged with fatigue.

"Yes."

"Ah . . . are you the Margaret Harrison who called Mr. Tracy's office three days ago? About the . . . the elf?"

"Yes, I tried to, but something happened."

"You were asked to speak a name, to verify your call."

"Yes, I said . . ."

"Please don't say it again. Not on the telephone. We have about two million dollars' worth of fiber-optic relays in the basement that are now two dollars' worth of junk. We have had a hard time finding you again."

"I'm sorry. Did I do that?"

"Yes, ma'am. But never mind. You are at your home now? This isn't an extended line?"

"I'm at home."

"Ah . . . would you mind staying there, ma'am? General Flanders would like to visit with you."

"Who?"

"General Flanders. Look, when you called, you said that one of the elves—Elefein . . ."

"Aaelefein."

"Careful, please! Yes, him . . . you said he was looking for you."

"Yes. You see, he's trying to find Nataea, and she's with me. More exactly, she is me . . . sort of. You see, she was killed when they arrived on Earth, and . . . "

"Yes, ma'am. We know about that. I guess. Anyway, General Flanders wants to come and see you. It will be a while . . . a few hours, probably. We could send someone to pick you up, but he requests that you just stay where you are in case the . . . ah, the elf you mentioned . . . comes there. We're only trying to help, ma'am. I assure you."

The otherness behind her brow nudged, echoing her dread and her hope.

"He isn't dead, then?" she asked.

"Who?"

"Aaelefein. Are you saying he's alive?"

"I don't know anything about that, ma'am. Maybe if you'll just wait for General Flanders . . ."

"I'll be here. Can I talk to the general now?"

"He isn't here, ma'am. He's . . . well, I don't know where he is, but he'll be in touch with you. Please wait for him."

As she hung up, Henry appeared at the top of the stairs, fully dressed. "Does anybody realize what time it is?" he asked. "Or does anybody care?"

Hazel had the coffee on. She turned to Meg. "Was that the people you were trying to get in touch with? To tell them about the person with you?"

"Yes. They want me to wait here for them."

"Do you think they'll believe you?"

"Oh, I think they already do, Mother. It all has to do with those elves. This one with me, Nataea, she's one of them. I told you."

"Yes, but people can be so dense sometimes. Would you like for us to wait with you?"

"No, Mother. I know you are anxious to get started. Where did they say that place is?"

"They don't really know," Henry said. "But we heard on television that there are thousands and thousands of people going there. You heard it . . . no, you didn't. You were outside. They said that elf girl is leading them. There were pictures."

"Sefraeonia," Margaret murmured. Within her Nataea radiated joy at the name. They had both been so preoccupied since his plaintive call . . .

"And that other one, his name's Haralan. He's been released, and they think he's going there, too." Her father took her hands. "We want to go, too, Meg. We want to see it."

Infrasonics flowed, and the communication was vivid. Of course they wanted to see it. Their lives had been profoundly changed, just by a taste of the people from elsewhere. She understood perfectly.

"We're being impulsive," Hazel chuckled. "We've never been very impulsive before . . ."

"Speak for yourself, woman."

"But we decided to just up and go."

Meg noticed again the radiance in her mother's eyes and smiled, an analogy in her mind that she didn't want to voice. Her parents were eloping. Again she took her father's hand, and again that dazzling wash of perception flowed between them. Don't dawdle, Dad. Look at your wife. Look at her eyes. Don't let that be spoiled. Don't make her wait. Yes, go. Now. Go to Elvenroost.

See those fantastic people and hear their song.

I wish you would come, too, his warm hand told her.

I have to stay. He may come. And a flash of thought between herself and the presence within her: *He is alive! I know he is! But how can we know? No, how can we doubt?*

Look at mother's eyes. She has seen the world now, as they see it, just as you have. Both of you are so beautiful.

And if he does come here?

Whatever happens will be right.

Hazel had come to them, and her hand was on theirs.

Yes, it will be right. Just know that we love you, Meg.

They shared that love, and it sang within them. And subtly, behind it, was a sadness, a realization of tragedy.

It could always have been like this, couldn't it? If only the elves had come before. All of human history could have been so different, just for the merest touch of . . . this.

It was done, then. It was all said, and they turned away.

"It's still hours until dawn," Hazel said.

"Wee hours of the morning," Henry agreed.

"Silly time to start a trip."

"It is, isn't it? Let's go."

33

Now, from an ancient past, from the silence and the veils of eight thousand millennia, the waiting crystal spoke. Winifraeda Feya, crouched in dimness behind crates in the basement of a museum, cradled it in sensitive hands and sang the harmonies that would awaken it. In awed silence, Jacob Laurel sat on a dusty box and watched.

The Ramapur Stone was flawed. Webs of tiny cracks patterned its surface. Laurel considered the sensation that would ensue when it was learned that the old oddity was in fact an implement, an artifact of a civilization so incredibly old that . . . but no, as things stood now, all the old cornerstone theories had already been knocked into oblivion. The origin of the Ramapur would be just another revelation to add to the revelations. Like his beloved elf tracks in cretaceous chalk, the old crystal now would be only another dry bit of corroborating evidence.

The Feya sang again and, subtly, the crystal changed its hue. Grudgingly, weighted by its age, the stone came alive. Laurel's scalp, around the fringes where hair remained, tingled. The place behind his brow pulsed. The stone was singing. It stopped. Winifraeda scowled, sang silent harmonics again, and once again the crystal responded briefly.

Lustrous elf-eyes turned to Laurel. "It is so old, Jacob. Things have happened to it through the ages. Its patterns have been interrupted. This will be difficult."

"Can I help you, Winifraeda?"

"You can try. Sit here by me, put your hands over mine. No, don't try to think harmonics, Jacob. You don't know how. Just support me. Lend me your strength as I need it." She tried again, and now Laurel felt through her the vast splendors of faerie song, the enthralling, heart-breaking glory of the ages of an ancient race. She sang, and again the stone responded. He could read no meaning from it, but was enraptured by the very human spirit he felt captured in its depths. It was a stubborn, masculine pattern with strength in its rhythms and heat in its lyric. He saw a dim spark grow within the stone and flutter into grudging life. It pulsed, faltered, and pulsed again, then settled into a steady glow that fluctuated with the resonance modulating outward through old crystal. He sensed intent interest through Winifraeda's tiny hands, a rush of meaning. Her eyes had taken on new luster.

"Rigil," she breathed. "Rigil Fen-Belen. Of course. It had to be his. He was the only one left behind. Jacob, this is his testament."

"Rigil . . . the one you told me about? The legend, the one who refused to leave Caiendon?"

"The very same. Listen . . ."

Once resonated, the crystal continued to sing. Winifraeda buried herself in its message, as awed for once as was Laurel. So many millions of Earth years ago, a lonely old warrior elf had done this thing, had committed his lore to a teardrop crystal which he could only assume no one would ever read. She felt her eyes misting, felt Laurel's hands warm on hers as he sensed her sentiment.

Though he could not read the message, the rapport between them had become strong. She looked up. His eyes were moist, too.

"It is like a book, Jacob. A journal, but done by lore a long time after he saw his race depart. Rigil Fen-Belen. Oh . . ." she concentrated anew on the crystal. "He was lonely, Jacob. Alone among the lonely ones . . . the Raporoi . . . He was so terribly lonely that if he could, he would have called back his decision. But then it was too late. His soul cried out. He wept. But there was no one to know. The darkness shrouded him. With Cai-kind gone, no one to sing with, it was infinitely worse for him. Ah . . . I knew it. The pixies came to comfort him. Even the lowest of the kindred rallied to him and surrounded him with their love. And though they could not help, their presence shielded him. Jacob, he tells of the world and how it was in the last days of Caian-essence.

Oh, you will adore this, you with your ravenous, disciplined mind. There is so much here in the crystal. Did you know there remained great lizards in the time of your ancestors? Not so many, he says, but there were a few. They were no match, poor, mindless things, for the savagery of your ancestors. Oh, he saw wonders, Jacob. The last Caian on a hostile world, and still he considered the colors of a sunrise. Jacob, can you feel the Caidom there? Does it awe you? That is what it is to be elf."

Laurel's breath was ragged, his eyes moist with wonder. "Go on, Winifraeda. Your words tell me what the feelings mean. Please go on."

"It covers a very long time, Jacob. Rigil Fen-Belen lived a long time after our . . . what you call elvendom . . . departed this world. And it is very hard to read. I will have to rest sometimes."

"Then we will rest, Feya, together. But let us continue

when you can."

*　　*　　*　　*　　*

In noonday sun, General Morey Flanders walked the path that led to the great rock at the edge of Sugar Creek. Aides followed him. Throughout the park and for miles downstream, Army specialists thronged the stream and its fringes, searching, seining, grappling, seeking.

"This is where he stood?" Flanders asked for the fourth time, clambering atop the rock. "Right here, exactly where I am now?"

"Yes, sir," a worried Special Forces sergeant said. "We both saw him, Private Williams and me. There was moonlight. He was very clear. And the trace-light was out, sir. That meant the—phenomenon—had started again. He was 'singing,' as they say. We had our orders. Sir, Private Williams was just doing as—"

"Can it, Sergeant!" The general waved an abrupt hand. "I know all that. You don't have to defend your men to me. But you are sure he stood right here?"

"Certain, sir. Right where you're standing. Private Williams fired, and he just sort of pitched forward, right out into the water there."

"Into the water. You heard him hit the water?"

"Yes, sir. I did. Right below where you're standing, it had to be."

"And you didn't see him surface? You didn't see him at all after that?"

"No, sir. You see, the moon was right about there. Those trees pretty well shaded the stream. He'd have to have come up just a few feet from this bank for us to see him, and he didn't, sir. We watched."

"What would you say is the possibility that Private Williams might have missed?"

"None at all, sir!" The sergeant straightened his shoulders. "Not Private Williams. Besides, I saw it. I know when a man's hit, sir, and this one was clean."

"Then it's your estimate that the elf is dead."

"Yes, sir." The sergeant nodded emphatically. "There ain't no way he could be not dead."

"In that case," Flanders turned away, shaking his head, "where is the body?"

"I talked with a park officer, sir," one of the aides said. "This is considered a hazardous stream. There are occasional drownings. Two last summer. One little girl wasn't found for three days. He says the stream bed is erratic and it causes currents and flow variations. They'll find him, sir."

The general nodded, waved them all away. Alone, he stood atop the rock, watching murky waters swirl eight feet below. The poor elf, he thought. The poor, heartbroken goddamned elf, out here singing in the night to find an elf-girl who was already dead eight weeks earlier. Now he's dead, too, and there's not a miserable thing we can do but find him . . . and then try to explain it to the others. He shuddered at the thought of how big Haralan might react. But oddly, that wasn't really what he found bothering him. The image in his mind was of himself, looking into the eyes of Sefraeonia, telling her that the United States Army had killed her last hope of survival. And even worse, trying to explain that to the little Feya. He felt suddenly very sorry for Tracy. Tracy had actually met the Feya.

*   *   *   *   *

Fortunately, the goal of the spontaneous pilgrimage was not far from Denver. People might have suffered horribly from their own pressing numbers had help not been near. But an emergency order by the governor of Colorado, with assurances of remuneration and more from the White House, brought the resources of state agencies into play. Army and Air Force resources backed them up.

From Denver, Boulder, and Colorado Springs, massive airlifts hopped the jammed roads to bring provisions to the Cassion Peak area. Food, make-shift shelters, portable toilets by the thousands, generators and medical supplies reached the ever-growing camp of the pilgrims, which spread now to the limits of a five-mile-long valley accessible by logging roads from both Eldora and Rollinsville. USCGS and CYCOM scans, translated to data screens, showed an eight-state octopus of converging traffic jams, and the airlifts were stepped up and spread to adjacent portions of four states. At the core of the octopus, two thousand feet above the writhing plain, teams of scientists and technicians worked in relays to implant buss bars in a strata of quartz. Insulated cables from a long bank of variable generators interfaced with resonators would feed the buss bars. Each resonator had its own computer port and each port was tied back to Cyber-205.

An Army engineer paced along the bank, shaking his head.

"They're crazy," he muttered. "Absolutely crazy. Modulation will bring that whole mountain down."

"Sure, it's crazy," another concurred. "But the scientists have got hold of this thing now. It's an event they're not about to drop until they've seen it."

An Air Force colonel disagreed. "The science event is

a ploy. Look out there. This is an event, all right. A media event. Hell, every news camera in the country is focused on this thing. Nobody's minding the store."

"Somebody is, Hank. This thing is being encouraged hard, by somebody high up. If this whole mess is a deceptive tactic, it's a lulu. I'm telling you, we're not just going to make this mountain sing, we're going to make it dance."

"Have you seen those elves, Joe?"

"Nah. Just pictures. Lord, I don't know, maybe they are real. But why all this?"

"Why? I guess we'll know when somebody tells us."

*   *   *   *   *

The old Ute trail up Cassion's northwest flank would not have been a difficult trail for an equipped climber. It would have been a hike in daylight. But now, in the darkness, it was torment to the lone girl who struggled upward along it. Her fingers were sore, her clothing torn, and her knee was skinned from a fall. Using abilities learned by observation, she had penetrated the tight cordon at Cassion's base and begun the long climb. She was still startled that the thing she had tried—several times—had worked for her. She hadn't expected it to work. She was no elf, only a human, and she wasn't at all sure she believed all that about elves anyway. But she remembered well the gentle words, "People are easily distracted . . . it's hard to concentrate on someone you don't know." And the odd, sidling eye-thing that she had seen done so often. It had worked. The soldiers were behind her. Only the mountain now barred her way.

They say he is an elf, she thought. And they say the elves are up there.

She meant to get up there and find him. He would take care of her. Since that night when the sky sang and her suffering grandfather died in peace, she knew she had to see him again, the gentle person she had known as Alvin Frost. He was like a song that once heard must be heard again—a light in the darkness.

34

Ten minutes after ten, full dark of summer night. Roy Holloway stared at the television set in dull fury that drained slowly toward defeat. From a promontory, the camera panned across a broad, twilit valley packed with people: young and old, the hearty and the sick, babies; cars, vans, campers, jeeps. The slow pan rested on a road disappearing into distance. More people. Hundreds, thousands of vehicles creeping forward.

Scene change: People pressed about a clear space where raw-looking toughs formed a defense ring around a blue Blazer. On its top was the "elf-girl:" exotic, strangely beautiful in arc-assisted half-light. The fabulous elf-girl. She stood slim atop the vehicle, staring up and away. The camera followed, long lens zooming as the view climbed upward on the peak. There, magnified but still tiny, red cloak streaming in last rays, the one they had called Centurion, the one they now called Haralan.

Precarious above a precipice he clung, wielding a bright thing. On a scaffold near him men clustered, watching intently. Some of them wore military uniforms.

Roy had the sound turned down. He had heard all he could stand. But still he stared, his face bleak. They had gone crazy. Everybody had gone crazy. Alone in his clut-

tered apartment, he slumped, eyes red-rimmed and
sunken as he watched altered people gather before a hor-
rible shrine. It had been bound to happen. He had seen
it coming for a long time. But nobody would listen.
Nobody ever listened. A cult in the California desert
brainwashed girls and used them, gathered drugs and
used them, garnered slogans and used them, and
nobody paid attention. Then that cult ran amok and
started killing people. It was a ten-day wonder.

A cult in Michigan festered on a college campus, pros-
elytizing kids, brainwashing, converting, altering, ply-
ing them with drugs until the kids ran amok, blank-eyed
zombies shedding blood in a quiet town. Another ten-
day wonder. A media event.

An orator in dark glasses, with drugs, thugs, and mystical words, mesmerized whole families of people, hundreds of them, into a flock of mindless sheep and led
them to Central America where he led them in an orgy of
murder and suicide. Sheep-people strewn dead among
vats of grape drink laced with poison. Roy's eyes in their
dark sockets closed for a moment in anguish. Sheep-
people. The poor, misguided, vulnerable, stupid people
of the world, so many pounds of dumb flesh waiting to
be slaughtered by raving lunatics who had found the
way. The cults. It was only a matter of time.

Teddy was gone. Drugs and junkies, pushers and their
flocks of miserable, stupid little sheep. Teddy . . . there
was no more Teddy. Dorothy was gone, a secondary victim but no less a victim. Then out of darkness had come
sunshine when he found Margaret . . . and now they had
Margaret. She was still there, but not Margaret anymore.
Altered was altered. He wasn't blind.

On the silent screen, an Air Force general was talking
to a newsman's microphone. An Army general and some

miscellaneous other brass stood behind him, with some civilians mixed in.

A matter of time. They hadn't been content. Somehow, this time they had gone for the whole hog, and got it. Roy Holloway loved his country. Now, deep down, he mourned it. What the cults took was never returned. It would have been better if the United States had gone out in flames, with bullets and bombs and waving flags. Hell, this wasn't even a whimper. They didn't even realize what was happening to them, the poor sheep-people.

All the hurt, all the pain of all the losses hung heavy on him now. He found he was not looking at the television any more, but at the open closet door and the toe of the shotgun stock that peeked out there. The old gun was dirty. He hadn't hunted now in years. But its oiled stock still shone lustrous beneath a pall of dust.

He couldn't take it any more. He saw what was happening and he didn't want to see any more of it. He didn't want to be the survivor any more. There was nothing left to survive for.

Musing, distant in his growing disinterest, he went to the closet and lifted the gun out. Remington model 11-48, autoloading, its empty action stood open and dusty. He wiped at it with a thumb. On the shelf behind his hard hat, goggles, and some old boots were several boxes of shells. Mostly they were birdshot. But there was one box of buckshot, 12-gauge shells loaded with heavy, .30-caliber balls, a devastating charge. Absently Roy fingered three shells from the box, slipped one into the shotgun's chamber and snapped the action shut on it. The other two he fed into the magazine. A touch of a finger and the safety was off.

He went back to the couch. For a time he held the gun loosely across his lap, then he set its butt on the floor.

The muzzle was above his head. You've had too much to drink, he told himself. You can't do anything right. Do what right, he wondered. By sliding the gun butt away with his foot, he angled it down until he could look into the staring muzzle. Down that dark hole was an end to it all. He slipped the muzzle under his chin and sat hunkered there, arm outstretched, toying with the trigger guard.

Now what? he asked himself. Do I know what I'm doing? No. Apparently not. I put three shells in this thing. If I fire one, who's going to fire the other two? The bleak humor of it stopped him. Do I know what I'm doing? The question hung there. For that matter, does anybody know what he's doing now? On the silent television before him, a camera high on the peak showed Haralan, close-up, at work on a spire of clear quartz. The flashing blade he wielded swung and cut, swung and cut, shards of rock falling away. The top of the spire now was a shaped pinnacle of crystal, a tapering basilisk with chiseled top like a pyramid. The elf's face was set and expressionless, but light from the refracting blade flashed in large, almond eyes . . . eyes that were other than human.

They're all inhuman, Holloway thought. They take and take and nothing ever comes back. These have some tricks and an appearance. He thought of the oil painting Margaret had done, that serene, cold elf-face staring at him from canvas, and tears welled in his eyes. His finger sought the trigger in its guard. Margaret was gone . . . like Teddy was gone, like Dorothy was gone, like everything was gone now. Do I know what I'm doing?

Yes. Slowly he drew his hand away, pushed the gun barrel from his throat, stood and reversed the weapon. He thumbed the safety on. Yes, he thought, I know what

I'm doing. Dimly he knew that there was one of them—
the one in the picture—who must never take again.
Elves, are they? Cults. The jackal cults among sheep-
people. I am no sheep, he told the hall mirror. Then he
said it aloud, "I am no sheep!" When he left, the door
slammed behind him.

*   *   *   *   *

"Here, Jacob, sense and listen." New energy now
quickened the Feya's tired voice. "He says, 'And then
one day there came a man.' Man, Jacob! Not Raporoi,
but human, like your kind. The song is very clear."

"The second culminant species emerged." Laurel nodded. He wasn't sure how tired the little Feya was, but he
was exhausted. They had been at this old stone now for
at least twelve hours with only occasional breaks for rest.
And yet, there was no sleep in him. His analytical mind
hummed with the excitement of learning. Here, in this
old crystal, was a detailed history of prehistory, an
anthropologist's dream. Rigil Fen-Belen, lonely old elf,
had encapsuled it all. In this testament stone, he told of
the vanishing kindred, the changes in the essence of the
world as the energies of elvenkind went dim and the
energies of another race flowed through Earth's mantle
. . . the rise of a different kind of human creature,
another thinker, sentient as elves and yet not elves. Similar in so many ways, yet terribly different. "What they
lack in modulation," Winifraeda translated from the
stone, "they supplant with determination. Their ways
are not so strange when I consider that they cannot see
the colors of night, hear the song of their mother world
or the harmonies of the stars, nor ever sense the fabric of
the life from which they come.

"My sadness is in their sadness. They are whole things with minds straining to burst forth, yet they have no means to share, even among themselves, what they are . . . even *that* they are. I love them, I think. And I mourn for them. I would be one of them if I could, so I could make that one to see, to be one of me.

"And then one day there came a man . . ." Winifraeda paused, her great eyes glowing. "There is another flaw here, Jacob. I miss something. It is so very old. It has been untended for so long." With probing senses she searched the stone for continuity, found a later thread:

". . . with man's children. They know of me and I of them. I have helped them in their need, have sung for them when their world was darkest, and they survive. They are strong despite their blindness. The pixies are few here. The lands are drifting part, and most of the pixies now are beyond new seas. But there is a strange comfort to me in the presence of the children of Raporoi. My resonance and theirs are not alike, yet coupled they make a wondrous harmony. Their darkness hurts me as it always did, yet I find among them a comfort akin to hope."

In silence she bridged another flaw, picked up the thread once more: ". . . so I crafted for him a blade of bronze, a thing of beauty to him as all of its colors are within his range. He held it before him and wept . . . not joy as I had thought, but sympathy. He wept for me. In his terrible loneliness, he wept instead for my loneliness. Always we wept for them. But now he wept for me."

"Oh, God," Laurel choked. They looked at each other with liquid eyes. "Go on, please," he whispered. She concentrated again, probed past another flaw.

". . . being Cai and alone is to have lived too long. He knew my need. Even the pain of his sword-thrust was gentle . . ." Laurel stopped here, confused. "The man killed him? Literally?"

"So it says here, Jacob. Rigil Fen-Belen is telling of his own death."

"But how could he? Please, Winifraeda, go on."

"I don't know." She probed, sensed, picked up a thread of meaning: "And after the darkness . . ." She looked up at Laurel. "But how can that be, Jacob? There is no 'after the darkness' for a Cai on this world. The darkness is here. Oh, I cannot find it. This is so very old, and untended. Here—'I will live among them now, free of the burdens of both Cai and man until such time as they are able . . . my two people should never have separated . . . were there one more, I would reunite us as the essence always intended . . . I leave this as Caidom left the moon here, a token of hope. Let both peoples know that there is hope . . .'"

Laurel urged, "Isn't there more? There must be."

"There may be. I am too tired now to find it. What does it mean, Jacob? The resonances have become so human. I find it is beyond me."

Laurel stood and paced the basement cubbyhole. His eyes roved the stacks and boxes in the dim light, but he did not see them. His mind sang with intuition so profound that Winifraeda felt its emanations and was awed.

"I have spoken of culminants," he said. "Predestined evolution producing the same creature twice. But I do believe I missed the whole point of my own logic. Winifraeda, supposing I am right, that there is an evolutionary matrix about this world, a sort of . . . terrestrial genetic code that preprograms what evolves here. I theorized it, you remember, that our two species were programmed as culminants, that any species culminating here would be like us? The point is, it did occur twice,

Winifraeda. I think that is part of the matrix, too. Somehow, I believe it was always supposed to have occurred twice. Elves and humans—two culminants, not just one. There were supposed to be two such races. But . . . oh, my addled brain! That just makes it worse. Two lines carried to the point of discontent—past the point of sentience—and then just dropped there. Why?"

"Jacob," her voice was tired, disappointed, "I had hoped the testament would lead us to the Corad-bane."

Her great eyes were so sad, Laurel mentally kicked himself. While he was obsessed with unraveling his own mysteries, she was trying to save her people. He rubbed tired eyes and put his mind to it. He owed her that, he supposed.

"We really don't know what it has told us, Winifraeda. There is so much to digest. But let's consider something again: what all did your race take with them when they departed this world? Search your lore, my Feya. There has to be something they left behind."

He left her there while he went looking for a telephone. They had done all they could do alone. It was time to enlist some human help.

*   *   *   *   *

Jacob Laurel's call to Dr. Seth Hyatt, director of the Wilkinson Foundation, produced results that were, to Laurel, confusing and mystifying. Somehow, since the night the elf had carried Laurel from his house, it had slipped his mind that there might be people looking for him. Hyatt's thunderous, "Dr. Laurel? Where in hell have you been?" was an abrupt return to reality.

A barrage of questions followed. Where was he? What was he doing there? Was the Feya with him? Why hadn't he contacted somebody? Sheepishly, he answered the questions. Then, in a tone that brooked no argument, Hyatt ordered him to remain exactly where he was.

Three minutes later the telephone rang and the questions began again, this time from someone with the Department of the Army. By the time he was off the telephone, there were officious men all around him, with more questions. Winifraeda came from the basement to see what was keeping him, and promptly took charge. She detailed a party of them to go and fetch the Ramapur Stone. It was heavy, and they were large and strong, and they might as well make themselves useful.

By the time the testament of Rigil Fen-Belen had been retrieved and safely packed, an army officer was there with a handful of authorizations and precise orders.

"I have a car waiting outside, Dr. Laurel," he said. "I am to take you and . . . ah . . ."

"Winifraeda. She's a Feya."

"Ah . . . yes. I am to deliver you to Meigs Field, to Colonel Blake. He will escort you by air transport to South Bend. General Flanders's aid will have a helicopter waiting to take you to him."

"Who is General Flanders?"

The officer's eyes widened. How could anyone not know General Morey Flanders? Civilians!

"Apparently he is someone who wants to speak with us, Jacob," the Feya explained. Then to the officer, "Where is he?"

"I don't know, ah . . . ma'am. But he knows where he is, and he wants you there on the double. Your pilot will have his instructions."

"Very well. But be sure and bring that testament along. I expect he will want to see it, too."

35

For a long time he flowed with the waters, mute and hidden, varying from oblivion to a dreamlike state that was not far removed from it. Barely alive, he rested in this, his second natural element, while resonances born of pure will sought to repair some of the violence done to his body. The damage was massive, much of it irreversible. But cool, dark times passed and the senester throbbed quietly with his resonance, acting almost on its own.

Once it seemed to him, deep in dream-trance, that the dark ones were all about him, reaching for him with hooks and shafts and nets, groping blindly, and then gentle hands had him and were sliding him aside, away from the danger. He dreamed of Nataea, her large, dark eyes bright upon him, her song a song of pure love. He dreamed comfort, and it seemed there were those about him who responded to the harmonies and echoed them back to him, faltering and unsure, acting on some ancient instinct older than humanity, older even than the Cai. Pixies? In his dreams he wondered. Could there be pixies?

The senester soothed him with harmonics . . . his own instinctive harmonics of healing, pulsed to him by seven perfect crystals acutely attuned to him. Slowly, tissues closed themselves, bound themselves together, regenerated where they could.

Fire in iron—the tools of the people of this world. They had found him, and the devastation done to him was enormous. But finally, some harmonies were restored.

For a time, at least, he could last.

With the slow return of consciousness, he was aware of presences around him—humanity and its searing, grinding darkness. Their awful sadness infiltrated him, dispersing his dreams of pixies, of the songs of bright Nendacaida, of a lovely scintillant with pixie eyes, of himself being whole and free to sing.

Aaelefein slowly surfaced from the dreams and the healing water. Almond eyes crested moonlit water. The bank close at hand was night-dimmed and shielded with rushes. Across were bright luminances above and below where men moved about. There were boats on the water. Through its fluid he felt the scuff of grappling hooks on sand bottom. He rested. His will was intact, and his senses. But he felt an urgency. Some of the tissues torn by fire and iron were too damaged to mend. Only his will and the soothing song of the senester kept him functioning. Below his submerged chin, the seven perfect crystals of the senester glowed faintly in the water. He had little time left. What had been premonition now was certainty. These eyes would not again see Nendacaida, these hands would never touch the lovely liveness of its bright soil.

The senester kept him alive now by constant resonance. But once out of water its song would be heard by the machines of the humans. He would be found. Are you near, my Nataea? The thought gave him strength. The boats were closer. Bright beams played on busy rip-

ples. Turning, he eased through rushes to the solid bank.
With a backward glance he pulled himself up and rolled
into the shelter of leafy vines. Somewhere in the sky, he
knew, their devices had already picked up the senester's
harmonics. Even now a mindless machine was advising
another mindless machine of the phenomenon, and
somewhere a machine that was a mind would know what
it meant. How long would it take to tell them?

Dulling his pain, ignoring it, Aaelefein crept through
shrubbery away from the stream. Past a rise, he knelt and
willed his song to the senester. Desperate, pleading,
searching, the multiple harmonics sang forth to the
world about him, a blaze of modulation, a resonant
glory. A single trill he sang, but with the variety of elven-
call in its weave.

Then in the silence, clear and beautiful, near at hand,
there came an answer. The tones were odd, strained as
before and in a voice he did not know, but the song was
that of Nataea in full, laced through with the brilliances
that were hers alone. His heart leaped with joy. She was
there. There! Nothing else mattered. Nataea was there.

* * * * *

Under Cheyenne Mountain, Cyber-205 was busy. The
redesigning of a mountain's crystal heart to produce an
instrument of spectral harmonics had added immensely
to the load of its thousands of other simultaneous duties.
But no programs had been withdrawn, and neither man
nor elf ever had fully tested the capacities of the great
computer. Scanner receptors at a dozen points received
the signal from orbit and fed its characteristics to the
data network for assimilation. A pattern presented itself
to Cyber-205, and the machine responded as pro-

grammed. Relays tripped and signals went out.

An orderly handed a printout sheaf to General Morey Flanders, encamped in Turkey Run Park. He opened it, read, and stood.

"Colonel, call them in. God only knows how, but our victim is moving again. Bring in those all-band scanners, and we'll see if we can track."

* * * * *

Through long hours she lay awake, a duality in darkness, half-frightened with human fear of the unknown and unknowable, half-rejoicing that he was there, he was coming, he would find her soon. The girl whose body they shared and the elf spirit who awaited her mate remained a dichotomy, though Margaret had long since become willing to achieve the final, harmonic blending that she somehow understood should have occurred . . . would have, were she of the race of the one who had come to her. The separateness hurt them both, a barrier insurmountable, leaving them two separate beings in one body. It was a thing incomplete. Somehow, by now, they should have become one.

There had been a time . . . she could hardly remember it . . . when Nataea had had to plead with her to be allowed to stay. So much had changed, so fast.

And then there had been the fear—the almost certainty—that Aaelefein was gone. But now the call had come again, and they had responded in delirious concert.

For two days she had tried to console the forlorn spirit after that night when the call had come and ended. But now he sang again, and with a throat that had long since stopped aching from alteration she had responded, the human part of her as giddy with joy as was the elven part. She knew where he was. The presence behind her brow tingled at his approach and her scalp tingled his whereabouts. Finally she could stand it no longer.

Quietly she got dressed, padded through the hall and down dark stairs, glad now that her parents had gone, glad to be alone to meet him when he came. Tremulous that he might not approve her human self. *He will!* Nataea assured her. *Oh, he will!*

She made her way to the front door, opened it, slipped out, and closed it quietly behind her. She stood in night shadow, sensory empathy rippling outward. A massive darkness across the street hurt her, and she withdrew, startled. There was hatred there, terrible blindness. Tentatively she let her senses explore. There, crouched in shadow, Roy waited. Hard pity welled within her. Oh, Roy, why can't you understand? she thought. But there was no reaching him. She went back in the house, through to the sunporch, and out the back way. At the end of the block, she emerged from the alley, turned north and walked, then ran, toward the sound that teased her hair.

In the hour past moonset, she stood uncertain in a darkened park, elf-touched eyes seeing the dim figure that came toward her. Just out of sensory reach he paused, seemed as uncertain as she. He's tall, the human girl noted, and strangely dressed. *It is Aaelefein,* the elf girl almost screamed inside her. *It is him!* She took a few hesitant steps, still holding frightened senses in check. Yes, it was the face of her dreams, the face of her painting, the one they called "the Singer." There was no doubt. She wanted to go to him. She wanted to turn and run away. Her hold on senses slipped. Love washed over her, joy and desperation, a bittersweet knowing that was complete. He was hurt. She sensed it, and the elf in her took control.

"Aaelefein! Aaelefein, I am here."

Then he stood over her, great almond eyes looking down at her with a depth of meaning she could never have imagined. He took her hand, and she knew him, saw through pouring tears the one she loved, the one she knew better than anyone could, the one she knew but had never seen before. She saw the dull glow of the senester at his throat and knew what it meant. The elf girl sobbed her grief. The human girl pressed herself against him and held him in gentle arms.

"Nataea." The word was elvensong and she/they heard all of it. Then he held her away, looking at her with eyes that approved. In human speech, he said, "You even look like her . . . Margaret. As much as you possibly could. But why are you separate? Can you not blend?"

Taking strength from his touch, she tried. Without reservation now, she opened herself to the elf-part in her and felt it respond eagerly. She felt him, his resonances, helping. But even as they tried to blend, tried to be what he wanted, they knew they could not. Margaret and Nataea . . . two people. A mix, a homogen but not a meld.

She/they stopped as he faltered. She helped him sit beside a tree. He was drained, sick, and exhausted. Through touch, they knew how seriously. "Cai can leap to human, Aaelefein," they sang softly for him, needlessly. The scintillance added, "I knew it could be done."

"You are not complete, my pixies," he said sadly. "I want you to be."

"We will try again in a moment," they told him. Margaret asked, "What can we do to help you?"

"Nothing." His song was a whisper. "I just need to rest a little. Here is a good place."

"Are you dying, Aaelefein?" Nataea sobbed.

"No, my pixie-one. Of course not. I will heal. Maybe the Feya will find us here. She has ways beyond ours."

"She will come," they told him, knowing his lie and theirs. "We will wait here."

"A moment," he said. "Then you must try again to blend. Your two resonances are sweet, but they do not make a whole. I'd like"—he slipped into human speech—"to know you as a total . . . while there is time."

A block away a hard darkness moved in shadows, crouched and stalking, a hatred intense as human passion. But they were lost in concentration on each other. They did not sense its coming.

36

The mission was far into the crowded valley before it revealed itself. Its eighty-three members, men and women, looked bleakly around them as they gathered into a tight phalanx among the massed pilgrims below Cassion Peak. Up on the peak itself, batteries of light illuminated the work in progress. Down here, though, the only lights were lanterns, flashlights, and an occasional campfire. It was well past midnight.

The eighty-three people unwrapped their bundles . . . heavy wooden signs and cloth-wrapped wooden bats. One among them opened a can of kerosene, and they dipped their bats into it. The Reverend Quist stood a moment in silent prayer, then turned to them.

"Very well, brothers and sisters. It is the appointed hour. Let the Lord's name be praised!" Matches were struck, and torches burst into guttering flame. The placards were raised aloft.

"Repent," they cried in unison, and sleeping crowds came awake around them. "Repent of your Grievous Sins!"

In tight order the group of eighty-three marched forward, torches dispersing the darkness, placards on high: DIVINE RETRIBUTION IS UPON YOU. CAST NOT THY LOT WITH THE SPAWN OF SATAN. REPENT!

The Reverend Quist's sonorous voice rolled forth, "Let us bind them unto their iniquities! Rise up, Brothers and Sisters, rise up! Praise the Almighty and cast out these who are Satan's own spawn! Rise up!"

People scurried from their path as they pressed forward, awesome in their righteousness and fire. Sentries ran to intercept them, but each was confronted by a deployed placard-waver, fending for the phalanx. The Reverend Quiest had drilled his flock well.

In the clear area around Buddy Chance's Blazer, Mel Thompson raised his head, got to his feet. "What's 'at?"

Benny Sinclair and Tom Curry scrambled from the back of Curry's pickup. "Looks like trouble," Curry growled.

Beside the Blazer, Buddy, Chance got to his feet. Powerful shoulders hunched, and he felt his hackles rise. One thing that had never let him down was his instinct for trouble. He looked up at the elf-girl sitting atop the car, watching with curious eyes as the procession of fire approached. "You just stay put, missy, an' don't worry. We'll tend to them."

"It's pretty," she said. "All that fire . . . it is so human."

"That ain't human, missy. That's trouble, if I ever seen it." Hoisting a wrench, he stalked across to where his boys were lining up to face the marchers. He pushed through them, waved his wrench at a clot of sleepy people before him. "You all get back, you hear? Go on, get out of the way. We'll handle this."

Off to his right, a soldier hoisted a field pack and another switched on its radio. "Major, you better get some men up here. We have a disturbance. Yes, sir. It looks serious."

The chanting could be distinguished at one hundred yards, a sing-song medley of righteous voices accompanied by the waving signs and flaring torches: "Cast out Satan. Praise the Almighty. Cast out Satan. Praise the Almighty . . ."

"Fan out, boys," Chance said.

Queries rippled through the miles of waiting people in the valley. But at hand, the crowds grew silent. The chanting grew in volume. All of Chance's crew now carried implements of various kinds. The marchers approached, and the former thugs stood their ground. As firelight found them, the Reverend Quist raised an imperious hand. "Stand back there. Stand aside in the name of the Almighty!"

Chance called back, "Where do you think you're goin', preacher?"

"We go in the Almighty's name to cast out the devils among us." The voice was sure, authoritative, but as he got a better view of the glowering Chance, his steps faltered. "Brother, be not guilty of harboring Satan's lot. Repent. Follow in the Lord's way."

"You just back on off and preach someplace else, brother. We're here to see nobody hurts no elves. Now just turn around and leave while you can."

Vagrant light had found the Blazer. A stern-faced female near the Reverend Quist went pale. "Oh, Almighty protect us, there she is . . . Lilith!"

The preacher peered, then raised a hand to calm the quailing in his ranks. "Be strong in the Way, children. Forward to the Almighty's holy work!" The mission pressed forward, its members a weight of fire and darkness against Chance's dozen men. Benny Sinclair lashed out with a tire iron, and a heavy man fell out of line, clutching his arm. The torch he dropped bounced off a woman's shoulder. The mob scurried back.

"I told you all to go away," Chance boomed, pressing the advantage. "Now git!"

"Please, Buddy." The musical voice beside him froze his advance. "Do not hurt each other."

"It's her!" the Reverend Quist shouted. "He has delivered the sinner to retribution!"

Chance glanced around to see Sefraeonia at his side. "Missy, I told you—" He cut off at a grunt of effort, half-turned to see a heavy placard arching downward at the elf-girl. "No!" he shouted, throwing himself in its path. The timber caught him across the shoulder. He felt the bone break as he pushed Sefraeonia aside. They swarmed across him as he fell. Dazed with shock, he tried to get up and heard harsh voices all around, calling out orders. A burst of gunfire, screams, and running feet, then Sefraeonia was bending over him.

"Oh, Buddy, they hurt you." Dimly in the uncertain light, he saw uniforms in tight cordon around them, dispersing people. "Did they shoot the bastard, missy?"

"They fired into the sky, Buddy. Please, don't move so much. Here . . . Buddy, you have a broken bone. Damn it, hold still!"

Even through his shock and pain, the words caught him. He looked up at her elven face, gaped at her, and then laughter erupted. He could not hold it in. "Missy, did I teach you that?"

"Situation under control here, sir," a soldier said into a field phone. "But I wouldn't count on it. It's touchy down here. Can we send the . . . girl topside, sir?"

Chance turned his head, winced at the pain. "Soldier, this here elf ain't going no place without me. You hear?"

*   *   *   *   *

On Elvenroost, a perimeter guard turned at a sound, then did a double-take. The girl pulling herself up onto the shelf had blood on her fingers, a bruise across her dark face. She was panting and wheezing, about to faint.

"Here!" he challenged. "You aren't supposed to be up here!"

She got to her feet, wavering, and he hurried to catch her before she fell. "Marvin! Go get an officer. We got an infiltrator here."

She sagged against him, trying to catch her breath. Finally she managed, "Please . . . is Alvin here?"

"I don't know any Alvin, Miss. There now, you just take it easy. You'll be all right." He turned his head, still holding her. "Sir, this girl just came over the ledge here. She's looking for somebody named Alvin."

The officer stared at her. "You climbed all the way up here, Miss? Like that? How the hell did you manage?"

"I have to find Alvin. Please. I thought he must be here."

"And who is Alvin?"

"He's . . . he's an elf, sir. I know him. He took care of me."

"Well, I'm sorry, but he isn't here, and you'll have to go back. This is a secured area, Miss. You two"—he gestured—"get her on a hoist and take her down to the perimeter. Turn her over to field security for questioning. They'll want to know how she got past the line down there."

"No! Please, I have to find Alvin. I have to tell him . . . tell him . . ." She broke into great sobs.

The officer shook his head. A pretty little nut, but a nut just the same. "Go ahead. Take her away."

As they closed around her, she screamed, in the way

Alvin himself had once pronounced it, though she had only heard part of it: "A-l-e-f-a-n-e!"

There was a stir somewhere above, sudden clamor of voices, a thump that seemed to jar the ground. Then the soldiers were thrust aside, and all she could see was a broad back in a red cloak, a huge man shielding her, crouched and ready to defend. She smelled cinnamon and cloves.

"Haralan!" the officer barked. "It's all right. She's a—"

"Leave her alone," a deep voice threatened. A moment passed, and she saw wide shoulders relax. He turned. The face she saw above her was not Alvin. But it was . . . like Alvin's face. The great gold eyes were soft with concern. "Did they hurt you?"

"N-no. Who are you?"

"Haralan. Who are you?"

"Carrie Hummingbird. I'm trying to find Alvin."

"You called Aaelefein."

"Yes. Is he here?"

"Aaelefein is out there, somewhere. He seeks Nataea."

She closed her eyes, lowered her head. Through the exhaustion and the pain in her, she suddenly felt terribly embarrassed. She had forgotten . . . Alvin loved someone . . . someone else. She felt a large hand close over hers and suddenly the weariness, the longing, the desperation were gone. When she looked up, the great gold eyes were the most beautiful she had ever seen.

"I know," he said quietly. "But it will be all right. You can stay."

"You are . . . like Alvin," she murmured.

He looked at her, elven senses exploring her. "And you are like Rose Simmons."

From that moment she clung to him, tagged after him, darting diffident glances at the soldiers who watched her, puzzled, but made no move to interfere. When Haralan went back atop the spire, she watched, entranced, as he completed his crystal cut.

In false dawn, a helicopter rose above the croft and settled in the brilliance of the arc-lighted cove. Soldiers helped two people out. There was a large, fierce man with a bandaged arm and—Carrie's mouth dropped open—the elf-girl. She looked as she had on television, but more dazzling, more real. The helicopter lifted away. Haralan scurried down from the spire, and Carrie felt her heart sink as he strode toward the breathtaking creature who waited there for him.

Haralan had not seen Sefraeonia—or any of the others—since that night at the roadblock. Now he assured himself that she was well, then glanced past her at the scowling, bandaged man a pace behind her. In the man's emanations were fierce protectiveness and something else. Jealousy? Haralan considered it. "Sefraeonia, you are well."

"I am well, Haralan. I have had an interesting journey."

"As have I," he told her. "The people of this world are strange, but I would wish to know them better were it not for this enfeebling darkness of theirs."

Sefraeonia glanced across at the dark girl who watched Haralan with eyes of deep music. "Yes," she smiled, "I know. They are more akin to us than one could have imagined."

"Not akin," Haralan corrected. "Our Feya would say no more akin than the clear sky and the dark clouds it carries."

"Our Feya," Sefraeonia mused, "might also speculate

whether either is complete without the other. We will have to return to Nendacaida, Haralan, when the Feya finds the Corad-bane. But if I could, I would stay . . . with this human."

"And if Aaelefein finds Nataea. I know. Winifraeda said, 'trust Aaelefein.' But I would stay, too, Sefraeonia, if we could."

As they touched hands, they found similar changes in each other, similar longings that had not been part of them before, each for another and each couched in a free and open love for something that was not Caian but was altogether beautiful—a tragic race of blind, determined souls too much like them and too vastly different to allow disinterest. Until we go back, each told the other, there is one who needs me here.

Wistfully, close as chord-mates, they shared the thought. If it only could be . . . there is room for two castles on Elvenroost.

"We will take one thing at a time," Haralan said. "This morning the spire will sing for you."

She thought of the people in the valley below, the seeking masses of them, wanting. "It will sing for *them*, Haralan. You have shaped it. I will resonate it. It will sing for them. With this crystal, I will sing the essence of Caiendon. It is all I know to give them."

"Sing well, Sefraeonia chord-mate."

At the edge of the light, Carrie Hummingbird stood alone and afraid. Then her heart lifted, and her eyes gained a new lustre. The elves had turned from each other. Haralan was walking toward her, and a smile tipped the corners of his upturned mouth.

37

Dawn touched the top of Cassion Peak as they fed the final factors to Cyber-205. Confirmation was immediate. Elvenroost was ready. The eyes of waiting researchers gleamed in anticipation. The heart of General James Edgar pulsed with dread. He knew what was about to happen, but no one knew what would come of it. He was patched through to General Morey Flanders in Indiana. The background was a beat of chopper blades. Flanders was airborne.

"We're ready here, General. You can still call this thing off, you know."

"Why should I call it off?"

"Because we don't know what we're going to let loose. Because this is without precedent. Because there doesn't seem to be any clear reason for doing it at all. Because I've got a feeling we're into something bigger than we know about. Pick a reason."

There was a pause. "Anything more than a hunch, Jim?"

"No. I guess not. I'd just as soon go out and do something that's been tried before, though."

"Look, Jim, you are about to pull off—at the very least—the biggest PR maneuver any officer of any military unit has ever done. You're about to make several million taxpayers extremely happy. And you're about to make the National Science Foundation delirious. Do it."

"General, I know damn well you have a better reason for this circus than any of the above."

"Yes, and I can't tell you about it. Not while you have Haralan and the girl in tow. Look, I've got things cooking here that will make or break us with the elves. I'm doing my damnedest to keep the lid on until I know. Your part is to keep public attention on that mountain. Give them their show."

"It's go ahead then, sir?"

"Damn right. Get on with it."

Edgar clicked off. "A goddamned media event," he muttered. At cove command, a harried-looking specialist gave him a quick thumbs-up. Everything was ready. He looked around. The elves and their various escorts were waiting. He nodded at his exec and jammed his hands into his pockets. "Okay. Let 'er rip."

Down at the ledge, banked levers were thrown. Powered resonators interfaced with quartz outcrop came to life with a warmup hum, quickly subsiding. Edgar had the feeling the mountain had throbbed. Then there was silence. Out across the dawning valley, people looked up, waiting for something they could not explain.

"Sefraeonia," Edgar said. As she came forward, he felt a lump in his throat. God, she was beautiful! "We're all set up. I guess it's yours whenever you're ready."

"I can give them song?"

He smiled into the gorgeous eyes. He had no clear idea what that meant, but . . . "Yes. You can give them song."

Amid silence, she walked across to the base of the cut spire. The spire stood tall above her. She reached out a tentative hand, touched it, and the mountain throbbed again, this time a deep thrill of infrasonics.

"The quartz is in resonation," a technologist at banked receptors whispered. "But no single resonance. This seems to be a wide band of multiple variation, a whole pattern of subaudible harmonics."

"So much for wave theory." Another shook his head.

Earphones reported, "Cyber-205 says the stone has just been programmed. Undulating infrasonic pitches in a repeating cycle like wide-range carrier bands."

"She gives the crystal her essence," Haralan said.

At the spire Sefraeonia opened her mouth. Cameras saw pulses in her throat. From the towering spire leaped a ripple of eerie, soundless beauty, a blend of ultrasonics climbing into the middle ranges. Unheard joy touched the very fiber of the waiting humans.

A single trill, cut short, then reverberating silence. She tested the stone. Again she trilled, a dancing cascade of bright tones up and down the spectrum, and the trill in massive intensity rippled up and down the mountain as its crystal core responded, waves of harmony pulsing outward on the morning air. Still it was beyond the range of human sound, but no sound was needed. It was an orchestrated ripple of unleashed harmonics, a splash of bright velvet pulse greeting the morning. Edgar felt it through his scalp, through the backs of his hands, through his brow, and his throat went tight with the terrible beauty of it.

Again there was momentary, echoing silence. Sefraeonia looked around at him, at all of them, and her smile was as sweet as the huge, silent music for which it thanked them. Then, with fingers on the crystal spire, head held high, she sang.

Sefraeonia the percept, adept at recognizing the blend of harmonics that was the essence of Caidom, sang

for humanity the thing she knew best. Into the funda-
mental rhythms that were the living mantle of Earth, she
wove tapestries of lyric tone—the ancient, bright harmonics of her kind—and the awesome arts of humans
powered the mountain as it built amplification upon
amplification of her song. Miles away, the thing that was
Cyber-205 responded as to programming, pulsing supporting lyric to Elvenroost's crystal heart until the quartz
fed back and back upon itself. Never in the millennia
had the children of the haunted ones known glory, but
now they came awake in untried senses as the starburst
beauty of elvendom unfurled, a singing, soaring,
ascending fullness of ancient essence leaping the spectrum from end to end. All the lesser harmonies tem-
pered, modulated to blend into this cascade of ringing,
soul-borne life.

Sefraeonia sang, the mountain sang, and those on the
mountain, those in the valley below, those progressively
farther away as Elvenroost took up and fed back the
mounting resonances, knew for the first time what Earth
had lost before their earliest ancestors opened eyes that
were aware . . . the essence of old Caiendon, of Faerie.
Resonance built upon resonance, thunder upon thunder
through the infrasonics, subsonics, sonics, and into the
vast ranges beyond. Sleeping senses millennia-lost
surged awake and caught the harmonies as they built.
Sefraeonia sang and an ancient sleeping world awakened
about her, a world of brilliance beyond human experience.

Below the croft, Haralan frowned. Something was
wrong. Sefraeonia's song was not complete. There was a
hole in it, a range of silence where there should have
been music. Quickly he went to her, drew and resonated
his blade, and plunged it half-length into the standing

quartz. Now the EHF took up the song as well, and the spectrum was complete.

Under Cheyenne Mountain, a technician, shaken out of his trance by the blaring of a discordant claxon, touched a recept button and jumped from his chair. "Turn it off!" he shouted. "My God, turn it off!"

It was too late. The mountain, fully resonated, had set up base modulations in subsurface strata. The resonance of elvendom was in control—the power humanity had tinkered with but had not understood. It grew. It overrode. It pitched and pitched anew, carrying that irreducible, sweet song ever outward in waves above and beneath Earth's living mantle. In the valley, massed people knelt and wept, laughed and sang, hugged and prayed. And then in the radius beyond, and in the radius beyond that.

Driven now by its own latent resonance, long hushed but now unleashed by human magics, Caiendon sang anew on Elvenroost with a richness beyond any that Nendacaida could have produced. The lost resonance of an ancient world awakened and smiled for the world that had forgotten it.

Sefraeonia the percept sang the song she knew best, and Faerie was reborn on Elvenroost. Its mother was an elf-girl. Its father was Cyber-205.

Outward and outward the harmonics poured. On a farm in Oklahoma, a ranch in South Dakota, a street in Nevada, people stood in silent wonder as beauty beyond hearing, beyond sight, danced about them. On a prairie in Saskatchewan, on a mountain in California, on a mesa in Chihuahua, glory reigned.

*   *   *   *   *

In the bubble of a helicopter racing southward from South Bend, Winifraeda Feya clutched Jacob Laurel's arm. "Jacob, do you hear it? Do you feel it?"

"My God, yes! What is it?"

The pilot, wide-eyed, echoed him. "My God."

"Sefraeonia," the Feya said proudly. "She sings. But there is such power . . . I don't understand, Jacob. No elf has such power."

Out and out the pulses flew: Alaska, the Yucatan, Hawaii, Maine, Siberia, Peru, Peking, London, Pretoria, Venice, Moscow, Leningrad, Perth. Expanding ripples of spectral orchestration overlapped then, met and fed back, crescendoed . . . Blanketing the globe, matrix-deep harmonics met and blended and came alive, a song that fed upon itself and had no end.

For a long time after Sefraeonia stopped singing, there was stunned silence on Elvenroost, broken only by the satisfied soft resonance that lingered—would linger always now—in the living crystal of Cassion Peak and throughout the mantle of the Earth of which it was part. Pleased at what she had done, Sefraeonia touched the spire, and the humming ebbed to faerie resonance barely discernible but unabated. Elvenroost lived. Caiendon lived. Haralan smiled his approval for her. She had done well. Then his eyes widened. He looked around.

"Sefraeonia . . . feel it! Can you sense any darkness?"

She raised her head and sensed wide. Distantly, out there, some of the darkness that was the human condition pressed down. But not here. On Elvenroost it was gone. And nowhere on Earth now was it dominant.

One by one the humans on the mountain began to move about, wide-eyed, dazed with awe. General James Edgar stood up, uncaring of the dust on his tailored knees, and looked around him with eyes that would never again see limits. Carrie Hummingbird, sobbing with pure joy, clung to Haralan and knew what he was . . . and what she was as well. Buddy Chance wiped away the wetness on his cheeks and began to inspect a world the king of Star City could never have perceived. John Tracy stood humbled, shaken, and somehow fulfilled. He knew now why he had felt such rapport with the elves. They had shown him beauty.

In the valley, stunned thousands milled, seeking one another to recapture and cherish the miracle they had experienced. For them and those beyond them the memory of incredible moments would last a lifetime. But for those humans on the peak, it would not be memory. Faerie reborn was part of them. They would carry the song of Earth's double matrix.

Morning sun touched the peak and flashed in the spire of Elvenroost. The mountain sang to greet it.

38

First dawn pinked the sky above shade trees in the park. In dimness below, Margaret Harrison who was also Nataea knelt beside the failing body of Aaelefein. The tears on her cheeks were both human and elf.

"Caiendon is too long gone on this sad world," Aaelefein breathed. "There is no song left to support empathy, so you, my pixies, cannot achieve rapport. I am sorry, Margaret, that I must leave you. And I grieve, Nataea my own, that I ever brought you here. You have your immortality, but only to share a person, not to be one. Forgive me."

"Aaelefein," they sobbed, "the Feya will come. There will be something she can do. Cling to life, will of the chord. Cling."

"I try, my sweet ones, but it grows dim about me. I find I cannot see or hear you very well, and I cannot parse at all. It is as well. I feel no darkness. For the first time since we chorded here that burden is not on me. I had a premonition, lovelies. I knew these eyes would not again see Nendacaida, these hands not—"

Dawn's fingers probed. In the distance, in two directions it seemed, was the clatter and thrum of approaching machines. But here was soft silence, the hush of morning.

"Aaelefein," they wept, clinging to the fitful spark of life that faltered in him. Darkness moved near, and now they sensed it. Even as she turned her head, Margaret heard a footstep, a brutal sound in the softness. They looked up to see the sunken eyes, the uncombed hair of Roy Holloway, dull and impervious. His eyes saw everything and nothing.

"I found him," he said tonelessly. "He took you, Teddy . . ." He looked at her, unblinking. "Dorothy . . . Meg. Nothin' left to lose, is there?"

She scrambled up, driven back by the hard darkness that drove him. He stared at her, then at the fallen elf.

Something was happening around him, and dull senses registered it. There was an unheard trill in the Earth, an unseen shimmer in the air. The elf by the tree opened misting, almost-gold eyes that wavered as they focused. "Hello," the dim voice whispered. "Hello, man."

The shimmer was growing, like distant music building about them. Holloway stared at the dying elf. "What are you doing? What are you trying to do now?" With a burst of dull fury, he raised the shotgun. "Never again," he muttered as Margaret screamed. The gun's blast was thunderous in the shrouded, singing silence. Its charge ripped into the elf, flung his limp body against the tree. Aaelefein's body hung there for an instant while gold eyes went muddy. Holloway's nerveless fingers emptied the shotgun into Aaelefein. But the gun's roar was drowned by great, unseen musics that grew and resonated . . . music in the Earth and sky . . . everywhere. Roy dropped the shotgun, sagged, and closed his eyes.

They stood in shock, the two who shared Margaret's body. Stunned by the rage, battered by the horror of it, they clung to each other as the faerie music grew about them, and something happened. Glory crescendoed, and the two of them became one.

Margaret stepped to the man standing bleakly over the elf and took his hand.

The creature that was Roy Holloway suddenly knew a compassion so intense, so caring, so bittersweet that it staggered him. As she took his hand, awareness hit him, a wave of knowing burst through his dark mind, shook his bleak soul like tender thunder. He opened his eyes, looked at the shattered body lying before him, and felt its life flicker out. Grief surged through him, the compounded grief of all the tragedies, of knowing the senseless thing he had done, grief that something beautiful was gone, and in a panic of yearning he sought it, opened himself to it, pleaded for it to be yet alive . . . to be. In an agony of anguish he willed that the senseless thing he had done be somehow undone. Vaguely he sensed profound change occurring around him. The air, the sunrise, the ground beneath him . . . sang.

Abruptly then, as though answering his silent cry, a gentle strength touched him. It penetrated, permeated him, lodged in him. A will that had not been his own soothed the chaos of his guilt. Senses Roy Holloway had never known sprang to full life, and a soothing, strong voice that was his own voice whispered, "Hello, man."

He looked up from the wrecked body. Glories presented themselves, and he accepted them, cherished them. Unearthly radiances, unsung harmonies, tones and lusters beyond comprehension were about him, and he comprehended them. He was alive as no human man ever had been alive, seeing as no human man ever had seen, and rapport was achieved in an instant of pure resonance. He knew.

She pressed his hand, and he turned to her. Tactile senses beyond man or elf passed between them. Their eyes locked, and they explored each other. With coupled minds that were more than human, more than elf, they knew the blindness of humanity, the terrible thing that had made it great; the emptiness of elvendom, ancient and purposeless except to exist and to yearn; the profound beauty each held for the other; and the tragedy of millennia of apartness that should never have been.

They knew and shared their knowing of the awesome artistry of a world that had produced twin races complete but apart, guided them to need each other, then left them to find their alter-halves—mirror-image races, alike and opposite, each the missing portion of the other, each destined to yearn until completion was achieved.

Minds that were human and elf and far more than both coupled and shared what they knew. Elf and human, male and female, the four that were two that were one and complete rejoiced in being. He turned, knelt, and gazed for a silent moment at the dead form that had been Aaelefein Fe-Ruast. Gently he removed the senester from its throat. The seven perfect crystals glowed warmly as he touched them. He dropped the senester into a pocket of his shirt. He sang his essence to her—an essence that was all that Aaelefein had been and all that Roy Holloway had been, and more. She sang to him, and she was Margaret and Nataea and so much more. Their harmonies blended, and a new music was born.

A helicopter had landed in a nearby clearing. A small, silver figure hurried toward them, followed by an aging man with bristling whiskers. As they approached, they hesitated, eyes of two races questioning what they saw. Then Margaret/Nataea sang a welcome to the Feya, and Winifraeda's great eyes widened. She stared at them and knew them, but only a little. In form they were human, a tall man and a small, pixie-pretty woman. In aura they were elf. The Feya's gentle heart leaped as she recognized Aaelefein and Nataea. But then confusion took her. The resonances about the pair were more beautiful, more profound than anything Winifraeda could ever have imagined. She felt she was perceiving only a part of them. Haltingly, on tiny feet, the Feya went and peered up at them. They reached down and took her hands for a long moment.

A huge tear formed at the corner of Winifraeda's eye. She turned. "It is all right, Jacob. Everything is all right."

The old man stood back, staring in awe at the serene pair and in horror at the mutilated body that had been an elf. The Feya went to him.

"Believe me, Jacob. All is right. I will explain it all."

Other motors were approaching.

"Go to Elvenroost, Winifraeda," Margaret/Nataea said. "Go there and tell them."

"I will," she sang. Then she dropped to her knees. Without quite knowing why, Jacob Laurel knelt beside her. "Oh," the Feya said to the four who were now two, "you are so beautiful." Her great eyes drank them in. "So beautiful."

The two joined hands. They looked into each other's eyes and smiled. Human and elf, male and female, ultimate, together and complete, their harmonies welled, and the senester responded. The part of him that was Aaelefein wove the intricate lyric of will, and the part that was Roy Holloway responded with steady rhythm. The part of her that was Margaret blended into the medley a richness of human heart unleashed, and the part that was Nataea sprinkled the weave with scintillance.

They were four and they were two and they were all. The matrix was complete. Of elves, a chord required five. Of ultimates, only two. Then, Earth saw none, as in a ringing radiance, the chord entered transference to Nendacaida.

Laurel staggered as he got to his feet. His comprehension had been stretched too far. He felt stunned. The two . . . he could think only of the word "angels" . . . were gone. He lifted the Feya to her feet.

"You were right, Jacob," she bubbled, "about culminants and ultimates, even about the Corad-bane. You were right about everything."

He stared at her dumbly. "I don't know what you're talking about, Winifraeda. I don't even know what I just saw."

"Oh, Jacob, follow your own logic. I did. About the double matrix . . . you were right. Evolution . . . creation of species, it was never completed. Our two races of culminants were never end results, don't you see? We are both parts of what was intended, not all of it. You spoke of double evolution, Jacob . . . of two human races separately evolved and neither quite complete. Of course we are not complete. We are culminants, yes. But not ultimates, Jacob. Those two . . . you saw them, you felt their aura. Those are people, Jacob. You and I—human and Caian—we evolved so that we could blend and produce them. They are what this world—this astonishing, surprising world—was always supposed to produce."

"I saw them," he breathed. "I don't even know what they are."

"They are the children of our two races, Jacob . . . not born of us, as I am sure new generations will be, but created by the blend that came from leaping. In death, Nataea leaped to that human girl. And in death, Aaelefein leaped to that human man. And the resonance from Sefraeonia's song . . . I don't understand how she did that, Jacob. There must have been human magic involved in it. But her resonance—this world's old resonance, in both its forms now—conjoined them, and they became complete. Oh, it is just beautiful." Her huge eyes were wide and moist, and just looking into them made Laurel's glasses fog.

He tried to digest it. Other machines were landing now, uniformed men emerging from them. There were shouts, a chaos that Jacob Laurel chose to ignore. "Ultimates," he mused. "Yes, it follows a certain, ah . . . elven logic. But where did they go, Winifraeda? They were here, and then there was . . . it was like the music of the stars . . . and then they were gone. Where are they?"

"They are a chord, Jacob. They are on their way to Nendacaida where they are needed. But they will return. They are needed here, too."

"But then, what about the Corad-bane? That's what you came here for, remember?"

"Oh, Jacob!" Her laugh was a ringing of silver bells, rippling through the spectra. "You are so . . . so pragmatically human. They *are* the Corad-bane. Their human essence."

"But how?"

"You asked me—do you remember?—what Caidom left behind on this world when the Cai transferred to Nendacaida. There was only one thing, Jacob. They left those harmonies that were not a part of their makeup. Those patterns of resonance that came later . . . or which were always latent here, but did not resound at first. The human essence, Jacob. The patterns of the Raporoi and their children, the human race. Caidom left those patterns behind. And it was that—the essential human mode of this world—that shielded it against the Corad."

"Then when those two reach Nendacaida . . ."

"I suspect they are already there. Their power is enormous."

"Then they will protect the planet?"

"They will . . . resonate it, Jacob. They will add their harmonics to its weave, and it will no longer be threatened."

People were all around them now, but Jacob was only vaguely aware of them. Taking Winifraeda's hand in his, he strove to grasp totalities, to revel in significances, to understand everything all at once.

People were kneeling over the body of the dead elf. Others were deploying, forming a perimeter, keeping other people back. A man with stars on his shoulders stood near, waiting for their attention. Winifraeda glanced at him and nodded. "Good morning, General."

"But Winifraeda," Jacob persisted, "what about you . . . and Haralan and Sefraeonia? Does this mean you must all leave, now?"

"Of course not." She squeezed his hand. "We can't leave now. With Aaelefein and Nataea gone—with whoever they are now gone—there are only three of us left here. We are only Cai, Jacob. Only elves. It takes five of us to chord."

"But can you tolerate staying?"

"Jacob, the darkness is gone—haven't you noticed? Oh, there are traces of it, but it is quite tolerable now." She pursed lovely lips in an expression so human that it tugged at Laurel's heart. "We must go and see how Sefraeonia achieved so much power. The song was hers, but the power of it!" Her eyes shone with wonder.

"It won't return? The darkness?"

"No. It is gone. This world sings with two voices now,

Jacob. Yours and ours, together. It is a strange mixture, but very appealing. I believe one could grow quite fond of it.

"But"—she straightened her tiny shoulders—"first things first." She smiled up at him. "Such strange logic. You must teach me to think that way, Jacob. First things first. Right now we must speak with the general. He is very confused, the poor man. He will want to know about the ultimates and about Rigil Fen-Belen's testament. It may all take some time. Then, I suppose, we should do something about you."

"About me?" He blinked at her.

"If you want to parse, Jacob, first you must have some hair. We need to attend to that. And your senses are really atrocious, you know. So limited. We should do something about that. You will need your senses if we find pixies."

"Pixies? Where?"

"You said you would like to meet a pixie. I agree. You would. Therefore, we shall see if we can find some."

"But, Winifraeda . . . here? On Earth?"

"I suspect so, Jacob. When we first came here—and since—Sefraeonia has perceived traces of Caiansong in remote places. On Elvenroost, for example, the resonance was quite strong. Someone has been maintaining the old harmonies. Residual patterns don't last that long untended, you know."

"But . . . *pixies?*"

"I can't think who else it might be. And it would be so like the sweet things—even after all this time—to keep a brightness here and there in case we should come home."